I0604964

**Also by Susan McCormick**


*The Fog Ladies*
*The Fog Ladies: Family Matters*
*The Fog Ladies: In the Soup*
*The Fog Ladies: Date with Death*

*The Antidote*

*Granny Can't Remember Me*

# THE ROOM AT THE END OF THE HALL

Susan McCormick

This is a work of fiction. Names, characters, places, organizations, incidents, products, and business establishments are either the product of the author's imagination or are used fictitiously. Any resemblance to actual persons living or dead, business establishments, events, or locales is entirely coincidental.

**The Room at the End of the Hall**



Carroll Press
Seattle, WA 98122
visit us at carrollpress.com

First Edition 2025 by Carroll Press
Library of Congress Control Number  2025911551
Print ISBN  978-0-9986-1877-7

Published in the United States of America

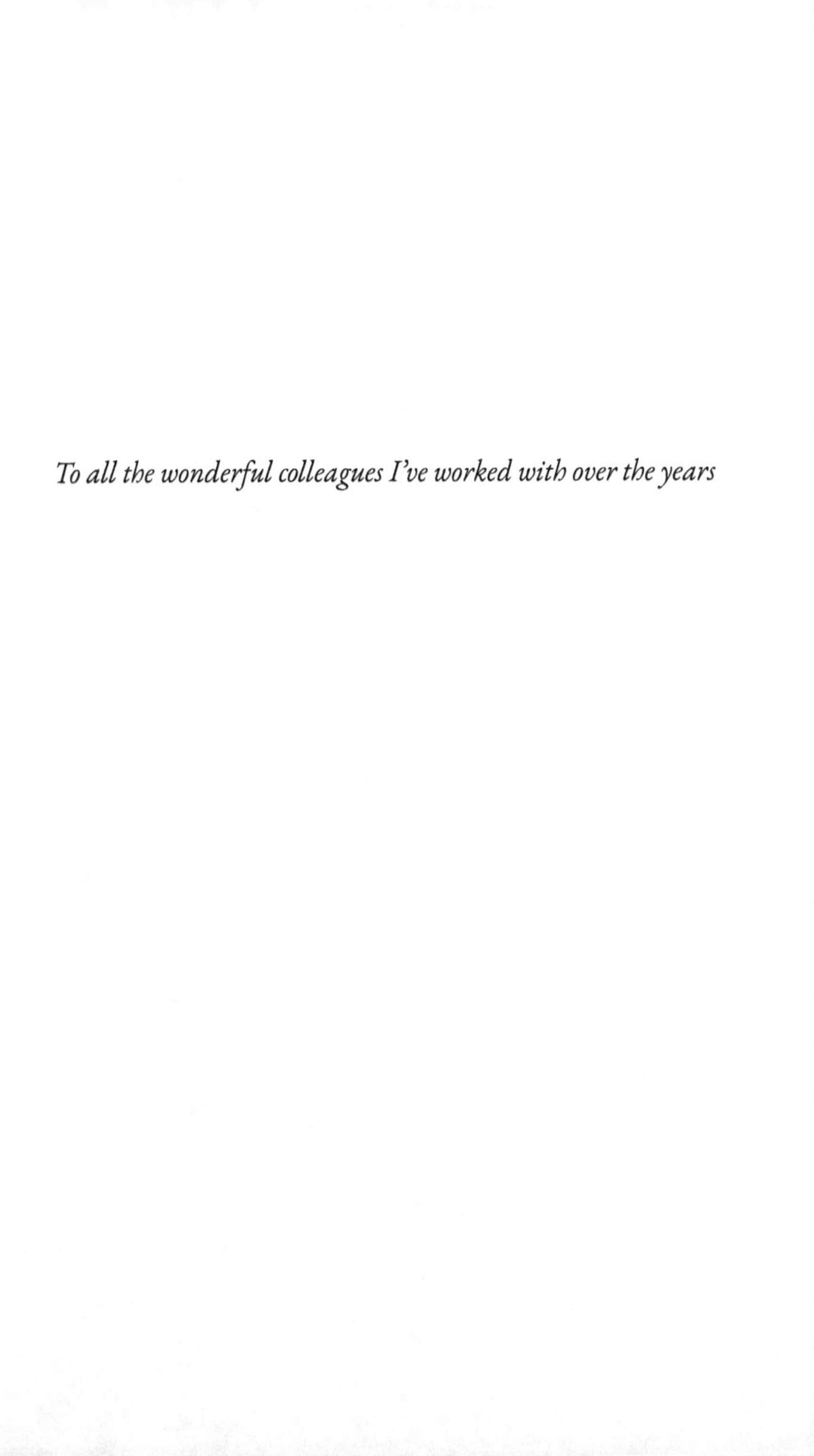

*To all the wonderful colleagues I've worked with over the years*

# Chapter 1

One note separated him from the room at the end of the hall.

Only seven o'clock, but the hospital floor was deserted. The empty hall, abandoned by the day shift, echoed with a rare footfall from the skeletal night crew.

Dr. Michael Baker had a final patient to see. He dreaded that room, not because of his patient, but because of her roommate. He had avoided the room all day, which was not his style. Usually he rounded on his patients early, before the day's surgeries began, then a second rounding in the evening before heading home. But this woman was a young, healthy thirty-two-year-old with a fractured femur. More than ten years younger than he was and the opposite of most of his list, who were frail and elderly, with broken hips or bone tumors plus countless co-morbidities.

"You're here late." One of the nurses, Mildred, swooshed by in her rubber-soled shoes. "Another complicated patient? I can spot your patients before they even roll off the elevator because of all the medical paraphernalia that rolls off first."

"Is that so?" Michael smiled and she smiled back.

"Not every broken hip has a cardiac monitor. Or oxygen. Or both," she said.

"The hips that break on my call days do," he said.

"A black cloud," she said, referring to the medical euphemism of some doctors having busy, difficult, unlucky days on call. "Better you than some of your partners, I guess. Maybe those sick patients wait to fall 'til you're on call. That's what I'm doing, if I ever break a hip."

This was high praise from Mildred, who'd worked at Cascadia Medical Center thirty years. Michael loved the OR, the technical part of his job, but he loved the joy part better, seeing his patients' lives improve, knowing he had helped. What other job could be as gratifying?

Mildred went on. "At least the patients get the best. Don't work too hard."

She waved, her arm circling cheerily like she was the queen, her wrist stiff in a short black brace. He'd seen her shaking out her hand after a few minutes' typing, he'd brought her the brace, suggested a new keyboard, and now she called him the best. Truthfully, *Mildred* was the best, perfect for his cadre of complicated patients.

His last patient, Chrissie Johnson was not complicated, thankfully. He'd poked his head in early this morning, long enough to make sure she didn't need anything, and said he'd be back in the afternoon. Now it was evening, and definitely time to go back.

He returned to his note. He could add nothing more. The note was done, more than done, the longest, most in-depth orthopedic follow up note he'd ever written. All because he didn't want to go into that room.

*She* was in that room.

The loudspeaker blared. The hospital operators only broadcast one call on the loudspeakers. Code blue.

"Code blue, code blue. Room 721."

Michael was on the seventh floor. He stood to answer the call. He missed the room number as his chair banged over backwards. The silent hallway was now full of people, one pushing the code cart, its wheel squeaking. He followed along, confident someone would lead the small crowd to the right place.

They rushed down the hall. He slowed, and others hurried past. The code cart disappeared. The squeaking stopped. He was alone.

Not that room. No, not that room.

The hubbub of sound and activity forced him to acknowledge what he already knew.

The code was in the room at the end of the hall.

# Chapter 2

What in the world?

Margaret McGillicuddy, Madge to her friends and anyone else courteous enough to ask her "preferred name," threw off the thin blue hospital blanket and peered around. She must have dozed off. The narcotics didn't help, fogging her brain and dulling her senses.

"Roll her on her back!"

All this noise, all these people. Why the kerfuffle? The only time Madge had ever seen this many people in a room at once was when her roommate Edith Murtle threw up all that blood and passed out cold. Everyone under the sun had piled into that room. She knew them all, knew their names and titles, had been around long enough that some of the medical resident doctors-in-training were now full-bore doctors, overseeing the care of oodles of patients.

Here was one now, leading the charge, Dr. Francine Mead. Dr. Francine gave orders, and the other doctors scurried around. Madge silently cheered her on, remembering how timid and meek the girl was a mere few years ago as a new intern, counseling Madge on her alcohol intake.

Well, maybe more than a few years. Francine certainly wasn't a girl anymore, and she was long past the training stage. She was running the doctor show tonight as a hospitalist attending like she did most nights. She must be mid-thirties by now. Time wandered when you were in your seventies. And on narcotics. And had had a few falls to the head.

"No pulse," Francine shouted. "Start chest compressions."

Madge blinked and shook her head. Hold on, hold on.

This was serious. Since Madge, age seventy-five but looking "older than stated age" as the doctors always said, lay here feeling fine and dreaming of a dinner she was not allowed to eat, then what was happening? Madge knew sick people, and her roommate wasn't sick. Had they switched roommates on her?

Her current roommate, Chrissie Johnson, cute as a cockapoo, funny, smart, and a perfect match for her picky son, was a young thing with a broken leg. You can't die of a broken leg.

Though when Madge last saw her, before the dream about the Reuben sandwich, Chrissie hadn't looked that good.

# Chapter 3

Michael paused at the doorway threshold. A curtain on metal rings blocked his view, drawn for privacy, though no one was in the hall but him. Shouts and a flurry of movement drifted through the beige opaque drape, muted and softened and belying the horror on the other side.

"Pulseless electrical activity!"

"Continue chest compressions! Epinephrine."

Two patients resided in the room at the end of the hall. Chrissie Johnson and...

Michael breathed in deeply to steady himself.

This code was not for Chrissie. She was young and healthy and had a broken leg. This code was for the other person in the room.

He yanked back the curtain. The metal rings clanked and jolted him back to doctor mode. He squared his shoulders and strode in but stopped short, at the wrong bed.

"Stinky! I was wondering where you were."

She reclined on two pillows, her frilly pink nightgown breaking one hospital policy, her strong perfume breaking another. Her coarse gray hair matted on one side, and her red lipstick missed its mark. He cringed at the nickname even while he grabbed the bedrail to keep from pitching over in relief.

His mother, Margaret McGillicuddy, was fine.

Then what...who... Oh, no. It wasn't possible.

He spun toward the other bed, the bed with the frenzied activity. Chrissie lay there, pale, a nurse and a bag valve mask squeezing air into her lungs, pads on her chest to monitor her heart. The anesthesiologist nodded to the nurse, who removed the mask as he intubated.

The hospitalist, Francine Mead, cocked her head. "This is your patient, right, Michael? We saw the chart."

He stood immobile for a split second, then his shock abated. "Yes. Fractured femur status post surgery."

"Yes. Look." She waved toward Chrissie's face and chest. Michael forced his eyes to Chrissie's impossibly gray face. Tiny red-brown spots covered her cheeks and chest, a tell-tale petechial rash he'd last seen on his first board exam more than a decade ago. He'd never seen it in person.

"Fat embolism," Francine said.

A globule of fat from the fractured bone that caused lung blockage or inflammation. It was rare, and sometimes deadly.

"Don't know how long she's been down," Francine continued. "When did you last see her?"

"This morning. Around six thirty. Briefly," he admitted. He had snuck in while his mother was still asleep and he'd spoken to Chrissie in whispers.

"Long day," Francine said.

Francine ran the code. Michael rotated in doing chest compressions, arms straight, full weight forcing Chrissie's chest down, then waiting for the recoil, then down again. He hadn't performed CPR since his ACLS recertification class a year ago. His patients didn't code.

How could this happen to Chrissie?

He pushed on her chest in a fast, steady rhythm. *Come on! Beat on your own!*

Time suspended, and he was surprised when a tap on his shoulder told him it was time to switch out.

There wasn't much the team could do. They covered all the bases, they tried the extra measures, but Chrissie was as dead then as she was when the nurse found her on evening rounds.

# Chapter 4

That poor girl was dead and all this very young hospital chaplain could say to Madge was "That must have been so scary for you." For her? What about for Chrissie!

Madge stiffened her back and squared her shoulders. The effect would be better if she were standing, her tall frame towering over this slender man, but at the moment she had no hope of standing without a strong arm of support. Propped up on the squishy hospital bed, she feared she looked nothing short of feeble.

When had she gone from strong to weak? From smart to confused? From capable to needing care?

She wanted to tell him she was fine, that she'd seen more than one hospital roommate die in her day. Like Edith Murtle. She threw up all that blood and, despite a room full of experts and life-saving procedures, died anyway.

But Edith Murtle was seventy.

She wanted to tell him she knew all about hospitals, that the nurses called Madge a "frequent flyer," given how many times she was in and out. Oh, not to her face. But Madge had ears. A frequent flyer. So be it. It meant she knew to bring her own pillow and her favorite pink nightgown. Chrissie wore the hospital-issued drab green gown with ties on the back and had to suffer the thin, plastic hospital pillows. Though the thing ended up on the floor when they started pushing on her chest.

She wanted to tell him she trusted the doctors and knew they were getting the best of care at Cascadia Medical Center. Especially with her son there now.

Finally, her son had come home. Mikey.

The young chaplain repeated, "That must have been so scary for you."

Madge would never admit it to this wet-behind-the-ears man. But it was scary.

Chrissie had had the best team tonight, the most trusted of doctors, Madge's favorite doctor, Francine Mead, and Mikey, of course. But Chrissie was still dead.

Madge had watched the frantic efforts to revive young Chrissie and hid under her blanket as the team limped out of the room, leaving her with a still, silent body covered with a sheet.

All Chrissie had was a broken leg. Leaned too far off her second story balcony looking for an escaped pet and toppled off. She and Chrissie laughed about it just yesterday. Lucky she'd only broken a leg and not her whole body. You can't die of a broken leg. That's what they'd said.

But Chrissie had.

# Chapter 5

Michael filled in information while Francine typed the report. He confirmed there were no next of kin, only a friend as the emergency contact, and he would call her. His hand froze on the telephone as the empty gurney with Chrissie's body in the large hidden compartment rolled down the hall, its too deep shape screaming of what lay within.

Francine laid her hand on his arm. "These things happen. Don't beat yourself up." She didn't say, "Of course, there will be an M & M and you'll get plenty of beating up then." But she and he both knew it. He'd have to present the case at that month's Surgery Morbidity and Mortality Conference, notorious for its Monday morning quarterbacks pointing out what you could have done better.

And she didn't say what he thought she might be thinking, "I had a lovely time, I thought you did, too, when can we do it again?" He *had* had a lovely time. He'd let down his guard at the spring party and broke his own rule of never again getting involved with someone in the hospital. He left her that day with every intention of calling and explaining why dating would be a mistake. But that would mean talking about Janet. He didn't want to talk about Janet, so he never said a word. That was a week ago.

Francine left him at the computer where he started, with one more patient to see, one who was now dead. How could

Chrissie Johnson be dead?

Was his mother the last one to see Chrissie alive? By some perverted twist of fate, a full house had placed his mother in a room with his own patient. He pushed up against the desk and headed back down the hall.

Another perverted twist of fate had thrust him back to Seattle, back to a coast he'd left a quarter of a century ago, back to his mother's tangled and messy life. They hadn't spoken in a year, for good reason, until he was forced home. She was the sole reason for the move. In and out of the hospital so many times that he and the social worker recognized each other's phone numbers. Each time his phone flashed with the 206 area code, his gut clenched. Acute alcoholic pancreatitis. Fall with concussion. Pseudocyst. Secondary diabetes. Biliary obstruction. Fall with subdural hematoma. Pancreatitis again.

Which was the illness responsible for her current admission. Her first hospitalization since he'd arrived four months ago. So that was something.

The quiet hallway stretched on forever without the hustle and bustle of the daytime crew. The fluorescent light sputtered, momentarily pitching the corridor into gloom, then brightness again, then solid gloom. An occasional flicker from a television inside a room cast a blue hue on the walls, but otherwise he walked in dreariness, slowly, to the end of the hall.

His patient was dead. Last night she'd joked that she wished Frank could visit her in the hospital.

"Frank?" He pictured a broad-shouldered boyfriend. "Of course he can visit."

"Doubt it," she said. "I bet the hospital has a rule against four-legged critters."

Not a boyfriend. Her pet.

Who would take care of Frank now?

# Chapter 6

Michael inhaled his mother's distinctive perfume as he slipped into her room.

"Stinky! Thank heavens you're back." A bad nickname from a toddler encounter with a skunk, his mother stuck to the name like she'd chosen it for his birth certificate.

"She was right there! She died right there!" Her arms flailed aimlessly, but finally one bony, bent finger pointed to the empty bed.

His chest tightened in its familiar vise, and the yellowed tiles of the ceiling pressed down on his head as if he had increased intracranial pressure himself, like his mother with her falls.

He leaned in and hugged her, encircling her whole body with one arm. God, she was thin. Alcohol had ravaged her body and her mind. She could not stop drinking, not when he was a kid and not now. She landed in the hospital over and over. She was unfit to live alone, per the social worker. Someone had to take control. Someone had to watch over her.

In Boston he'd been on the verge of promotion, next in line for the assistant chair, a quick stepping-stone to chairmanship itself. Quite a coup, given such a large and prestigious hospital. He'd given up the promotion and moved west.

He didn't want the position for the power. He wanted it for the patient. Healthcare was complicated. Healthcare was stressful. The sick or injured patient was already in a miserable place. He wanted to ease their burden with the best medical result and as painless and seamless an experience as possible.

Now here he was at a small Seattle hospital on the other side of the country. He was in line for chairmanship, with a mere formality meeting next week and the new position starting soon after when the current chair retired. But chairmanship of what? At Cascadia Medical Center, it meant a group of doctors younger than he was and a current chairman as old as his mother. Well, Boston or Seattle, he could still do right by the patient, excellent outcomes and excellent service, just on a lesser scale.

Except his healthiest patient had died.

To be honest, he hadn't moved solely to take care of his mother. He was not entirely altruistic. He had a secondary reason for returning. Self-preservation. Who knew what words might slip from his mother's mouth as her filter eroded?

"She was so young, Stinky."

He shut his eyes to erase the image of Chrissie's face, marred by petechiae. "Please don't call me that," he said. "Especially at work."

"Right, right," she said. She wouldn't remember, though she could recount everything else that went on in that hospital. And then some. She dreamed up torrid affairs between the director of Central Services and the head nurse or the transport tech and the radiology tech. Once she motioned Michael in close only to blurt out in front of Nurse Bob, "He just got out of jail!" None of this was true, except in her alcohol-addled brain.

"That Francine Mead was the one to run the code," she said. How did she know this lingo? "She's on the night team and yesterday she let slip that you had an evening out. She wouldn't say, but I gather you never called her back. That's not how I raised you."

An evening out? Was that what Francine called it, or was his mother being delicate? He'd never known her to beat around the bush, so it must be Francine who was discreet.

"Mom—"

"Give her a call, Mikey. She'd be good for you. You dated Janet in Boston. You can date Francine here."

"I'm not doing that again." Would she never get out of his life?

It was as if the past twenty-five years he'd lived on his own didn't count, had melted away, and he was sucked inseparably back into her chaotic existence.

He'd set up shop in a condominium with a peekaboo view of Lake Washington just down the hill from his childhood home, and he stopped in to see her before work and after, often so early she wasn't yet awake. At least he could make sure she had food, and he could discard liquor bottles that continued to materialize. At night she tried to wait up in her chair, an old horror movie playing on the television even if she was snoring, a nasally snorting sound that set his teeth on edge.

"I'm the one who called the nurses." His mother gripped his wrist with her frigid hand. Her large ring dug into his flesh. "About Chrissie. I'm the one who knew something was wrong."

"What? What happened?"

"They didn't come right away, of course. They never do. I rang my bell and called out to them, but it took a full five minutes. They thought I wanted dinner. I know I can't have dinner. I only asked them twice to be sure."

His mother made a harrumph noise. She was NPO, nothing by mouth, and would be until she stopped vomiting every time she swallowed. That didn't stop her pestering the nurses.

"Why did you ring your bell? What happened?" He extricated his arm from her clutch.

"What happened? What happened? I'll tell you if you stop interrupting. We watched a quiz show together last night, and we were going to watch it again tonight. I reminded her when I got back from my CT scan. Her dinner was there but she'd only had one small bite. She looked awful. Her color was all off. I asked her if I could have her Reuben, since she wasn't eating it. She laughed, but that's about all she could do. I think she was having leg pain. No offense to you and your surgery skills, Stinky. She was breathing fast, and her face was that pasty color you turn when I catch you in a lie, like when you told me Molly Esteban's parents knew she was spending the afternoon studying with you. You get that red spot on your cheek, too. She didn't have the red spot."

Molly Esteban? Tenth grade? Where did she come up with this stuff? "Mom, what happened when you rang your bell?"

"I rang my bell to tell them Chrissie didn't look good and she wasn't eating, probably time for more pain medicine. By the time they finally got here, all I could think about was that Reuben, and I asked if I could have it. So maybe it's my fault." At least his mom had the insight to hang her head sheepishly. "Because the nurse huffed out without so much as a glance at Chrissie. Our show came on, and I must have fallen asleep. It's the pain meds. They hit you at the darnedest times. The next thing I knew, Dr. Francine was pulling the sheet over her face."

It had been Michael himself who drew the sheet, so his mother had that part wrong. But how much did she have right?

# Chapter 7

Madge lay still with her eyes closed because, sleep or not, those darn nurses would be in at the crack of dawn with the whining, squeezing blood pressure machine and chipper morning greetings.

Poor Chrissie. She was chipper, too. Such a lovely young girl. Poor Stinky. He always took on the weight of the world, and something like this must weigh a ton. Not that he should feel responsible. Just because Chrissie was healthy and chasing her pet around one day and dead the next. What had he called it? A fat embolus? That could happen to anybody. Not his fault in the slightest.

What would happen to the pet? Frank. She'd better ask Stinky. No, not Stinky. He didn't like that name. Mikey. Madge would only call him Stinky when he wasn't around.

He was touchy these days, ever since that Mother's Day episode last year. At least he deigned to talk to her now.

She only wanted the best for him. That's all she'd ever wanted.

Well, not all. She wanted what every mother wanted. She wanted love. She wanted respect.

Madge squeezed her eyes tighter. *Don't think about that. Try to fall asleep.*

What time was it? Ten at night? How could anyone sleep in this place, with IV lines tugging every time you turned over and the noisy, crinkly mattress cover and nothing to eat? She wasn't hungry exactly, but her mouth wanted food, something to chew on, something to swallow. Like Chrissie's Reuben sandwich. Corned beef. Melty cheese. Rye bread. Maybe even sauerkraut. The thing smelled delicious. What had happened to it?

Madge peeked at the bed by the window, stripped to the green vinyl mattress. The bed table was bare, and the windowsill was bare. Not that Chrissie had much on there. Some patients had gobs of get well sentiment stuffed into every cranny of their tiny space. Cards, flowers, balloons, stuffed animals. The most Madge ever had was one card or a small bouquet from Stinky. Mikey. Chrissie only had a tiny box of chocolates and a red "Get Well" balloon brought by her friend Gloria, who visited for twenty minutes and left with a casual "see you around."

What ever happened to those chocolates? Madge loved chocolate. If Mikey wanted to bring her something useful, he could bring her chocolates. Much better than flowers. Flowers were okay, but flowers weren't chocolate.

Chrissie didn't have flowers because she didn't have family to send them. No parents. Car crash in a snowstorm a few years ago. No husband. Not even a boyfriend. No one to wonder why she died. If Mikey suddenly died after a simple leg surgery, Madge would want answers. This fat embolus thing sounded hokey.

What if Chrissie had died from something else?

If Madge could get the Reuben sandwich out of her mind, she could think more clearly. Hmm. The Reuben sandwich. Chrissie was fine when Madge went off to the CT scanner, which had taken forever due to a clogged IV and the need for the IV therapy team to put in a new one. When Madge returned, Chrissie was gray and breathless. And she'd eaten a bite of the Reuben.

Was something wrong with the Reuben? Bad meat? Spores in the sauerkraut? Good thing Madge hadn't gotten her hands on that Reuben. If one small bite could kill a healthy young woman, how much would it take to kill a sick old lady? Madge would have finished the whole sandwich off in no time.

Was the meat bad? Madge had always enjoyed the food at Cascadia Medical Center, much better than cooking for herself, but maybe she should be more cautious. Good thing she, Madge, was NPO.

Speaking of which, it was time for some of those lovely green swishy mouth swabs. She could also mention her concerns about the bad meat. Maybe it was botulism. Because it sure wasn't Stinky.

She shifted around to reach the alarm on her bedrail. Why did they put it in such an awkward place? Did they think she had arms like a gorilla? She oonched her left side down, then her right, but the bedcovers tangled around her and pinned her arms. She was out of breath, but the alarm was no closer.

The kitchen was contaminated, and she was too weak to sound the alarm, too trapped to tell.

"Nurse! Nurse!" Her voice was high and thin. Her door was almost closed. Her room was at the end of the hall. No one would hear her. "Nurse! Nurse!" It was useless. She was a feeble old lady, and she could die here and no one would know. Like Chrissie.

Wait a minute. One bite of bad meat would never kill someone. Madge knew from experience that bad meat could be eaten without problem most of the time. And food left on the counter might cause a little bowel embarrassment, but rarely more. You'd need something stronger. What if... What if...

"Nurse! Nurse!"

The door flew open, and Nurse Bob swooped in. He always moved so fast. He was tall, and his clogs lifted him higher, so he towered over her bed. He wore a scrubs jacket loose around his shoulders like a cape, and in the dark he looked like a vampire, gliding in and hovering over her bed ready for the bite. She was afraid of him anyway because he told Chrissie he liked to hunt rabbits and any man who killed fluffy bunnies was scary.

Why couldn't this be Nurse Mildred with her sensible white nurse's shoes and gentle manner? Or even new Nurse Evan, all "Let's fluff up our pillow so we sleep well tonight" and "Do we need help getting to the potty? Do we need to go wee wee?" Nurse Bob was not the sort to bother with pillows and wee wee.

"Miss McGillicuddy. What is it?" His voice was smooth, but then so was a vampire's.

She knew enough not to look at him. Vampires could hypnotize you with their eyes. She scrunched her shoulders to hide her neck.

"You're all tangled up," the cool vampire said. "Let's get your sheets straightened out."

Centuries of dust and darkness seeped from his cape, musty and dank. His breath was fetid, wafting down from a mouth reeking of the blood of the innocent.

He leaned in for the kill, his face next to hers.

Madge opened her mouth and screamed, not thin, not feeble, but a shriek so loud Nurse Mildred, Nurse Evan, and even Stinky appeared.

# Chapter 8

Michael recognized the scream at once. His mother's scream was fixed in his brain from the time she discovered a rat in the basement, from the time she caught a kitchen towel on fire broiling sausage, from the time she fell down the front porch stairs. The one time she hadn't screamed, when he was ten, was the worst time of all.

He raced down the hall, Evan right behind, and Mildred surprisingly passing them both. Evan flipped the light switch as they entered the room. His mother's screams ceased. She cowered in the bed with one arm stuck straight up in the air, her crooked fingers stretched out.

Bob stood safely out of reach, an angry scratch on his cheek.

Michael's mother shouted "Vampire!" She blathered on about a wooden stake and a cross.

How his mother loved her horror movies. The scarier, the better. Did she think she was in a horror movie now? Right here in the hospital? She'd accused a man of being a vampire, for God's sake.

The three nurses turned to Michael, and their faces wore the same expression.

Great. He'd seen these looks before, from each nurse and doctor who discovered Margaret McGillicuddy, infamous Margaret McGillicuddy, was his mother. When she was admitted the week before, few at the hospital knew. Their last names didn't match, as she went back to her maiden name after his father left. They didn't look alike, never had, and especially not now with her face so puffy and her nose red from drinking. But word traveled the seventh floor quickly, and one by one he'd seen these looks.

Everyone had a mother, and some were likely as bad as his, but most were hidden away safely in their own home, preferably in another state, not parading into your workplace with their craziness on full display.

She was invading his work life. With his mother in Chrissie's room, he'd spent less than five minutes at the bedside that morning. He'd reviewed the chart, noted the vitals, the labs, the notes. Everything was stable, everything was fine. No need to see someone so young and healthy before his other patients. He would see her later, last.

All because of his mother.

Would he have noticed something the nurses had not? So many people saw Chrissie, nurses, nurses' aides, the physical therapist, the pain doctor. Not one noted anything wrong. Would he have been any different?

Only his mother noticed, and she didn't have the brain power to let anyone know. His mother was the reason he had not seen Chrissie and his mother was the one who could have saved her.

That wasn't fair, he knew. If they had diagnosed it earlier, they could have given oxygen and put her on a vent, and she still might have died, given how severe this embolus must have been. At least they could have tried. Because of his mother, they hadn't had the chance.

Now she was shouting that Nurse Bob was a vampire.

Mildred adjusted her face and smiled sympathetically. She murmured about how difficult it was to be away from your own home, your own familiar surroundings. Evan was more direct and said "sundowning." Bob just gave Michael the look and flounced out.

"Maybe we'd like a pill to help us sleep," Evan said.

"Maybe I'll sit with you and make sure you feel safe until you're tired," Mildred said.

"The sandwich was poisoned," his mother said.

# Chapter 9

What could anyone reply to this? Michael laid his hand on his mother's arm in hopes she'd say no more.

Evan averted his eyes and exited quickly. Mildred clucked and adjusted the bedclothes and said, "Just yesterday you said the ice chips tasted like soap. The ice was fine, the sandwich was fine, you are fine. It's just scary being in the hospital."

His mother harrumphed, but Mildred was already gone.

Michael stayed longer, soothing his mother and assuring her about Chrissie and the fat embolism. A young woman was dead and nothing was to blame but bad luck. He explained it over and over, and each word conjured Chrissie's smiling face and her laughing prediction that she'd be back to kickboxing in no time.

Finally Madge fell asleep. Michael trudged downstairs to collect his jacket and briefcase from his office. The entire clinic area was empty, abandoned hours earlier when the afternoon clinic ended. It seemed like an eternity ago. Before Chrissie died.

A textured white envelope caught his eye, addressed to him and left on the front desk of the clinic. It looked like a card. A patient must have left it. He set his briefcase on the floor and ripped the envelope open.

"Michael Baker is not the good doctor you think he is."

Wait, what? Michael grabbed the envelope and read it

again. His name was on it all right, in big block letters. But it did not just say, "Michael Baker." It said, "Re: Michael Baker." And in smaller print above, that he just noticed now, it said, "To: Head of Surgery."

He lifted the paper and read on. His hand shook.

"I would not trust him with my health. You should not trust him with your patients."

That was it. No signature. The whole thing was typed. An anonymous letter about him. About his abilities.

Michael set the letter and the envelope back on the counter. He leaned against the cool surface with both arms. Was this about Chrissie? She had just died. Could this possibly be about Chrissie already?

A fat embolism was a tragedy, but her death was not because he was not a "good doctor." Certainly no one could think that. His logical mind knew this.

But whoever wrote this note clearly felt otherwise. *You should not trust him with your patients.* If not Chrissie, then what? He racked his brain but could not come up with any possible patient or situation that might have left someone unhappy. So much so that if this were a few weeks later, he would be the one receiving this letter as the Head of Surgery himself.

He straightened and glanced around the empty lobby. He placed the letter back in the envelope and smoothed the edge where he had ripped it.

Then he snatched it up and shoved it in his jacket pocket, picked up his briefcase, and strode out the door into the stairwell.

# Chapter 10

Finally home in his apartment, Michael read the note one more time.

"Michael Baker is not the good doctor you think he is. I would not trust him with my health. You should not trust him with your patients."

The whirring of the shredder filled his ears. He'd walked into his office and turned it on, so he must have made a decision, but not consciously, not that he would admit. He listened to the sound and fed the note in.

That night he dreamed about the whirring noise, but he woke to a silent apartment. He lay awake, his mind a swirl of Chrissie, unbelievably dead, the anonymous note, now in tiny pieces in his recycle bin, and, ever present these days, his mother.

Early the next morning, he ran into Bob the nurse in the parking garage. Michael nodded and murmured good morning. Bob pointedly turned away and walked several steps behind, then faced silently forward in the garage elevator. Michael couldn't blame him, after the vampire accusation.

On the hospital seventh floor later, a mere ten feet from Bob at the nurses' station, Michael studied an x-ray image on his computer screen. In the chairs around him, staff wrote notes at breakneck speed. Tony the big physical therapist sat so close his elbow bumped Michael's. On his other side,

Francine, who'd greeted him with a gentle smile, typed and answered pages at the same time. Michael's fingers moved slower.

How quickly had someone typed that note? His shredder had sliced up the words but not the fact that someone believed them.

What was the letter about?

Chrissie? He knew every intimate detail of her life, thanks to his mother. Chrissie had no family. Her parents died in a car crash. She had a friend named Gloria who visited once and very briefly. Chrissie had never married but turned down two suitors, and they were long out of her life. Not that Michael would use the word suitor, but that's how his mother presented it, so that's what he knew. Chrissie worked at the aquarium and ate lunch outside on the pier, rain or shine. She hated cooking but loved cookies and made a mean lemon bar. Michael loved lemon bars, so this detail was not lost on him.

Yes, he knew all about her. But no one his mother described seemed likely to write that letter, would even know that Chrissie was dead.

Someone at the hospital then? Someone at Chrissie's code?

Who had been in the room during Chrissie's code?

Francine here. Tony the physical therapist, too, who heard the overhead announcement and was just down the hall. He'd spelled Michael with the chest compressions. Two nurses, including Bob, now huddled at the nurses' station. Were they whispering about him? The anesthesiologist and the anesthesiology resident. The medical resident. Who hadn't been at the code?

This was ridiculous. None of these people could think he was a bad doctor. Chrissie had died of an unfortunate, unpredictable, freak complication.

Yet someone clearly believed otherwise.

Francine tapped the keyboard with finality and pushed her chair back. She looked exactly the same as she had the night before, crisp white shirt, short brown hair neatly combed, lipstick perfect. She had worked all night and looked as fresh as if she were just beginning. Michael hadn't even shaved.

"How are you doing?" Francine's voice was low. "Rough night?"

Was it that obvious? Did she have to point it out?

God, he was irritable. He knew she was only concerned. Francine didn't have a mean bone in her body.

"Fine, thanks for asking," he said.

"Your mom did well, slept all night, no problems."

Did Francine know about the vampire incident? The sandwich? Maybe not. Michael himself never knew about his mother's nighttime shenanigans unless the head nurse took him aside the next day.

He didn't want to talk. "Thanks." He turned back to the computer.

Francine got the message and didn't press further. She stood and left. Evan, who was newer to Cascadia than Michael and just out of nursing school, sidled over and hovered near her vacated seat.

Evan had been at the code. Could he have written the note? Michael doubted it.

On Evan's first day at the hospital Michael found him wandering in the maze of short hallways where the old hospital building and the new one connected. He was tall and thin but managed to pick scrubs way too short, and his bare ankles showed above his low socks and black street shoes.

"Easy to get lost here," Michael said. "Can I point you in the right direction?"

"I'm looking for the...ah...the..."

"The bathroom?" Michael guessed. Evan blushed and nodded. "The staff bathroom is around the next corner."

Not long after, Michael heard him discussing bowel movement consistencies with a patient as if it were the most natural thing in the world. Go figure.

On Evan's second day, Michael led him to the floor's scrub supply closet and pointed out the tall sizes, stored paradoxically on the bottom shelf. Now Evan wore scrubs that fit and also sneakers on his feet.

Michael hoped their relationship was one of mutual respect. Not one with behind-the-back accusations.

Evan stood above him now, silent but clearly uneasy. "Do you need something?" Michael asked. The guy was practically wringing his hands. Was this something about the note?

Evan motioned him away so they were out of earshot of the others. The long computer desks sat in a U shape behind the nurses' station, with three computers to a desk and fat chairs on wheels. Each chair was occupied this morning, and the area was crowded. Evan was nothing if not discreet.

"I don't want to bother you, Dr. Baker, but your mom's IV came out and she's refusing another. Do you think you could talk her into it?"

Michael exhaled loudly. This wasn't about the note. It was about his mother.

So Michael strode down the hall, Evan at his heels, to tell his mother to get the damned IV. In the room, Mildred straightened and brushed her hands together. "All done," she said.

His mother grinned. "I heard Nurse Mildred in the hall, and I asked if she could do it. You know how hard my veins are, Mikey, and Nurse Evan just doesn't have the magic touch. He poked me three times last time."

Poor Evan blushed and backed out, his face an embarrassed mess. Michael grimaced at his mother, thanked Mildred for her expertise, and chased down Evan to say he was sorry his mother was so difficult.

"It's okay." Evan's cheeks were still red. "We tend to get feisty in the morning."

Feisty was an understatement. His mother was back to her normal self, as normal as she could be. Her normal ornery, rude, self-absorbed self.

That wasn't kind. She was sick, so of course she wasn't at her best. Michael smiled. Her best wasn't too far from this.

Michael sat back at the computer, but his notes were slow going. Evan's stricken expression floated in his mind. He signed a note and glanced at his watch.

Shoot. Only ten minutes before clinic. He wasn't done, but there was no way around it. He'd have to see his mother for her morning visit and finish his notes between clinic patients. The quick IV stop didn't count. She wanted chitchat, she wanted him to hear her complaints, her aches. She wanted company, and it didn't matter that he was at work. If he didn't go now, she was likely to ask Evan to page him. She'd done it before. Evan hadn't learned to stand up to her yet.

Michael stepped from the bright hallway with its gleaming linoleum floors into the shadows of her room. Despite the early hour, the morning light was blocked by a building across the street. All the rooms on this end of the hospital were dark, but strong fluorescent bulbs overhead solved the problem. His mother hated the lights. They hurt her eyes and buzzed a noise only she could hear. As she loudly proclaimed to anyone who presumed to turn them on. Maybe his mother was the vampire.

He braced himself and breathed deeply, gagging on her heavy perfume. Even in the dim light, the lipstick on her teeth was noticeable. At least most of it was on her lips this morning and not the corner of her mouth or her cheek.

He asked if she remembered the night before, being afraid of a vampire. She scoffed and said, "There are no vampires in Seattle."

"True enough," was all he could manage.

"Besides, if a nurse wanted blood, he could steal it from the lab. He wouldn't need me." She said this with a straight face. Her sense of humor was so dry he couldn't tell if this was a joke or not, especially since she continued with a discussion of whether it would be better to be bitten by a vampire or a werewolf.

Her nausea was improving, and the day doctor, Hal Dexter, had told him she might be eating in the next few days. Michael kept this to himself. Michael and Hal had grown up together in Seattle, and his mother liked him and trusted him. But the nurses would never forgive Michael if his mom badgered them about "when, when, when?" The head nurse had warned him that his mother rang her buzzer far more than any other patient, and that they didn't have the staffing to be at her beck and call. She recommended he ask a friend to come sit with her. His mother had long ago burned through her friends.

"Hal says you're doing well," he said.

"Do you think he still plays the drums? Remember that afro, bouncing away? It's so short now. I liked it long. Should I tell him?" Madge said.

Hal played drums in the high school jazz band, and Michael played sax. Hal never gave Michael the look about his mother because Hal already knew. Madge had once shown up to a band concert drunk and loud, and the whole performance halted when she screamed at her seatmate and had to be escorted out. Another time, crying and wobbly, she pulled Michael off the basketball court down the street, and Hal helped him hold her up until she vomited in the gutter and he sent Hal away.

"It's great you get to work together. In Seattle. Dr. Hal stayed right here, college, medical school, residency, job. Right here, Stinky."

His mother trotted out this line about Hal every time his name came up. It was not lost on her that the school Michael chose was not the University of Washington, or any school in Washington, Oregon, or California, but one on the East Coast, across the entire country. Depending on her mood, she might add, "First chance you get, and you hightail it out of here. Some sort of thanks I get."

She was right. He stayed East for college, medical school, residency, work. All by choice. For twenty-five years he'd managed to stay away. Until now.

Hal had wanted to go away, too, Michael knew. The two of them vied against each other for a locally sponsored college scholarship. Michael was the lucky winner. Hal never mentioned it, but he went to the University of Washington and not his first choice, Penn, because of cost. Then med school and residency, all at UW.

Hal was close to his mother in high school, but who wouldn't be? Hal's mom was lovely, had run the band's money-making citrus drive and chaperoned overnight trips, all without one embarrassing peep out of her. Michael should be so fortunate.

When he and Hal played pickup basketball on Thursday nights, Hal had the grace to avoid the subject of mothers. Last week he and Hal laughed about Hal's latest disastrous attempt to meet a man who wanted a commitment, not a fling.

"Does Dr. Hal date anyone?" His mother was off and running. "Do I know them? Do you think he'll ever get married? I thought you and Janet would get married, but maybe you and Dr. Hal could find nice women here. Or men. Doesn't Hal like men? Maybe if he grew his hair out again. He looked better with the afro. What do you think, Mikey?"

Mikey. He hated that name almost as much as Stinky. He'd always be four to his mother.

"Maybe. Mom, I have to go to clinic." He was already late.

"I have to tell you something about Chrissie."

He glanced involuntarily at the empty bed. Chrissie had lain there just yesterday.

Was this going to be about the sandwich again?

"Mikey, Chrissie has a pet at home. A cat, I think, because she said he had a beautiful tail but he didn't like anyone petting it. She told me he had enough food to last three or four days." His mom's voice sped up. "Her friend, Gloria, doesn't like him, maybe she's allergic or something, so Chrissie said she hoped she'd be home in time. You have to save Frank, Mikey. You can watch him until someone else turns up."

He'd wondered about Frank, too, in the sleepless night he'd just had. He imagined Chrissie and her life before she leaned too far and broke her leg. The cat was inadvertently responsible for her death. Without the fracture, there would be no fat embolus. Much easier for Frank to be responsible than Michael.

But even last night, in that long, dark, sleepless night, Michael knew he, the attending physician and no one else, was the last stop.

Whoever wrote that note thought so, too.

# Chapter 11

Michael had to save Frank, as his mother said. He looked up Chrissie's address in her records. Only a few blocks from his own apartment. Hopefully the cat could wait until the end of the day.

It was later than he'd hoped, but he stopped at Chrissie's on his way home and rang the bell for the building manager.

"I'm a friend of Chrissie's," he fibbed, feeling the blood leave his face, "and I've come to collect her cat."

"Damn shame, what happened." The manager was short and stout and wore a denim shirt too tight across the chest. "Don't trust hospitals, never have, and this just goes to prove it. Her friend called this morning to tell me. Said she'd try to hunt up a great aunt or something to come clear her stuff. But there's no pet. Building doesn't allow it."

Michael actually knew this. Chrissie told him that's why she was so desperate to see where Frank was when he escaped. Then, lying one balcony below with her leg askew, she watched him slip back onto her own balcony. Frank was safe and she was not, and all she could do was wait for someone to find her.

"Would you mind if I looked?"

"Suit yourself. I have to come with you, of course."

They trooped upstairs and the manager opened the door. The radio was on, with soft music echoing, making the dark, empty apartment seem emptier.

A flash streaked across the room as the lights went on. "Huh," the manager said. "I'll be damned. She does have a cat."

Did, thought Michael. She did have a cat, and now that cat was his.

Michael followed the streak to the bedroom, noting how similar Chrissie's apartment was to his. Not in size—her rooms were much smaller and her kitchen was a wall of her living room. Not in style—his furniture was modern and hers a hodgepodge of hand-me-downs. But the feel was the same, neat and tidy without excess stuff, no shoes of a roommate on the floor to trip over, no leftover dishes from a dinner for two. A single picture of her parents on the table next to the couch, a picture of the three of them on her bedside table, no other pictures, no boyfriend with an arm around her, no gaggle of women friends preening for the camera. The place felt barren. No one home but Chrissie. Now not even that.

A loaf of bread waited on the kitchen counter. Chrissie would never eat that. An open book lay face down on one side of the bed. Chrissie would never know the ending. A book of crosswords sat on the desk with a pencil marking the place she'd left off. Chrissie would never finish those.

*Stop,* he told himself. *You are not responsible. Now find the cat. That's how you can help.*

The bedroom appeared empty. The closet door was ajar. He eased it further, slowly, so as not to scare the poor thing.

Two eyes shined in the light from the bedroom. Michael's own eyes adjusted, and he made out a ghastly head twitching side to side and a monstrous body, ready to pounce. A massive black and white creature stared at him, then a long tail whipped through the air, narrowly missing Michael's head. The monster disappeared into the shadows of the closet.

Michael's heart raced. Chrissie did not have a cat. For all the world, Frank looked to be a miniature Tyrannosaurus rex.

"You find him?" the manager called from the doorway.

"I found him," Michael said.

"Good thing you came. Cat can't survive alone. You're going to take him with you, right? 'Til the great aunt shows?"

Michael inched the door open. The closet was large but filled with a glass and plastic cage. A screen top leaned next to it. A shelf above held bottles, one labeled "Calcium for Reptiles."

Frank was an enormous lizard. And was perched on the shelf next to the vitamin bottles, eye to eye with Michael.

The landlord took one look and fled. "You're on your own. I'm not touching him. We don't even allow cats. What the hell is this thing? Ring the buzzer when you leave and I'll lock up."

Getting Frank home was a logistical nightmare. Not the lizard himself, who was docile enough, after some soft words and gentle touching, to let Michael lift him into what had to be a carrying case. Michael loaded the vitamins, a harness, a leash, two heating lights, and a bag of substrate mulch for the cage into the trunk of the car. Wrestling the cage was another matter, unhinging it and folding the gigantic thing. Good thing Michael had a spare bedroom, currently devoid of all furnishings except a black metal desk, a project waiting for another time.

A black metal desk and a paper shredder. His fingers tightened on the steering wheel, remembering the note.

In Michael's apartment, Frank remained in the carrying case. Michael felt for him. This must be quite a shock—a new person, a new place. "You'll come out when you're ready." The cage itself would take some time to set up anyway. And it would take up a good chunk of the room.

"I'm still here, Frank." Michael crossed to his bedroom and changed out of his work clothes, tossing his shirt and tie on the chair and kicking his shoes into the closet. He passed the case on the way to the kitchen. The lizard was still inside.

Michael's apartment was modern and sleek, with thick white carpeting, a black leather sofa, a painting with splashes of red, and a low, black-edged glass coffee table that matched the black-edged glass dining table. He had no clutter, no mess. Just like Chrissie. It was the opposite of his mother's house, with her furniture from fifty years earlier and every flat surface brimming with photos or papers or books. Her carpet was multicolored but didn't hide the constant spills.

Of course, who knew what his place would look like in a week, with a huge lizard prowling around. Probably exactly the same as it did now, given Chrissie's neat apartment.

If Frank ever materialized, that was. Michael had never had a reptile, but his neighbor in med school had, a tegu lizard, and Michael was certain Frank was a tegu. Michael had watched his neighbor handle his and feed him. It wasn't rocket science, or even hip replacement. Michael could figure this out. Give Frank time.

Michael sizzled bacon in the skillet, and the crackling and the salty aroma filled the kitchen. He set the dining table, one glass, one napkin, one knife. One pretty lonely existence, his mother would say.

It had been this way for more than a year now, and he was used to it. If the tegu didn't join him, the table faced a window with a partial view of the lake, and tonight's sailboat races would be entertainment enough. The white-sailed boats were already gathering, crisp and bright against the dark blue water.

If his schedule ever calmed down at the hospital, he might take up sailing again. Growing up in Seattle, sailing lessons on Lake Washington with the Parks and Rec had been part of his summers. It helped that Molly Esteban took lessons, too. They'd had a lot of fun in those little dinghies.

There was no sign of Frank. "I'm quite the cook, you know," Michael called on his way to the kitchen. "Let me razzle dazzle you. I don't want to oversell it, since this is just a BLT, but wait until you taste the secret sauce."

Michael washed lettuce and sliced a tomato, humming mindlessly. He turned to pop bread into the toaster and tripped. Frank lay at his feet, solid as a rock. The bread flew in the air, and Michael slammed his wrist on the counter grabbing for support. He swore, then clamped his lips tight so he didn't scare Frank. Too late. The lizard sprinted away, running on two feet with his mouth open. So much for giving him time.

Frank stayed hidden, and Michael carried the BLT to the dining room. Chrissie's apartment had the radio left on, so on a hunch, Michael hummed again, a tune that had percolated in his mind since his return to Seattle. The lizard's head poked around the doorway, his long tongue flicking in and out. Then Frank scurried into the room and out of sight under the table. He was so fast, Michael hadn't had a good look at him yet.

That was okay. He and Frank had all the time in the world. No one else would come for the tegu lizard.

The bacon smelled wonderful. Would a lizard like bacon? Would it make him sick? Maybe lettuce? Michael had better read up.

Frank slithered out, and Michael gulped. Frank was gargantuan, three and a half feet at least from head to the end of his powerful-looking tail. He was striped black and yellow, and the yellow bands were speckled. His black eyes regarded Michael, unblinking, calm. From the side, the natural curve of his mouth looked like a human smile.

Michael tentatively rested a few fingers on Frank's head. The lizard pushed up against them until Michael's whole hand covered his crown.

Michael had always wanted a dog. It was out of the question when he was a kid. And a dog would never work with his long hours as a doctor. But a companion would be nice.

Frank wasn't a dog, but...

Frank had no one. And, frankly, neither did Michael.

"Are you hungry, Frank?" Michael lifted his hand and tore a piece of bacon from the BLT, but the lizard was not interested.

"All the more for me," Michael told him. "I'll have to figure out what Chrissie fed you. Maybe not the same food she ate."

The sandwich was halfway to Michael's mouth. He dropped it abruptly. A tomato slice plopped onto the table.

His mother said Chrissie's sandwich was poisoned. Was there anything to that?

# Chapter 12

The next morning, Michael rounded on his least favorite patient first. Reginald Stark. Michael would be relieved to see him go. The hospital staff, too. Hopefully he'd be discharged soon. Mr. Stark yelled at his wife and was rude to the nurses. "He had the nerve to say I was too old to be a nurse and he wanted someone with a shorter skirt," Mildred said. "I sent in Bob." Mr. Stark called the nurses' aides "darling" and the head nurse "honey." The staff complained about him as much as they complained about Michael's mother.

The guy was a seventy-three-year-old professor emeritus who'd had a new knee the week before. In clinic, Michael had heard his story. He was in the military and went to school on the GI bill. He'd sat ramrod straight, his sparse hair shaved close, his skin leathery from cigarettes, his voice a gruff bark. "Those pussy students didn't think I belonged there. Well, I showed them." He became a professor of geography at a small midwestern college and retired to Seattle to be near his son.

He should have been out of the hospital in no time, but he stayed on because his cardiac rhythm changed postop. He was set to go home three days ago when, smoker with bad lungs that he was, he developed pneumonia. Untreated, a pneumonia could kill a man like him. But he'd turned around quickly on antibiotics. Michael would switch him from IV to oral today, and the guy would be home in no time.

Michael reviewed Mr. Stark's early morning vital signs. A slight fever—that was unusual. His heart rate was up. Not much, but higher than his norm. The night nurse noted that his cough was worse.

"Mr. Stark. How are you?"

The man was pitched forward in bed holding both handrails. He tilted his head up but didn't answer. He couldn't answer. He was breathing too hard.

"Mr. Stark?" Michael whipped out his stethoscope. The noises on the side with the pneumonia were ominous. Michael felt Reginald Stark's pulse. It was racing.

Michael ran to the door. Nurse Bob was just leaving the room next door, pushing the vitals monitor cart in front of him. Of course it would have to be him.

"Bob! In here!"

Mr. Stark's blood pressure was low. Dangerously low. His oxygen saturation, too.

"Looks like septic shock. Get fluids," Michael said. "I'll start oxygen."

The mask and tubing were in a plastic bag next to the bed. Michael ripped it open and twisted the tubing onto the wall oxygen.

"Mr. Stark, I'm going to put this oxygen mask on."

Mr. Stark's eyes were wild. He shook his head back and forth. He might not be mentating, not thinking well due to lack of blood and oxygen to the brain. Michael got the mask on and tightened the straps. "You'll feel better," he said.

Mr. Stark looked like he was about to die. His skin was gray. His hands were blue, clamped onto the bedrails, and ice cold when Michael took his pulse. With each breath his intercostal muscles sucked inward, retracting due to the pneumonia. He wouldn't last long this way.

The man looked so good yesterday. He was supposed to go home soon. What happened?

# Chapter 13

Madge hadn't seen Mikey yet, but Dr. Hal was just outside her door leading rounds. She leaned forward in bed to eavesdrop. They were talking about her, after all. Nothing wrong with listening in.

Madge's ears were sharp still, and she strained to hear his spiel, especially when she heard the words "necrotic pancreatitis." She knew what necrotic pancreatitis was, the bad kind, with inflammation that could last a while and push on her stomach and make it hard to eat. What she wanted to know was, was it getting better or not? Could she eat or not?

Dr. Hal droned on and on. Get to the point. Enough about fluid in and fluid out, I's and O's to the nurses as they recorded every cc from her catheter. Nurse Mildred's voice was too soft for even Madge's keen ears. They'd be in the room soon enough, but Madge wanted to know now. Could. She. Eat?

She heard the unmistakable clogs of Nurse Bob, in a rush as always. He wasn't really a vampire, she understood that now in the light of day, but sometimes her mind got away from her. She couldn't always trust her own brain. But even if Bob wasn't a vampire, there was something disquieting about him that bore watching.

Bob said something to the team, but Madge missed it as she shifted and her hermetically sealed mattress rustled. Then her whole team was gone, clamoring after Bob to a room closer to the nurses' station. They didn't return until midday, and by then there was no talk of lunch, merely a quick in and out and "please don't talk while I listen to your lungs." Nurse Mildred explained that one of the other patients wasn't doing well, and Dr. Hal had spent all morning giving fluid resuscitation and transferring him to the ICU.

This was nothing new. Madge had been around the base-ball diamond enough to know that one sick patient could suck an entire day out of a team. She'd been that patient, many a time. Madge knew about fluid resuscitation, too, because she'd had it herself once with a bad case of pancreatitis causing low blood pressure.

Sit back and wait, that's what being in the hospital was all about. She inhaled, taking in the hospital scents of hand sanitizer and disinfectant wipes. It didn't bother her.

She sniffed again. Hmm. She herself was a little fragrant. A bath by the nurse in a bed was nothing like a real shower. She retrieved her perfume from her over-the-bed table and gave herself a spritz. Much better.

Before Stinky came home, she truly enjoyed being in the hospital, with roommates to talk to, nurses to coddle her, and doctors to befuddle. She could always ask a pertinent question or predict their diagnosis, thanks to multiple hospitalizations, a son who was a doctor, and a modicum of memory.

"It's pancreatitis," she could say when she arrived in the ED. "My phlegmon's infected," she predicted if she spiked a temperature, though she knew this was an old-fashioned term and they preferred "acute necrotic collection." Too much of a mouthful for her.

Now that Stinky was home, being in the hospital was even better. She saw him regularly, and she could throw his name around if the nurse was abrupt or the transport too slow. Or if she just wanted to bask in his glow. Everybody knew him.

"He's the best," Mildred said. "He saw me shaking out my hand and brought me a wrist brace and recommended a new keyboard. Who else would think to do that?"

"He made Doctor of the Quarter, and he's brand new here," Dr. Francine gushed. Madge had seen Francine's own picture on the wall last year, but pride in your doctor and pride in your son were two different things entirely. Now Madge's heart jumped when she passed through the lobby, seeing Mikey's handsome face smiling with those expensive braces-straightened teeth and that blond hair laying perfectly as if she hadn't fussed over it needlessly when he was a boy, fretting that his thick hair would always stick up. And his blue eyes. As deep as the day he was born, never turning brown like hers, with a few dignified crinkly lines to show his age and wisdom.

"He'll bring a new energy to the department once he takes over." This from a surgical colleague, a doctor named Katherine Pierce, so quite a compliment.

Yes, everybody knew him, and everybody loved him.

But he wasn't here now. Madge was alone. Sitting back and waiting in the hospital would be easier if they gave her a new roomie. The bed had been empty since Chrissie two nights before. Or if they had better television. At home her favorite show was *Creature Friday*, now shown daily on channel 15 and recorded on her high-tech television recording system. She'd been recording for twenty years and hadn't missed a *Creature Friday* since. She skipped the unrealistic giant slimy creature episodes, but she'd watch anything else. Monster, zombie, vampire, alien, unassuming man next door turned psycho killer. All of it. On her own TV she could watch whenever she wanted. Here she had to wait until three p.m. and hope they didn't whisk her away right as the spooky music started. Today's show was about ghosts. She loved a good ghost story.

Did hospitals have ghosts? Did the souls of those who died live on in the walls and halls? Or only in the minds of the nurses and the doctors and all who tried to help?

Was Chrissie's spirit in the room even now? Would her death haunt Madge's son forever?

Not if Madge could help it.

# Chapter 14

Michael raced to the OR once Hal took over the transfer of Reginald Stark to the ICU. Michael's morning cases had piled up, and he worked through lunch due to the late start and finished the morning in the afternoon. The surgeon with the afternoon cases would have to work into the evening now. Michael stopped to apologize before heading up to the ICU.

Reginald Stark's wife was in the ICU waiting room with a younger woman and a crying child. The two women held hands. Michael would stop and speak with them after he saw Mr. Stark.

Michael sat at a corner computer to read the chart before going into the room. His stomach tightened with each line he read. Mr. Stark was on pressors now to support his low blood pressure. He was on high-flow oxygen and might need to be intubated, which could easily signal the end for a man with his lungs.

What had happened? The guy was fine yesterday and then crashed and burned over the course of the early morning. His pneumonia should have been getting better, not worse.

Michael reviewed the current medication records. Mr. Stark was on the same antibiotic Michael had started three days earlier.

Wait. Why did the ICU order say "start" antibiotic? The order should already have been there. Michael stared at the medication record. Why wasn't the antibiotic checked as having been given this morning? Or the day before, not one of the doses? That antibiotic was the one thing keeping the deadly pneumonia in check.

Had the nurse forgotten to give it? Michael's heart pounded as he scrolled through the medication records. This would be a critical error. Possibly a fatal error.

Evan had been the nurse yesterday. Evan was new. *Please don't let Evan have made a mistake.* Michael turned to Evan's note.

"Antibiotic stopped by MD." What? What had Evan written?

Michael hit the electronic orders record. He blinked his eyes. His mind went dark for an instant.

The record showed an order to stop the antibiotics. Yesterday morning. A day and a half after they were started.

The order was written by him.

# Chapter 15

At five minutes to three Madge punched the TV remote for *Creature Friday*. She settled back on two pillows, one stiff and plasticky, one plump and soft, courtesy of her own bed at home. How she could prop up for her show without two pillows, she did not know. The bed was supposedly adjustable, but each time she tried it, the overhead lights flared on or her feet ended up higher than her head. Those buttons on the rail were just too complicated.

Her back hurt and she squiggled to the left and squiggled to the right. It wasn't the bed's fault, a fluffy marshmallow affair with air pockets that inflated and deflated to keep her comfy. It was her back, old and stiff and off kilter since her last fall on the steps. As soon as her program started, she wouldn't be thinking about her back anymore. She'd be immersed in the phantom only the child could see.

So many commercials! She pressed mute to stop the blaring horn in an ad about homeowners' insurance while keeping her eyes on the screen so she wouldn't miss the intro.

"Hello, how are you feeling?"

Drat! Stinky. Why was he here in the middle of the day?

"One of my patients took a turn for the worse, so I'm just one floor up in the ICU. Thought I'd pop by."

Oh, no. Was that patient who decompensated Stinky's patient?

He looked awful, face as gray as Chrissie's. Well, not that bad. But none of his usual rosy tones. He looked tired, too, with dark circles under his beautiful blue eyes. He blocked her view of the television, and she craned her neck to see if the show had begun.

He dropped into the seat by the bed. He never did that. He always stood, ready for a quick getaway, busy or just wanting out. Her show had started, but she reluctantly hit power and the screen went dark. So much for her ghost show. Stinky needed her.

"I wrote the antibiotics," he said. "It's clear as day in the chart three days ago. Then I canceled them. I don't remember that. Why would I cancel the antibiotics?"

He didn't say any more. HIPPA, he said. But he said enough for her to gather a patient was in trouble and Stinky felt responsible. Again.

# Chapter 16

Michael sat at the nurses' station, bustling with afternoon change-of-shift activity. He heard nothing. All he could think of was Reginald Stark. What the hell had happened?

He'd found himself in his mother's room before he even thought about it. As if she could give him advice. That's how out of sorts he was.

Hal slipped into the seat next to him. "Stark's pneumonia antibiotics were stopped. That's why he went septic." Hal knew exactly who stopped them. Anyone looking at the chart would know.

"I know. I saw."

Hal glanced around the busy room, then leaned in close.

"Do you know what happened? Maybe you intended to change them and got distracted? You know, stop that one and start a different one, but you never wrote the second order?"

"Maybe," Michael said.

"Or maybe you were in the wrong patient's chart?" Hal's deep brown eyes held Michael's. This was a serious error, and they both knew it. A man could die.

"Call me if you need me," Hal said and was gone.

Hal was full of ideas about what happened. The problem was, none of them were right.

Michael just couldn't remember what was. He couldn't remember anything about the antibiotics at all, once he started them. He stared at the screen, at his unfathomable order on the computer.

He had never presented a case at Cascadia's M & M, and this week he had two for the Friday conference. Chrissie Johnson was bad enough, a young patient, completely healthy, now dead. But doctors could understand a fat embolus. A fluke. Now Reginald Stark, an emeritus professor, in the ICU, septic and hypotensive because his pneumonia antibiotics were stopped. By Michael.

Had Michael been distracted? That's what Hal asked. Hal knew about Chrissie. She died the night before the discontinuation order was written. Had he been distracted by Chrissie?

Hal had no idea about the anonymous note. The words cut into Michael, sharper now because they held some truth. *You should not trust him with your patients.* The note came right after Chrissie, the night before the order was written. Had he been distracted by the note?

"Mikey! Hi!" His head jerked. His mother, pink frilly nightgown and all, stepped carefully down the hall supported around the waist by a strap held by one of the physical therapists, Don. The guy was small but brawny and easily maneuvered the canvas strap with one hand and the IV pole and the Foley catheter bag with the other. He had the good sense to say, "Miss McGillicuddy, let's turn around here and get you back to your room."

His mother shuffled in a half circle, waving energetically. Michael lifted his hand, then turned back to the computer.

There it was, in clear black font in the record, mid-afternoon three days ago, his order to start the antibiotic, written within an hour of the x-ray report showing the infiltrate. Then inexplicably, yesterday morning, the discontinued order. Signed electronically by him, on his account, under his login information.

He'd done this racing to finish his notes on the ward or during his morning clinic, after he'd gone back into that room and seen his mother and the empty bed next to her, and he couldn't remember anything about it.

He'd been late to clinic yesterday, but his medical office assistant, Robin, covered for him, telling his patients he was delayed on the wards and he'd be there as soon as he could. Robin and the other medical assistants didn't know anything about his mother, and Michael intended to keep it that way. The hospital and the clinic buildings were attached, but the two realms were separate. The clinic staff—the medical office assistants and the clinic nurses—never ventured to the hospital and thankfully would never know about his mother. Only the doctors.

When he'd arrived at clinic, God knows how late, Robin was sitting in a room with a new patient, eighty-two-year-old Evelyn West, who was referred for total knee replacement. She was completely different in all ways from Mr. Stark and his new knee upstairs.

"Call me Evelyn," she said. "Makes me feel young. Mrs. West seems so old."

She was tiny, a white-haired wisp of a woman, and Robin was middle-aged, dark haired, and large. She towered over Evelyn like a Pacific Northwest old-growth giant tree. But her hands cupped Evelyn's, and the two of them were having a high old time, laughing about Evelyn's great-granddaughter who played volleyball and was almost as tall as Robin and wanted to be president one day.

"I wanted to be president one day," Robin said. "I married young instead. That didn't last long."

"I married young, too," said Evelyn West. "It lasted fifty years."

Despite this lovely first patient, the clinic was rushed and chaotic. Thanks to his mother and her concerns about vampires, werewolves, Hal Dexter's hair, Evan's prowess with an IV, and Chrissie's Frank.

Had he been distracted yesterday? Yes.

Had he inadvertently stopped the antibiotic? He couldn't remember.

# Chapter 17

The nurses' station was quieter now. Michael hadn't moved.

A soft bell chimed overhead. The baby bell. The social worker at the computer next to his paused and smiled. When a baby was born, the bell chimed, alerting hospital workers to this joyous event. In Boston, he'd loved the baby bell.

In Boston, he'd loved Janet.

They'd broken up one year and four months ago. Not that he was counting. She was his main scrub nurse in the OR, a cliché he told himself didn't apply to them. Two young people in love. Never mind that she was ten years his junior. They'd worked together forever, her shifts corresponding exactly to his OR days. It was inevitable, certainly, that they would end up together, with her bubbly personality, her winning smile, and that way she cocked her head when he spoke and laughed with a low chuckle at his jokes. When he spied her at a bookstore event for his favorite author, he asked her out for coffee. They talked for hours, until it was plain that they were now a couple.

She said she'd known he was the man for her since the day he crafted a splint for the teddy bear of a three-year-old whose mother had a broken arm. Then he brushed a spider to the side of her doorstep so it wouldn't get stepped on, and that won her heart. She worked around blood all day but abhorred violence.

She loved to laugh and she loved to tease. She teased him

when he sneezed three times and she teased him that he hated the smell of fried chicken. Nonetheless, she gave up eating it herself because it bothered him so. She even teased him about his mother. More importantly, she tolerated his mother.

If he and Janet were near when the baby bell rang, they'd exchange meaningful glances. Someday, someday, his glance meant. Now the bell was just another noisy intrusion on his concentration. A sad intrusion.

*Get your head together. Stop thinking about Janet.* Talk about distraction. He'd vowed never to date at work again, and he'd stuck to it.

Even after the breakup, with all that angst and emotion, his job was his job. Janet was in one compartment and his job in another. His work had never suffered.

Where was the compartment for a mother?

Doctors were pros at compartmentalization, and so was he. At least he was until now. Why was being home in Seattle so hard?

He knew why. His mother and his past were tied together, pushing up from the depths of his brain and demanding attention. He'd have to pound it all back down, at least at work.

His pager vibrated. What now?

It was Phil Perkins, the chair of the Surgery Department. The anonymous note had been meant for him.

"I'm in my office. Come see me." This was a summons. Michael had seen Perkins only yesterday, during the weekly meeting they started when Michael was onboarding and continued in anticipation of the upcoming chairmanship transition and Phil's retirement. Michael had sat there nervously, thinking about the note he had seized. Phil, oblivious, had clapped him on the back and said, "Heard about the Johnson case. Hell of a thing. Hell of a thing. Don't let it get to you."

Today, in Phil Perkins' bright corner office with a view of

blue Puget Sound from his large windows, Michael detected a shift in tone. Phil's back was to him in his swivel chair as he leaned over a file cabinet. Flat cardboard boxes lay against the wall, waiting for Phil to fill with his life's work. Books, diplomas, accolades, awards. Michael glanced at the sparkling water out the window, with the snow-covered Olympic Mountains framing the background and a large white and green ferry sailing into view. He thought of his windowless office down the hall. This would be a step up.

In Boston he would have ascended to the top floor, with a view of the city, but more importantly, a seat at the table of the chosen ones, on a trajectory that could only lead up, first assistant chair with the understanding of a rapid succession to chairman of the department, then chief of staff, then chief medical officer, then who knew? The current CEO had taken that exact route. Michael had worked toward this for years, and more to the point, he would be good at the job, dedicated, determined, creative. He could make the lives of the patients better, make their experience with the hospital better. He had the time and the energy. He was ready.

Here in Seattle, when he became chairman of surgery in less than a month, he would move down the hall to this larger office with a window. And that's it. Cascadia's chief of staff was young and energetic herself, and it was no wonder she'd been appointed to this role. Michael knew her from Boston, and she'd been just as effective there. Cascadia's chief medical officer was the brother-in-law of the CEO. Here in Seattle, Michael was going nowhere.

The department chair in this small place was in charge of all the surgeons, every type, orthopedics like him but also general surgery, thoracic, urology, vascular, everything. In a bigger hospital, department chair would be a major accomplishment. Not here. At Cascadia, he'd be Phil Perkins, stuck in the same position for twenty years.

Perkins finally swung around, a tight smile on his face. "Sit, sit." He indicated one of the soft leather wing chairs in front of the desk. He played with the end of his pen. Click, click. Click, click.

This wasn't good. Michael had heard this pen clicking before, each time presaging some unhappy event. Click, click. *Our department didn't make budget last quarter and Continuing Medical Education funds are frozen until further notice.* Click, click. *Mick the scrub nurse made an inappropriate comment in the OR and is no longer with us.*

The room was quiet except for the pen. Click, click.

Michael sat stiffly. He'd been here countless times, every week for four months, always easy, congenial, agreeable. Two doctors who enjoyed each other's company planning for the future of the department. They'd already implemented several of Michael's ideas, with staff and patient satisfaction as top priorities. Today's meeting was clearly not about the patient.

Uh-oh. Did Perkins know about the note? Michael licked his dry lips. Did Phil know Michael took the note? Was there a second note? *Michael Baker is not the good doctor you think he is.* The words were so ludicrous when he first read them. Now they seemed almost prescient.

Phil spoke. "Heard about the Stark case. Hell of a thing. What happened? Heard you stopped the antibiotics."

Michael stared at his hands and then out the window. The ferry was gone, and the blue water held no answers.

This wasn't about the note, but it may as well have been.

"What happened?" Perkins said again.

He was a man who did not tolerate excuses. He wanted a straight answer.

"I don't have a good explanation."

Phil's voice didn't change, but his pen told a different story. Click, click. "I'm sure there is an explanation. I look forward to hearing it at M & M on Friday."

# Chapter 18

"Beep."

Michael jumped. The traffic light was green. His mind was on the hospital. On Chrissie, Reginald Stark, plus the note denouncing his skills.

He glanced in his rearview mirror. The car behind him was old and angular, not like the sleek aerodynamic models of today. With requisite Seattle driving politeness, it idled silently.

"Beep." This cheerful, apologetic little horn beeping twice was from the electric vehicle one car back.

Two beeps. The driver must be from out of town. Maybe from Boston. The thought made Michael smile.

He lifted his foot from the brake. He arrived home.

So soon?

The drive from the hospital to his house included one of the most beautiful views in the world, Michael was certain. The hospital sat on a hill on the western side of the city, looking down on Puget Sound with the Olympic Mountains beyond. His neighborhood was only a few miles away on the eastern side. When he crested the final hill, the whole of Lake Washington spread out before him, with the Cascade Mountains huge and snowy on the far side. To the south, Mount Rainier, the enormous white glacier-covered volcano, rose impossibly high. Today would have been particularly stunning because of the blue sky, a luxury in Seattle.

But he hadn't seen it. The entire drive was a blank.

Like the antibiotic order.

*You should not trust him with your patients.*

Michael couldn't even trust his own memory.

There was no way around it. He had stopped the antibiotics. He had a lapse of attention, opened the wrong chart, and discontinued one order thinking it was another, just as Hal said. His mind had wandered and, like driving home on autopilot, which he'd just done, he couldn't remember anything.

Michael unhooked the door of Frank's huge glass crate, searching among the thick substrate shavings for the lizard, searching his mind for an answer. Whose antibiotics had he intended to stop? He ran his list of patients in his head. Only one was on antibiotics, and he had recently stopped them. Or so he thought. He rushed to the other room, opened his laptop, and logged in. Tracy Hopkins. Her antibiotics had been correctly discontinued yesterday. Thank God.

However he'd made the mistake, the results were the same.

Reginald Stark's pneumonia took hold and now he was fighting for his life in the ICU. A hospital-acquired pneumonia was bad enough. Being seventy-three with bad lungs and on no antibiotic treatment would be the wooden stake in his heart, to use his mother's language.

The guy was a fighter, Michael could tell. And a blowhard. At his presurgery appointment in the clinic, he said he retired to Seattle because of his son. "But I never see him. He can't make the time," he said mockingly.

"We do see our grandson," his wife said. She sat hunched beside him, both hands clutching the purse in her lap.

Mr. Stark gave her a withering look. "That kid is out of control. I tripped over his wagon, and I swear that's what put this knee over the edge. The mother doesn't lift a finger to rein him in. How my son puts up with it, I don't know."

"Now dear, the doctor doesn't want to hear about all that."

"I'll tell the doctor whatever I goddamned want."

His wife busied herself retrieving a tissue from her purse. Michael's medical office assistant, Robin, trying to take his blood pressure as Mr. Stark gesticulated, raised her eyebrows. Michael gave a slight nod of acknowledgement.

Robin said after, "My dad was like that. A real a-hole. He had a heart attack and died when I was young. We were better off without him."

He and Robin shared that, then. Mean, missing fathers.

Robin had gone on. "My mom really stepped up and took care of us. She made sure we had everything we needed and then some. Now I'm taking care of her."

Another thing they shared. The care of a mother. Robin looked to be about his same age, so her mother was likely about the same age as Michael's. Young enough to hang around forever, year after soul-sucking year.

He never spoke these words, saying only, "It can be quite a burden," but his tone must have given him away.

"No, really," she protested. "It's the least I can do ."

Robin's mother and Robin's situation sounded completely different from his.

Movement in the far corner of the apartment caught Michael's eye. The long tail of Frank flicked out from behind a plant and twitched. Michael eased himself onto the leather couch so it didn't creak and scare the lizard.

He hummed the tune from yesterday, the one Frank seemed to like. He felt a little foolish, but his old neighbor with the tegu had talked to his, so why not? Whatever made Frank comfortable.

Michael had written the song when he was ten and hadn't

thought of it since he'd left Seattle. Sure enough, the tail swept around and Frank crept into the room. He settled on his belly in front of the couch, his thick body nearly touching Michael's leg. Michael continued humming, the tegu lizard and the old song strangely comforting.

He switched from humming to singing, quietly, like he imagined he'd sing to a baby at night if he ever had a baby. "I know you and you know me. Will we be friends forever?" That was the first innocent line.

Frank seemed to enjoy it, or at least he stayed put.

Michael was not prepared to sing the rest, probably couldn't remember most of it. The song lurked deep in his mind, pushed far away long ago. Back in Seattle or not, now was not the time to delve into that particular past.

Frank pushed up on his legs and ambled off. Michael started singing again, and the lizard turned back.

"I have two cases for M & M," Michael improvised to the same tune. "The whole department will know then."

M & M, Morbidity and Mortality, was meant to be a learning experience so doctors could improve by other's mistakes and "systems errors" could be revealed and resolved. Michael had been involved in a few systems errors in Boston, the worst one being two years ago, when the wrong drug was administered by the anesthesiologist because the packages were similar sizes and colors. The anesthesiologist was at fault, of course, but the hospital realized the new packaging of one of the drugs was just as much to blame and immediately had Pharmacy add a warning sticker until they worked something out with the drug manufacturer to prevent a similar mishap in another hospital.

Reginald Stark's case, however, was not a "systems error." It was a Michael Baker error.

"I'll have to admit I made a mistake," he sang to the lizard. "They'll all know I'm not a doctor first rate." He sang the words to make a silly rhyme, but their meaning sank in, more true than not.

*Michael Baker is not the good doctor you think he is.*

He leaned back and stretched his legs in front of him. He examined the painting on the wall, a blank canvas with thick horizontal brushes of crimson red. He'd liked it when he found it in Boston. Now it seemed harsh and admonishing. He craned his neck and focused on the lake instead.

A good doctor. That was his whole identity. That's who he was. Who he thought he was.

For four months at Cascadia, hell, for his entire career as a doctor, he hadn't made a mistake like this. He'd had complications, sure, a wound infection here, a poorly healing bone there. A mistake was different from a known, possible, expected complication. A mistake was terrifying.

"Two M & Ms in one week is too many," Michael sang. "I can't help but notice that these two occurrences"—he made a show of taking a deep breath—"occurred at the exact same moment, at the exact same time"—he paused now for dramatic effect for Frank, who lifted his face in anticipation—"as the arrival in the hospital of my mother!"

He finished with a flourish, his hands thrown in the air for emphasis. He had Frank's attention now.

Michael dropped the singsong voice and spoke to the tegu, man to man. "You know what I'm talking about. Four months I've been there, working away without a hitch. She's been doing so well, out of the hospital all this time. Then she shows up and I lose my concentration. I get interrupted by nurses' complaints, by her walking in the hallway, by her screaming from her room. I'm slipping, Frank. God help my patients."

Frank dipped his round head, a nod of sympathy, Michael was certain. Michael touched the skin on his crown, bumpy and cool, and ran his hand down Frank's neck and back. The lizard stood still, his face relaxed. Michael curled his hand around Frank's muscular tail, stroking gently to the tip.

A knife slashed Michaels' arm. He jumped to his feet, barely out of the way as Frank's tail whipped a second time. A red welt appeared on his forearm, and he backed away from the lizard, bewildered. Frank's black eyes fastened on Michael's.

"Don't touch my tail," Frank said. At least that's what Michael heard.

# Chapter 19

Michael woke early, if woke was the word to use when he hadn't truly fallen asleep. How could he sleep? All he could see was Chrissie's face, pale and still. Or Reginald Stark, now intubated and on a ventilator.

A young woman was dead. An elderly man was near dead. Michael was the attending physician in both cases.

That anesthesiologist in Boston must know how this felt. He gave the wrong meds and the patient had had a stroke. How had that guy coped? Had he thought of it night after night, month after month?

At least there hadn't been a lawsuit, dragging the unfortunate outcome out forever, never letting the doctor forget, making the family relive every detail. The hospital spared everyone with a quick, quiet settlement.

Lawsuit or not, how did any doctor cope after a bad outcome? Something as bad as Reginald Stark, when you could not tell yourself that these things happened, all surgery was risky, sometimes there was a complication. No, that case in Boston and Michael's case with Mr. Stark were mistakes, human errors that should never have happened.

It was three hours later on the East Coast. He dialed the Boston hospital number and asked them to page Dr. David Eaves. "This is Dr. Michael Baker. I'll hold."

He didn't know David well. They hadn't had a lot of cases

together. But he knew the man well enough to know he would understand this type of a call. Any doctor would. They didn't reach out often for help, but when they did, help was there.

"I'm sorry, Dr. Baker. Dr. Eaves is no longer with us."

"He left? Where did he go? Do you have any contact information? I used to work there. I used to work with him."

"Yes, I know, Dr. Baker. I remember who you are. But I can't give you any more information."

Michael hung up the phone and started again. He dialed his old OR number, directly to the OR front desk. His hand was shaking.

"OR, this is Betsy."

"Betsy. It's Michael Baker."

"Dr. Baker! How are you? We miss you here."

"That's kind of you to say. I'm fine, fine. I have a question. I'm trying to get in touch with an anesthesiologist. David Eaves. He apparently doesn't work there anymore. I'm hoping to get some contact information, a phone number, or the name of the hospital where he works now. Do you know anything about him?"

Betsy was silent on the other end of the line.

"Betsy, you there?"

"Yes. Dr. Baker, Barbara is sitting right here. Why don't you talk to her?"

The phone was handed over, but Barbara, the head nurse, didn't come on for an excruciating amount of time. Michael gripped his phone so hard his knuckles turned white.

"Dr. Baker? It's Barbara."

"Hello, Barbara. I'm trying to reach David Eaves."

"Yes. I'm sorry to have to be the one to tell you. David Eaves is dead. He took his own life a few months ago."

# Chapter 20

The M & M was worse than Michael imagined. He sat on the edge of his hard wooden chair in the Surgery conference room, every muscle tense, his jaw aching from clenching.

David Eaves had taken his own life. That's how he had coped.

Michael tried to catch Phil Perkins' eye, but Phil looked everywhere but at Michael.

They discussed Chrissie Johnson first. They discussed surgical technique ("appropriate," the doctors agreed), timing of the surgery (delayed because it took her so long to summon help, prompt once she arrived at Cascadia), and diagnosis of the fat embolus. Chrissie had been seen on nurses' rounds three hours before she was found unresponsive and pulseless.

"You had not written a note that day," Phil Perkins said. It was a statement of fact, but his voice had an edge.

"Correct," Michael answered. "I saw her briefly in the morning and intended to see her again at the end of the day. She was doing well and tentatively scheduled for discharge the following day."

"She was not diagnosed with the fat embolus until the time of the code." Another statement of fact, again delivered with sharpness.

"Yes, Phil. There was no indication of anything amiss until then." Michael did not mention his mother's noting of the pasty skin and the shortness of breath. Or the potentially poisoned sandwich.

"The medical examiner, not unexpectedly, declined an autopsy because the case was so classic. I think this is a tragedy, but standard of care was met." Katherine Pierce was the reviewer on the case, and her eyes met Michael's. She was one of only two women surgeons in the room, her long blonde hair a contrast to the short hair of the men. She was petite, and she appeared extra small with all the men sitting around her, but her voice was confident and the other doctors at the table nodded.

Phil Perkins sat in the one leather chair, at the head of the table in the chairman's position. He picked up the pen in front of him and clicked the end. "Shame you don't have a note in the chart on the day of her death."

The room was silent for a moment, then he clicked his pen again.

"Right." Brent Williams frowned sympathetically at Michael. "Standard of care met." Brent was head of the M & M and made a notation in his ledger. Michael knew he'd thrown his hat in for the chairmanship, but he'd been nothing but courteous since Michael arrived.

Brent glanced at his notes. "Next is Reginald Stark. Also Dr. Baker's case. Dr. Pierce presenting."

Katherine Pierce stuck to the facts during her synopsis of the case. "Dr. Baker diagnosed pneumonia and started antibiotics in a timely fashion. He discontinued them less than thirty-six hours later. The nurse who took off the order is new and didn't think to question Dr. Baker about it. The next day Mr. Stark's condition deteriorated."

Michael kept his eyes on Katherine and wished he could drown out the noise of Phil Perkins' pen going crazy.

Katherine consulted her notes. "Mr. Stark was intubated yesterday and still remains on a ventilator today. With his underlying lung disease, the ICU doctors don't know if he'll ever come off. Plus, the ICU team notes he's at risk for multi-organ system failure."

"The man is a military veteran and an emeritus professor." Phil spoke from his throne.

*But not a nice person,* Michael thought. Not that he deserved to be in the ICU. That was all Michael's doing.

The table turned toward him. He was ready to say it. "I made a mistake. I inadvertently stopped the antibiotics. I was distracted." He opened his mouth.

Click, click. Phil Perkins twirled the pen in his hand and clicked again. An old-time surgeon, he bemoaned the softening of the younger generation of doctors, those who didn't dedicate their entire life to medicine and medicine alone. Phil regarded Michael, single and childless, as his ally and his example of what a surgeon should be. Michael was certain that was one of the reasons Phil had marked him as the next chairman. Phil was divorced. Small wonder.

Many of the surgeons in the room knew about Michael's mother. Phil Perkins knew. If Michael said "I was distracted," they would assume he meant "distracted by my mother." Which he was. No way Michael was saying anything about the anonymous note.

God, could one of his colleagues, one of the doctors in this room, have written that note? Someone who thought he wasn't on top of his game? Distracted?

Michael kept his eyes down, avoiding their questioning faces. Whatever the cause, to Phil Perkins, saying "distracted" was akin to saying "I am not up to the task."

Michael closed his mouth. Why should he admit to something he didn't remember?

"I didn't do it." As Michael said the words, he realized it was true. Distracted or not, he was absolutely certain he had not written that order.

The room was quiet for a moment. Katherine looked at the doctors on either side of her.

"You mean you don't remember doing it," Brent Williams suggested.

"Maybe you meant to stop that antibiotic and start another," Katherine said. "That's what I thought might have happened." Hal had said the same thing, Michael remembered.

"No." Michael's voice was more irritated than he wanted, but days of pent-up worry and anger flew out. He was angry at his mother. He was angry at himself. "I mean I didn't do it."

Several doctors spoke at once. The voices blended together. Michael's ears were ringing, and the words sounded muffled.

One voice broke through, and the other doctors quieted.

Phil Perkins rose to his feet. "We will discuss this case further next month. Standard of care was not met. You signed the order, Michael. You signed the patient's note just before, then you signed the order. You *did* do it."

# Chapter 21

Madge straightened her blanket and searched her son's face. Stinky said he didn't do it, and that meant he didn't do it. Madge was certain. He was a lot of things, but he was not a liar. The few times he tried, he turned pasty and got that red spot on his right cheek. He had a "tell." No, Stinky was not lying.

She had worried about that most, all those years ago when he was ten. If anyone had asked him outright, he could never have kept their secret. She made sure no one asked.

He stood next to her bed with a straight face, flushed even, no sign of any untruths. He came late in the day, after this Morbidity and Mortality mumbo jumbo. He wasn't saying much, but he was clearly upset. "I didn't do it. I just don't know how it happened. They think I'm lying. Or forgetful." About what, she did not know. Something about Chrissie? Or the patient with the antibiotics? Or something involving Dr. Francine? She tried to find out, but he kissed her forehead and slipped from the room.

Hmm. Francine. Michael told Madge he didn't mix work and dating, not since Janet, but Madge could still try.

"He likes lemon bars, you know," she'd said the last time she saw Francine. Or, once when Francine asked if she cooked for herself, "Mikey brings me meals sometimes. He's a really good cook. Not all men enjoy cooking, but he does. You should try his chicken mole sometime."

Mikey was in his forties, long overdue for a wife. Madge was long overdue for grandchildren. She heard that baby bell ring, marking the birth of another bouncing bundle of joy, and each time she wished it were for her Mikey. At this rate, sick and in and out of the hospital, she'd be dead before she saw him married. Look what happened to Chrissie.

Was Chrissie the reason Mikey was in trouble? Did they think he was lying about Chrissie? Well, he wasn't.

What about Chrissie, anyway? *Think, think.* There was something wrong about Chrissie's death.

Madge knew a thing or two about deaths. Before she started on horror movies, she watched murder mysteries. Sunday nights on public television were her favorites. She knew enough about solving a crime to make a timeline of the deceased's activities and a list of anyone remotely connected to the victim. These would be her suspects.

A hunch was good enough. She didn't need ironclad evidence. Leave that to the police, the lawyers.

She would have been a lawyer herself, if it weren't for Stinky. No point in thinking about that. Water under the overpass. What mattered now was easing Stinky's mind.

Paper and pencil, that's what she needed. She didn't have a menu, let alone a blank sheet of paper. She didn't even have a purse. They made Stinky take it home after she was admitted.

Madge twisted her upper body toward the bedrail. That darn call button was so far. She reached forward, nearly losing her balance and cracking her head on the guard rail. That would be something. Concussion by bedrail. Injured by the very item that was there to protect her.

She jammed the button with such vigor one pillow fell to the floor. She relaxed back on the other. Thankfully, it was her puffy pillow from home. She might be waiting a while. She didn't expect miracles. The nurses would take their time. Maybe send the nurses' aide, who would do in a pinch. All

Madge needed was paper and pencil, after all. It wasn't like that night with Chrissie.

She could see Chrissie clearly, as if she were a ghost in the next bed right now, sitting up in the darkened room. The room had been brighter that night, but without a roommate, Madge kept the bright lights off. Chrissie's face had been pale, and it wasn't a trick of those fluorescent bulbs. The girl had looked awful.

Madge closed her eyes to picture the scene better. Oh, if only she had her paper and pencil to write it all down. Chrissie was breathing fast, talking in short bursts, then breathing in between. The Reuben sandwich was on a glass plate on the bed table alongside a green sheet of paper decorated with a crutch, plus a carton of orange juice leftover from lunch. The sandwich had one bite in a corner, a tiny bite, nothing like the huge chunk Madge would tear off if she could sink her teeth into the thing.

"Sure smells tasty," Madge had said.

"Want it?" Chrissie gasped.

"I'm NPO." She saw the girl's puzzled expression. "Nil per os. Nothing by mouth. Can't eat anything."

Chrissie didn't say anything. She braced her arms against her thighs.

"You feeling okay?" She clearly wasn't. She didn't answer.

"Is it the pain? Do you need some more medicine?" Chrissie had had an extra dose of pain killer before her physical therapy session. That was hours ago. The girl was too stoic. When Madge was in pain, she demanded medicine.

Chrissie shook her head. "It's not..." She took a breath. "They said this is pretty normal."

She'd told Madge she was worried about getting addicted to pain medicine and wanted to be careful. Madge never worried about addiction, and, for heaven's sakes, the girl had just had surgery. She needed *something*.

Chrissie sat there huffing, and Madge rang her bell for the nurse. While she waited, though, the melted cheese and corned beef smell wafted around the room. By the time the nurse arrived, all thought of Chrissie's pain was trounced by the Reuben.

The nurse scolded Madge and never glanced Chrissie's way in her hurry to exit. Then they turned on their show, Madge lounging back on her pillows and Chrissie leaning forward, and that's the last Madge remembered.

It was the narcotics, making her sleepy, playing with her mind. But they did help the pain. Yes, indeedy, without narcotics, this hospital visit would be a whole different story. As well she knew from past experience. Sometimes the nurses were so stingy with the pain meds. Doctor's orders, they said. My foot. She knew they had it in for her.

But back to Chrissie. Madge needed to get this all down. She might fall asleep again, lying here with her eyes closed in the dark room. What with her age and the meds, the picture might not be so clear tomorrow. Paper and pencil were all she asked. Where was that nurse?

Had the floor squeaked? Was someone there?

Madge opened her eyes. A large ghostly shadow loomed above her in the dark. The ghost held a pillow. Slowly the pillow lowered, until it was inches from her face.

# Chapter 22

Madge screamed but only a high-pitched squeak escaped. She opened her mouth to scream again. The pillow crashed down and covered her nose and mouth. She couldn't scream and she couldn't breathe.

Was this what happened to poor Chrissie? Unsuspecting hospital patient murdered by crazed killer on the loose? They were sitting ducklings in their fancy air mattress beds, weaklings waiting for the slaughter.

Well, not her. Not Margaret McGillicuddy.

Madge thrashed her arms and brushed the pillow to the side. She let out a piercing shriek, then another. The shadow sprang back.

Bright lights flipped on. Nurse Mildred rushed in. She gazed from Madge to the shadow, which had morphed into Nurse Bob.

"What in heaven's name?" Mildred said.

"He tried to kill me!" Madge screeched.

"Her pillow was on the floor," Nurse Bob muttered. "I was putting it back."

"On my face?!"

"I dropped it when you screamed." Big Bob hadn't budged from his place near the end of her bed. He held out his empty hands in a gesture of peace. "I'm sorry if I startled you."

"I want him out!" This man was trouble. She wasn't going to lie there like a victim and wait to die. "I don't want him taking care of me."

"There, there," Mildred soothed. "You'll feel better in the morning."

"Don't patronize me. I know what I want, and I want him out." Madge thrust her arm and pointed at the culprit.

Embarrassingly, her finger quivered. It always did this when she was first admitted, what with her drinking. The nurses used it as a sign to give her more anti-withdrawal meds to ward off a seizure, and she didn't mind that at all. But she was long past withdrawing, those delusional first days with a yellow IV bag full of vitamins and round-the-clock medicine providing blissful sleep. By now her finger should be steady as a rocket ship, heading straight for Nurse Bob's eyes. But it wobbled, and she closed her hand into a fist and dropped it to the bed.

She wasn't delusional now. She was in full control of her faculties. She glared at the two of them, huddled together at the foot of the bed.

Nurse Bob knew she meant business and scuttled from the room on his clackity clogs. Mildred wrinkled her nose and followed him out on her sensible rubber-soled shoes.

Drat! No paper and pencil. And she'd gone and fired her main nurse. She hadn't meant to. Things slipped out. Though she wasn't sorry he was gone.

No point in concentrating on Chrissie, then. If some nugget came to her, she was likely to forget it. She needed to write everything out. It had been this way for years. Well, decades.

She'd forgotten Mikey's birthday when he was eleven. When he was twelve, he planned his party himself, three guys and a movie in the rumpus room. She made the cake, though. She was good at cakes and presented it with a flourish in the middle of the movie, a cake with a yellow and black frosting superhero to go with the rented movie Mikey chose.

The boys didn't eat more than a bite, like Chrissie with the Reuben.

Was that why this memory popped into her head? Why was she thinking about Mikey's birthday? She hadn't thought of this since it happened, a memory safely tucked away in a part of her brain best left locked.

Because the cake was poisoned.

Thank goodness the boys didn't eat it.

She was upset with them in the moment. All the time she'd spent on that superhero, getting the bright yellow color just right. The boys were too polite to tell her it tasted funny. When they finally did, she thought they were being rude.

Then she tasted it herself. Inedible.

No wonder it hadn't risen properly. She'd mixed up the salt and the sugar. An easy mistake when her sugar cannister was full of salt. How that happened was a mystery to her, until she remembered her margarita craze. It was a fine idea at the time, a much easier method to salt the rim of her glass. The cannister was the perfect size and filling it with salt seemed ingenious. But she'd long switched from margaritas to rum and cola, and she hadn't used the sugar container since.

As if two cups of salt could poison a child. Mikey had made such a big deal over it. He never noticed the beautiful cake, the effort.

Why bother? Things never worked out anyway. That's what she told herself after that.

She should have put in more effort.

Poor Mikey. The last cake she'd made before the superhero fiasco was when he turned ten. When there had been three of them to celebrate. When they'd been a family.

Mikey returned the movie the next day without watching the end. He never had a party again.

Anyway, the boys' cake slices and Chrissie's sandwich had nary a nibble. All such a waste.

Was Chrissie's sandwich poisoned?

If it was, and if Madge could prove it, then everyone would realize that Mikey was not responsible for Chrissie's death. Madge had to find out. She couldn't give Mikey back his childhood birthdays, but she could give him this.

# Chapter 23

Michael spent Sunday morning at the hospital. This was such a regular part of his life, he never gave it a second thought. Rounding on patients, paperwork, research grant writing, lab results. There was never enough time in the week. But that was not why he was here today.

He'd seen his patients and visited his mother, and now it was time to get down to business. He had not stopped the antibiotic order. All he had to do was figure out what had happened. What glitch in the computer had sent through a faulty order. What "systems error" needed to be fixed.

He studied the electronic orders record again, this time without emotion. The antibiotic order was discontinued. His name was on the order, so it was definitely his account. Cascadia had a double-check system in place to prevent errors. A click of a button discontinued the order, but the system required the doctor to type out the words as well. Every order had to match. It was laborious, but it was effective.

It was there, the written-out order. "D/C antibiotic."

An icy finger crept up his spine. Michael leaned forward and squinted to make sure he was reading correctly.

"D/C antibiotic" had to have been typed in. Not by a "system." By a human.

The only problem was, that human was not him.

He never wrote "D/C." He wrote the whole word out,

"discontinue," not "D/C."

He'd heard that doctors practiced medicine most of their career much in the way they learned in training. Old habits were hard to change. He had been taught to avoid abbreviations, to avoid acronyms, to avoid anything at all that might cause confusion. He spelled everything out. He never took a short cut.

He would never write "D/C." He had not written the order.

But someone had.

# Chapter 24

Phil Perkins paged Michael again first thing Monday morning, which was not unexpected. It was another summons to his office "when convenient." When did "when convenient" ever mean anything but "right now" when it came from the chair of the department?

Michael shoved the pager back into the pocket of his white coat. He wanted to talk to Phil, too, but not yet. He couldn't blurt out what he'd found. Never using abbreviations was not proof. Phil would see it as making more excuses. Michael needed something concrete before he went to Phil.

Which he didn't have. All he'd done so far was change his computer password, just in case. Though Michael always used complex, nonsensical strings of numbers and symbols, impossible to guess or replicate. He used communal computers on the floors, but he was diligent about logging off the shared computers. Anyway, the floor computers logged out after thirty seconds of inactivity, which was annoying but safe. Could someone have used his computer within the thirty second window? Unlikely, especially since he always logged off himself.

He couldn't go to Phil yet.

Phil would have to wait in any case. Michael was late for the OR, courtesy of a barrage from the head nurse regarding weekday nursing staffing and his mother.

"I won't mince words just because you are a doctor. Your mother's complaints are affecting morale and now they are affecting staffing. I cannot cater to her every whim. I will only accommodate her when I am able, but I will not compromise my team."

His delusional mother had apparently fired Nurse Bob and was telling anyone who would listen that the man was a murderer. The only person she hadn't mentioned it to was Michael. At least she wasn't calling Bob a vampire anymore. The weekend crew worked around it, but Monday morning brought the head nurse, and she was not happy.

Michael wasn't happy either. He was late. The OR wouldn't be happy. Phil wouldn't be happy.

Michael wouldn't make it up to Phil's office for two hours minimum. Cellphones didn't work in this part of the hospital. The place had so many dead zones. Thick concrete walls, leaded rooms, stairways. He almost never used his cellphone at work. No one else did, either, because there were too many dropped calls. The pagers worked everywhere. Michael stopped at a computer in the recovery room, brought up Phil's pager, and tapped out a quick reply that he'd come after his first surgery.

"Yes," came the clipped response.

Exactly two hours later, finally ensconced in Phil's leather wing chair, Michael waited while the man sent a page.

"Matilda," Phil said. "She wanted to be here."

Matilda Walters was chief of staff. The job Michael would never have unless Matilda left Cascadia for bigger and better things. Ironic, because Matilda was partially responsible for Michael being at Cascadia in the first place. They'd worked together in Boston, where she was chief of anesthesiology. She'd left Boston over a year ago to take this job. When she saw Michael's application, she reached out to him personally and vouched for him to the Cascadia recruiting committee.

So he would be chair of surgery and she was chief of staff. Matilda lived for her job, didn't go away on the weekends in case there was an emergency, was on top of any whiff of a problem. She'd just received an award for working every day in a three month stretch. Every single day, physically in the hospital at some point, Monday through Friday and Saturday and Sunday, too. The CEO created the award just for her. Then told her to take some time off.

She was a classic workaholic. As was Michael, though not quite as bad as Matilda.

Michael searched Phil's face. He guessed the meeting was about Reginald Stark. Matilda's presence was not a good sign. Michael had already deflected responsibility at the M & M. They wouldn't want to hear Michael shift the blame today. He hadn't written the order, but who had? He couldn't make vague accusations without evidence. He wasn't his mother.

Phil's face was blank and his stare so intense that Michael averted his eyes and gazed out the window. Fog hid the waters of Puget Sound, but the sky was blue above. A seagull swooped down and landed on the windowsill. He cocked his head at Michael and cawed, his squawk sounding uncannily like "you're screwed."

Maybe the meeting wasn't about the M & M. Maybe the head nurse complained. About his mother and staffing and murderers.

If this meeting was about Michael's mother, Phil must be livid. He didn't deal well with family matters when they involved children or spouses. He certainly didn't want to deal with a mother.

Michael himself didn't want to deal with her.

Especially today. It was his birthday, and he hated his birthday, and the reason he hated his birthday was because of his mother.

She never remembered it, which was fine. *He* tried not

to remember. The last time he'd truly celebrated his birthday was when he was twelve. He invited friends over for a movie, a superhero movie he'd wanted to see for weeks. He'd loved superheroes and pretended sometimes he had a special power, always the same, the ability to turn back time. He'd turn back the clock on all the embarrassing things his mother did.

But more than anything, his child's mind wanted a superhero power to turn back the clock to the night when he was ten. The night his father left.

Anyway, he loved superheroes, and the birthday movie was everything he'd hoped for. He and his friends were on the edge of their seats when his mother barged in, a garish yellow and black monstrosity in her hands. She switched on the lights and insisted on singing. She carved up the cake, handed them each a hunk, and waited.

They all took a bite, and he knew something was terribly wrong. He was about to shout "Don't eat it!" but he didn't need to. Tom, Ronnie, and Dirk all spit out their mouthfuls and set the plates down, looking to him for what to do next. His mother screamed about ingrates and almost fell over when she tried to grab a piece for herself. Michael gathered up the cake, raced to the kitchen sink, and hurled it in. The boys left right after, and no one said anything the next day. Neither did his mother. She probably couldn't even remember.

Michael never saw the end of that movie. In fact, he never watched another superhero movie again.

Well, today was his birthday. Forty-five years old.

The fog was lifting but his mood was not. The seagull pooped on the window and soared off. Happy Birthday.

He and Phil waited silently, Phil's eyes on Michael, Michael's eyes on a container ship sitting low in the water.

"Sorry to be late." Michael jumped at Matilda's clear voice in the quiet room. He quickly recovered and pretended he was standing for her instead.

"Oh, sit, sit." She waved him back and took the wing chair next to his.

The three of them sat for a moment without speaking. Phil clicked his pen twice. Michael imagined all the things they might say. He prayed it wasn't about his mother.

The room was hot. His head suddenly spun, and he gripped the arms of the leather chair to keep from falling headfirst onto Phil's desk. Could his mother have slipped up? Could she have said something about...

No. In all these years, in all her drunken rants, she had never mentioned that night again.

That hadn't kept him from moving home, though.

He couldn't stand it any longer. He broke the silence. "Why did you want to see me?"

Matilda swiveled her whole body toward Phil, making it clear the floor was his.

Phil clicked his pen again. He set it carefully on his desk. He raised his eyes and met Michael's with that intense stare. "We've decided to broaden the pool for the department chair. The recruiting committee did their job, but ultimately the decision lies with Matilda and me. There are several other candidates we feel we should consider."

Michael's breath escaped with an audible gasp. He sat stunned. Phil didn't say anything more, and Matilda did not see the need to fill the empty space. The silence lengthened.

"What?" Michael finally said. "Why?"

Matilda turned gracefully back toward him. Her hair hung straight, black with streaks of silver. She wasn't much older than he was. He knew when he took the job he had little chance of advancing beyond Phil's department chair position. Matilda was the perfect chief of staff, competent, smooth, and charming, but right now she was direct and unsmiling.

"Michael. Two of your patients have done poorly this week. There is no shame in that." She paused. "However, Dr.

Perkins described your response at the M & M. He even had IT look into it. Your ID and password were used throughout the morning to write notes and orders. *Your* notes, on *your* patients. That order came shortly after the note on the same patient. The facts speak for themselves. Yet you did not take responsibility for your actions. I've known you some time, and I must admit I'm surprised. Phil and I are concerned you may not be the best choice for the next leader of this department. A leader leads by example, and trust from the team, once broken, is difficult to restore."

What could he say to that? I never use abbreviations, so the order isn't mine? Her stern eyes and downturned mouth told him this would not be the correct answer.

He should have fallen on his sword at the M & M. Said he didn't know how it happened, but he'd made the mistake. That's what they all wanted to hear. He made a mistake, he learned, it would never happen again.

In this stuffy room, with their eyes boring into him, Michael felt a tentacle of doubt.

*Had* he made a mistake? Were his restless sleep and twice daily rounds on Reginald Stark evidence of his guilt? Mr. Stark had no orthopedic problem anymore. His knee was healed. He was intubated and his kidney function was worsening, the first sign of organ failure. His knee didn't really matter now.

Still Michael visited and talked with his wife and learned he was the first in his family to go to university, and now his son had an MBA and was head of a small company. His grandson had stopped talking because he felt so bad about the wagon. "Though truly the wagon had nothing to do with it. That knee had been bothering him for a year," his wife said. The little boy sat quietly in the waiting room and tugged at Michael's heart. Was that guilt?

Phil and Matilda sat back and waited for his words of contrition.

Michael hadn't done it. The order wasn't his. Reginald Stark was his patient and he'd had a bad outcome, and any doctor would feel some level of responsibility.

But someone else had written the order.

"This is preposterous," Michael blurted. "I'm the best man for the job, and you know it. I tell you, I didn't cancel the antibiotics."

The expressions on their faces told him one thing.

Michael himself should stop talking.

# Chapter 25

Madge clasped the paper menu in her hands and studied it as if it were the winning lottery ticket. Today was the day. She'd started on clears and Dr. Hal said if she continued to do well, he would advance her diet. Full liquids tomorrow! Hallelujah.

Eating was relative. Clear liquids, then thicker liquids, then solids. Low fat only. She'd been down this path before. It might take a few days before she was truly eating.

But clear liquids meant gelatin and chicken broth and frozen fruit juice. She could still taste strawberry on her lips from lunch. For dinner she'd try orange. Maybe grape as well.

Wait a minute. What about Chrissie? What about the poisoned sandwich? Should she be worried about a poisoned popsicle?

She needed to talk to Gerta.

She should have thought of Gerta earlier. She delivered the meals, had worked there for decades. As long as Madge herself had graced the beds of Cascadia Medical Center. Gerta had delivered Madge's clear liquid lunch that very day. Gerta spent time in the kitchen. She would know about any hanky-panky with the lunchmeat.

"Time for a walk."

Darn. Tony the Terrible. A physical therapist who would not take "no" for an answer. Madge had seen her share of physical therapists over the years, keeping her muscles working so she didn't atrophy in the hospital, re-training her balance to try to prevent falls. And occupational therapists, watching her dress and eat and making sure she could take care of herself, assessing her home for trip hazards and making her remove her throw rugs and install grab bars in the shower.

Usually Madge could feign a nap and get them to go away. Especially if *Creature Friday* was on. Sometimes it simply hurt too much to move, her back stiff and her right knee screaming. Plus, her left big toe wasn't too happy ever since she slipped and slammed it into the shower tile the year before. And she had a crick in her neck more days than not. She could go on and on.

The more she lay there, the more she moldered, and no amount of PT was going to change that. So why bother?

Once she'd been in the ICU a week, and Don the physical therapist had to move her legs for her, and it took a month to get her up and walking again. She'd been ferried around in a wheelchair, no pain, no effort. It wasn't so bad.

In fact, her bad knee thanked her. How she had a bum knee when she never did any exercise—no glory days of football, no marathons in exotic places—was beyond her. She never mentioned the knee to her orthopedic son because he'd have her under the knife in no time, and really, the knee was fine if she never put weight on it.

Anyway, Tony was new and not like Don or even gym teacher physical therapist Carlotta. Madge had only worked with Tony twice, but he made it clear he'd get his way and that protest was useless. He never let her off without some torture involving stairs.

Chrissie had agreed, telling Madge she never hurt more than after her session with Tony, but that was probably a good thing. Madge wasn't so sure about that.

Chrissie was the one who called him Tony the Terrible. "He's going to bring me a pamphlet with extra exercises I'm supposed to do on my own. While I'm lying in bed. I can't just lounge here." Madge had to laugh at that.

She wasn't laughing now, when it was her turn with Tony.

"Where to today?" Tony hoisted her in one beefy arm and supported her with his body. Were her legs ever weak! Without Tony there, she would have toppled right over. He fastened the belt around her waist and held her in his strong grip.

"Do you know Gerta?" she asked. "She delivers the meals. Is she out there now?"

"Short gray-haired lady pushing a cart? I do believe she is right down the hall. Let's go."

One slow step at a time. She'd never get to the hall at this rate. She'd done better yesterday. Her strength was going backwards. What good was PT? Her knee hurt. Her back hurt. Her stomach hurt.

"Tony, it's too painful. Take me back to bed."

"Oh, no. You're doing fine. Just a little more and we'll be in the hallway, and you can see Gerta."

"Get the nurse to give me some pain medicine, then."

"You had a dose half an hour ago. You're good to go."

"I don't feel good to go. I don't feel well at all." Now her stomach was really hurting. She wobbled forward.

Tony tightened the belt to hold her steady. "You can do it," he said.

Madge turned her head and vomited all over him.

# Chapter 26

Michael sat in his office and tried to listen to Hal on the phone, but his mind was elsewhere. He'd just seen Reginald Stark in the ICU, and he was swollen with fluids because his kidneys had stopped working.

Discontinue. D/C. Discontinue. D/C.

"Missed you at basketball last week. We needed you, man," Hal said. "John was out, too. He's interviewing for that tech job in New York. Wonder if it's changed much since your college days. I've never been to New York. 'Course, I've never been anywhere but here."

"Mm?" On Thursday Michael had been prepping for M & M. Look how well that had gone. He should have played basketball.

He'd completely forgotten about the game. He'd never felt so distracted in his life. What else had he completely forgotten? Discontinuing the antibiotics?

*Michael Baker is not the good doctor you think he is.*

No. He hadn't done it.

"Calling about your mom," Hal continued. Who else? Talk about distraction. "She didn't tolerate the clears. She's vomiting again and her pain is back. I thought we'd have her eating by now. She's going to need a feeding tube. She's not going to like it."

Michael shut his eyes and concentrated. "You're right

about that. How's she feeling?"

"Well, that's the thing. She looks okay and her vitals are fine, no fever, but she's a little delusional. I don't know why. She thinks someone is poisoning her."

"What?"

"Yes. She says it's too much of a coincidence that Chrissie Johnson died after eating a sandwich and now she's sick after her first meal in the hospital. She's telling everyone within earshot. Want to come and talk to her?"

No. No, he did not want to talk to her. "On my way," he said.

"Maybe mention the feeding tube, too?" Hal said with a laugh.

"Sure," Michael said. Getting his mom to agree to a tube in her nose when she swore each time she'd never do it again... Talking about poison might be easier.

His medical office assistant, Robin, appeared in his doorway with a pink frosted cupcake.

"One left," she said. He'd seen them in the break room that morning, a dozen chocolate cupcakes capped with vibrant frosting, pink, blue, yellow.

"This is exactly what I need right now. Thank you." The cupcake would be the perfect substitute for lunch. He didn't tell her it was his birthday. He wanted to forget himself.

"I used pumpkin instead of oil, so they're healthy. You'd think oil was poison, the way some people go on."

Poison. That reminded him about his mother's fantasy. He'd better head up. He ate the cupcake between floors as he hurried up the stairs. It was delicious, pumpkin or not.

His mother was lying flat when he arrived at her room, pillows clutched to her abdomen.

"Oh, Stinky, it hurts. Tell them more pain medicine." She grabbed his wrist and pulled him down to her, surprisingly strong for someone appearing so frail.

"Mom—"

"Stinky, my food was poisoned. I ate that broth and now look. I'm sick, Stinky, sick."

He ran his hand through his hair. Where to start with this wacky poison theory? "Mom, I don't think..."

"Ask Gerta. See what she knows. First Chrissie, now me."

"Mom, it's the pancreatitis. There's still inflammation around the stomach. That's what's making you sick."

His mother had not been poisoned. On this he was clear. He had seen the CT scan. No one gave her pancreatitis but her. Despite his never-ending battle to keep her from drinking. How many liquor bottles had he removed? Where did they come from, since she didn't drive and wasn't much of a walker due to unsteadiness? He asked her once, and she just tilted her head and blinked innocently.

"They want you to consider a feeding tube to get some nutrition in you to help you heal."

"That tube in the nose? Okay."

"Okay?" Had she heard him? Had she really agreed so readily? She hated feeding tubes.

"Yes. Okay. If you talk to Gerta. Stinky, listen, it's not the pancreatitis. Because what about Chrissie?"

Chrissie had not been poisoned either. That tell-tale rash of the fat embolism was unmistakable.

"Mom, we've been over this. Anyway, who would want to kill Chrissie?"

"That's just it, Mikey."

"What, Mom? What's it?"

"We are both linked to you," his mother whispered. "Do you have any enemies?"

# Chapter 27

Michael finally arrived home, after an emergency afternoon case and evening rounds on his patients and his mother. Their discussion was short, as Mildred arrived at the same time for a sponge bath. He was thankful, because really he just wanted to get home.

*Do you have any enemies?*

His mother had it wrong. No one had been poisoned. No one but him. The proof of the poison lay shredded in the recycle bin in the other room.

Would Phil receive another note? Who had written those words? Who had changed the antibiotic order on Reginald Stark? Was it the same person?

He'd spent the afternoon assessing every interaction, reviewing every colleague. Where was the enemy?

He spied fellow surgeon Brent Williams in the locker room. Did ambitious Brent Williams think he'd make a better chairman? He was young, but he'd grown up in the Cascadia system, first as a resident then on staff. He had every reason to believe he might get the job even though he was too young.

Hal waved from down the hall. Did Hal hold a grudge because Michael won the scholarship to college and not Hal? Michael hadn't thought of this in twenty-five years, but Hal must have been as devastated as Michael would have been had the award gone to Hal.

He passed the administration offices and thought of Matilda. Was she sorry she'd recruited him from Boston and now wanted him gone pronto?

He could go on and on, driving himself insane.

Through it all, somehow, all he could think of was Janet. The person he longed to discuss this with, who could help him make sense of it. And, okay, the last person to be with him on his birthday, two years ago. By last year, she'd been gone.

He circled around his apartment, knowing exactly where he was going but telling himself he was not. He detoured to the office to let Frank out of his cage. Back in the living room, he unlatched the hook on the hutch in the corner and opened the door. His mother's confiscated liquor bottles stood inside, three almost empty bottles of different colors and different sizes, a variety of alcohol. Whisky, gin, and vodka. He hadn't thrown them out. He'd put them here.

He carried the bottles to the glass coffee table and set them in a line. He chose the whisky bottle and clinked two ice cubes into a short glass. He poured the brown liquid, watching it flow over the ice until the glass was a quarter full.

He flopped on the couch and rested his feet on the coffee table. He sipped the drink and grimaced. Frank appeared from the ethers and edged warily forward.

"You don't drink." Frank didn't say this, but Michael could see it in his eyes.

"It's my birthday. I've had a hard day. Come closer. I won't bite." Michael leaned down and patted the floor.

The lizard stepped forward and rolled on his back. Michael touched his soft belly, cool and smooth. Frank's body shimmied as if he enjoyed this petting. He flipped over and rotated his head and gazed up at Michael. His look could only say "Happy Birthday."

Michael lifted his glass. "Thank you, Frank."

He hadn't had a drink in a year. He hadn't seen Janet

in a year. They'd dated over two years, nothing secret about it, a full-on hospital romance that everyone knew about and everyone sanctioned. They went to the Christmas galas together, he in the same tuxedo he'd worn for over a decade, she in a stunning jade dress without a back or a long, straight red velvet skirt with a side slit. And the Department of Surgery picnics, manning the barbeque and serving up skewers of chicken and pork. They worked together and played together and lived together. A golden couple, happy and carefree and spreading sunshine. He adored her and she adored him. He thought they would always be together.

So did she.

He left Frank and wandered to the desk in the second bedroom. He reached far into the back of the drawer and found the photo. Janet smiled up, blonde hair back, heart-shaped face beaming with the excitement of her first lobster bake on the beach, seaweed and all. He settled back on the couch, the lizard again at his feet, and propped the photo against the gin bottle.

How did it get so screwed up?

Secrets. Janet had a secret. He had a secret. Hers involved future hopes and dreams. His involved blood.

He'd wake in the night, a little boy standing in warm sticky blood, blood in his hair, blood in his eyes. She'd hold him and soothe him, and she never knew why.

Yet it was her secret he let destroy them.

He'd broken things off, and he started to drink.

Thanks to his mother, he never drank in high school or college. Or medical school or residency. He didn't drink. Period. It was never an issue, and no one ever pushed the matter.

Then Janet left, cleared all her things out of his tiny Back Bay condo, and the place never seemed bigger. So much space. So much emptiness.

They continued to work together in the OR. She didn't change her days and he didn't change his. They saw each other at staff meetings and in the hall. He drank and he drank, in the evenings, on the weekends. He realized he had his mother's genes because he could not stop.

After three months Janet changed jobs, left the hospital, maybe even left Boston. She didn't tell him, and he didn't ask. She was gone and that's all it took for him to stop drinking.

It wasn't like he was an alcoholic. That was a year ago. Now he was just having a simple drink on his birthday.

And getting stink eye from the tegu lizard.

"Frank, you wouldn't understand." But Frank abandoned him for the solitude of the space under the couch.

"Happy Birthday to me," Michael sang, but the lizard stayed put.

He knew what Frank wanted.

Michael took another sip, then a gulp. The whiskey burned, and he gulped again. He set the glass on the coffee table.

"All right." He started to sing. "I know you and you know me. Will we be friends forever?" Frank stayed hidden.

"You know my secrets and I know yours. Will we be friends forever?" The forgotten lines bubbled up from the past. The lizard slithered out and stretched luxuriously, his body lengthening and flattening.

Michael assessed the lizard, Chrissie's tegu lizard. Chrissie was dead. Reginald Stark was barely hanging on. David Eaves, the anesthesiologist who'd dealt with this sort of thing, was dead.

Michael stood abruptly, and the lizard slipped back under the couch. Michael's head whooshed, a familiar sensation from his drinking days. He steadied himself against the coffee table. He located his laptop and typed in David Eaves.

"Doctor dies in fall from roof." This was the first brief

listing. "David Eaves, a 35-year-old anesthesiologist, was found dead yesterday morning in an apparent fall from the balcony of his fifth story Brookline apartment. His body was found by an early morning jogger in the parking lot behind the building, but police believe he fell late in the evening before. Foul play is not suspected."

A subsequent story told of a recent divorce, with his ex-wife confirming that he had been depressed over work. The police determined he died from his own hand.

David Eaves would not have any advice for him. He hadn't had any advice for himself.

Michael poured himself another drink. He drank it alone, the lizard preferring to stay hidden. A third drink emptied the bottle, and he switched to vodka.

Michael became aware of pressure on his chest and throbbing in his head. He opened his eyes and closed them immediately. Frank's face was inches from his, his scaly face still, his black eyes unblinking. Frank was standing on his chest.

What time was it? He turned his head slowly so as not to disturb the lizard, but Frank recoiled and bolted away. Morning light shone through the window. Oh, Lord. He was late.

He flew around the apartment looking for his shoes. He'd have to skip morning rounds, but he might just make it to the OR in time. He didn't even stop to brush his teeth.

Traffic was heavier than he was used to an hour earlier. Not so heavy that he didn't notice an old blue car a few cars back. He'd seen this car before, its sharp angles standing out from the others. He couldn't remember where, and it was too taxing to try. His head pulsed, each bump in the road sending daggers to his brain. His pager shrilled. His head split open.

"Dr. Baker returning a page."

"Thanks, Mike, it's me, Hal. Your mom pulled out her feeding tube. Francine didn't want to bother you overnight. I thought I'd see you this morning, but I must have missed you. Sorry to page. Your mom doesn't want it back in."

*God damn it, Hal, take care of it yourself. Pretend I don't exist and treat her like any other noncompliant patient. You handle it and leave me out.* This is what he wanted to say. Instead, he said, "Okay. I might not be up until later, but leave it to me."

Fuming, he rushed through the clinic building's lobby. He usually paused to admire the glass wall and the small greenspace beyond, typical Seattle with cedar trees and a hemlock, even though they were in the middle of a city. A trickle of sunshine illuminated the opposite wall, where his own smiling face jeered at him from his Doctor of the Quarter photo.

Worse, the lobby gift shop displayed a plenitude of Mother's Day gifts: crystal hearts engraved with "Mom," ceramic mugs with affectionate sayings, and beautiful vases to hold the flower arrangements a dutiful son was sure to bring. A simple holiday that wrapped his entire life in such mixed emotions. Guilt. Sadness. Embarrassment. Wishing things were different. Anger. The pastel papier-mâché flower bouquet in the window was all innocence and love.

He sprinted up the stairs, slowing only slightly when he reached the surgery clinic hallway. He passed Phil Perkin's open door.

"So you see our situation." This was Matilda's voice. What was Matilda, the chief of staff, doing back in Phil's office? Was this about him? He paused and strained to hear.

His pager bleated and he clamped his hand over it to deaden its shriek. It was the OR, saying they were ready. All voices in Phil's office ceased.

Michael tiptoed away. The door shut quietly.

Michael continued on to his office, dumped his bag, snatched the printed schedule Robin had left on his desk, and raced back down the hall.

And collided with fellow surgeon Katherine Pierce, trailing Matilda as they exited Phil's office.

Matilda didn't see and strode ahead. Katherine grabbed onto him to keep from falling over. Her eyes met his and then darted away. She pushed off him and stepped back. Then she studied him, her head tilting up and down as she did.

"Katherine, what—?"

She spoke at the same time. "You don't look so good, Michael."

He pondered his rumpled yesterday's clothes. His hair was uncombed. He suspected his eyes were bloodshot. He had unbrushed-teeth breath.

"Everything all right?" Her voice was kind. Her clothes were immaculate, her pink blouse and navy skirt the epitome of professionalism. A small black bow held her long blonde hair in a ponytail. He bet her teeth were brushed.

She waited as if she had all the time in the world and wasn't on a tight schedule just like he was.

"I'm late." His voice sounded gruff, even to him. He dashed off before she could respond. He didn't need an explanation. The search for the surgery chair was broadening, and Katherine was meeting with Phil Perkins and the chief of staff. As Matilda had said, the facts speak for themselves.

# Chapter 28

Madge eyed the hospital chaplain, who was back, this time talking about reflection.

What was the point of reflection? Where did that get you? Parading out your bygone mistakes for re-examination, digging up flaws you'd rather forget...

Really, why bother? Nothing changed, for all that mental unhappiness.

No amount of "reflection," as this very young clergyman suggested, would hasten her recovery or undo the past.

She wished she could throw off this thin, blue hospital blanket and trounce out the door. Even sitting in a chair with her perfect posture on full display would show him her mettle, but she needed assistance to the chair and the thing was damned uncomfortable anyway. All she could do was lay in the bed, swallowed by pillows and unable even to hoist herself to his eye level. At least she wasn't connected to the nasal tube anymore. That was something.

She was in the hospital, and she knew why. She and Mikey were not emotionally close, and she knew why.

Drat. This was reflection, exactly what she did not want to do. He tricked her, getting her mind to wander to these best-forgotten places.

She only wanted one thing. She'd only ever wanted one thing. Reflection would not help.

If she were able to get Mikey out of whatever mess he was in, she just might get it. Action was needed, not reflection.

Someone was sabotaging Mikey. He didn't understand, but she did. Mikey hadn't seen enough murder mysteries. He wasn't suspicious enough. Foul play was afoot, and Mikey was at the center.

"Could you leave me now, please? It's time for my television program."

The chaplain was polite. Not pushy. Too green yet to have the confidence and conviction to truly reach her. Thank the Lord.

"You need not come back," she added.

He backed out, apologizing and imploring her to think on it.

Think on it. Ha! Good riddance, that's what she said.

Mikey was lucky to have her. She would do anything for him. Why couldn't he see that?

Maybe some things had not gone as well as they could have in Momland, but the past was the past.

She had a crime to solve. She would fix Mikey's world. This was finally her chance to prove he could count on her. She would win his love.

# Chapter 29

Michael had ten minutes before he was due back in the OR for his last case before lunch. He sat in his office, the four windowless walls closing in.

Phil Perkins had lost confidence in him.

He should march down the hall and tell Phil he'd been hacked. He hadn't written the order and he absolutely knew it. Someone was out to get him, and they were willing to hurt an old man just to bring Michael down.

Or was it the old man they were after? Did Reginald Stark have enemies? Definitely. Even Mildred was against him.

Michael had to get back to the OR. If he was going to talk to Phil, he had to do it now.

He leaned back and contemplated the four white walls.

Two cardboard boxes were stacked neatly in the corner, waiting for the move down the hall. His certificates and diplomas were still in there. Since he'd only use this office a few months, he'd never bothered to unpack.

The blank walls stared back.

Phil would think he was nuts, and for good reason. There was no big conspiracy. No one was out to ruin him. No one was out to kill Reginald Stark. It wasn't Brent or Hal or Matilda. There was a much more likely explanation for what happened. It didn't involve poison and it didn't involve enemies.

Michael had forgotten to log off the computer on the floor. In that thirty seconds, someone sat down or moved over, thought they were in their own patient's note, and discontinued the antibiotics on Reginald Stark thinking they were stopping their own patient's antibiotics.

The computers were crammed together. Maybe someone slid their chair away, and when they slid back, they were at his terminal instead of their own. It was a costly mistake. His mistake for not logging off. Their mistake for not double-checking. A horrible, terrible, deadly mistake.

*I would not trust him with my health. You should not trust him with your patients.*

Whoever typed that note was correct.

Phil should not trust him. Michael couldn't even trust himself. He was as much to blame as the person who wrote the order. He'd been so certain he hadn't done it, he'd lost sight of the bigger picture. A man was in the ICU.

He should have taken responsibility right from the beginning. Some leader he was. Phil had every right to lose confidence.

Somewhere in Michael's boxes was a bright red glass award from the Boston hospital for Clinician of the Year, the highlight award at the yearly black-tie gala. Those colleagues had confidence in him. He'd had confidence in himself. Michael would like to hold the heavy sphere in his hands now, but he didn't have the energy to rummage in the cartons.

"Dr. Baker?"

Michael started. Robin stood in the doorway, her hands twisting together. "You're here. I thought you were in the OR. Someone wanted to see you and they're coming back during lunch."

Michael shook his head. "Sorry. I have to make rounds then. I didn't get to it this morning. I start right up in the OR again at one."

"I know. I told him. He was pretty insistent." Robin stepped into the office and stage-whispered. "It's that Reginald Stark's son. I told him you were in the OR, but he just got louder. He made quite a scene in the lobby. So I said come back at noon. I was going to page you."

Michael sank back. "Oh. All right. I'll round after that."

Great. Had Phil heard this "scene"? Good God. Phil hated scenes.

"I'm sorry. I couldn't dissuade him."

If Robin couldn't dissuade him, the guy was not dissuadable. That didn't bode well.

Michael nodded and headed out. He'd better get a move on. The OR did not tolerate lateness. He didn't need Phil on his back about that, too.

He turned the handle of the door to the stairs, and the door flew open and bashed him in the shoulder. A man catapulted out, his phone in his hand.

"No service in there!" he shouted.

"Right," Michael said. "It will be fine here." He indicated the full clinic lobby where several people spoke on their phones.

"If I wanted to talk in front of other people, don't you think I would have done that?"

Michael smiled sympathetically and tried to move around the man. He was a big guy, thick necked and barrel chested, and he blocked the door. He was taking an inordinate interest in Michael's name badge.

"You're Baker?" he bellowed. His commanding voice quieted the room and the faces in the lobby swiveled their way. "Your assistant told me you were in the OR. You are not in the OR. She was lying."

"She was not—I am headed to the OR. Excuse me."

The man held his ground. "We can talk now. Save me coming back. I am Hunter Stark. My father is Reginald Stark."

Of course. Michael glanced discreetly at his watch. The OR couldn't wait. But clearly neither could this man.

"You operated on my father. What should have been a simple surgery and recovery has turned into a nightmare. He is in the ICU on a breathing machine. A breathing machine! I hold you personally responsible. If my father dies…"

The audience in the lobby gave their full attention. They set down their phones and closed their waiting-room magazines and lowered their newspapers. Not one tried to pretend they weren't listening.

"Let's talk in here," Michael said. He leaned past Hunter Stark and opened the door to the stairs and tried to usher the man in.

"No! We're done here. I've said my piece." He stormed off in the opposite direction, shouting back. "This is on you."

# Chapter 30

Where was Stinky? Madge could ask the nurses to page him, of course, but she didn't like to bother him if he was saving lives. She could wait. A little while longer. Or maybe she should just ask Evan to page him. It was noon, after all.

"Hi, Mom. Sorry I didn't come earlier."

"Stinky!"

He looked tired. His beautiful blue eyes were a mass of red blood vessels and puffy lids. Poor boy. Saving lives was hard work.

"You don't look so good, Mikey," she said.

"Not you, too." He closed his eyes and sighed. "I'm fine."

"You look stressed."

"I am stressed. You're right. I overslept and missed my morning rounds. I was late to the OR. Never good. And I was chewed out by a man whose father is in the ICU."

"Ooh, Antibiotic Man!"

"What?"

"Did you find out anything about the poison? Do you think they could poison the liquid nutrition as easily as the broth? I pulled out the nose tube just in case."

This possibility clearly hadn't occurred to Mikey, she could tell. As it dawned on him, his mouth opened and his eyes widened like when she surprised him with his first saxophone. Well, not exactly like that.

"You did what?" His voice was louder than her ears needed.

"Pretty clever, huh? Whoever it is, they're not getting to me."

"Mom, the formula is from the pharmacy. No one's putting poison in the formula."

"Good to know, good to know. It's not from the kitchen. Got it. You might want to check if that antibiotic patient had anything to eat right before he turned sour. Maybe he was poisoned, too."

"It wasn't poison. It's pneumonia. Mom, you've got to stop talking like this."

"Right. You're right. Someone might hear us and know we're onto them. Smart thinking, Mikey. My lips are sealed."

Mikey pressed his fingertips to his forehead like he had a headache. She'd had headaches like this. He needed an ice pack.

"I've got to get back to the OR, Mom. Will you get another feeding tube?"

"For you, Mikey, anything. Now that I know it's safe."

He didn't saunter off like usual. He stepped out softly, as if each step jarred.

Hmm.

Oversleeping. Headaches. Bloodshot eyes. Puffy lids.

Stinky wasn't tired. Stinky was drinking again. A mother knew these things.

Stinky never drank. Then he showed up one Christmas and threw back almost as much mulled wine as she did. She'd made the mulled wine for herself. Stinky drank half. His spiced cider remained untouched, and in the end they added rum to the cider and it tasted quite cheery.

She didn't want Stinky to end up like her. And his no-good father. Two drunks, that's what they were.

It didn't start like that. She wasn't much of a drinker before Stinky was born. Neither was George. She didn't like the taste of beer, so drinking in high school and college didn't appeal. But oh, the hard stuff. She must have had a propensity toward drink. Her father did. He died young, a fall from a boat, maybe from drinking, for all Madge knew. She didn't have her own memories of him, but her mother sometimes alluded to his dark days. Her mother had been a complete teetotaler. Madge didn't get the sickness from her.

Once she and George started, they couldn't stop. They lost their jobs, maxed their credit cards, and ran out of excuses to borrow items from the neighbors. One day they didn't have money for diapers. Madge wrapped the toddler in George's undershirt held on with duct tape. George still managed to bring home a bottle. Which was why they didn't have money for diapers.

After the diaper day, they both buckled down and found steady jobs. Well, she did. George couldn't hold a job for long, but they managed. She worked two. They drank on the weekends, but she made it to work every day. Mostly. Especially after George left and it was just her.

She hadn't sacrificed her whole life, scrimping and saving and encouraging and setting her own dreams aside only to see Stinky drink his life away.

"What's up, Mikey?" she'd said that Christmas. And he told her Janet left him. There were no secrets between them. She didn't press him on why. The why didn't matter.

"If you love her, get her back." That was her advice.

He flew home again for Mother's Day. She was in the hospital, but no matter. He might have come even so.

By that time, Janet was gone. Stinky had somehow let her go. Janet had left the hospital and was completely out of his life. At least he was on the wagon. That was the one spot of bright news during his visit. Because the rest had been a disaster.

She'd fallen in the grocery store and hit her head so hard

she was unconscious. She awoke in the emergency room, and they wouldn't let her go home. She had some bleeding in the brain and they wanted to monitor.

A teeny, tiny subdural hematoma, Dr. Francine told her.

"You were drunk," Mikey said when he arrived.

Well, for his information, she wasn't drunk. She'd run out of alcohol. That's why she was in the grocery store. She wasn't withdrawing, hadn't had a seizure or anything like that. She was just a tad unsteady. Francine understood. But not Mikey. He wouldn't listen.

"You were driving, and you were drunk." That's all he cared about. True, she had a mildly high blood alcohol level when she was admitted, but she wasn't drunk. Mikey droned on and on about the driving. He didn't care that she had a *bleed.* In the *brain.*

He sold her car while she was in the hospital. Technically it was his car, he'd bought it, but still.

She was so angry. How dare he.

She trotted out a few choice expletives but finished with a zinger.

"You're killing me, Mikey. Just like you did your father."

It was the first and only time she'd ever said anything about his father. It was the last thing Mikey heard because he left the same day, and they hadn't spoken again until she had a bigger subdural and the social worker told him he had to come home.

While Janet was in the picture, Madge thought she might move to Boston and be closer to them. Without Janet, why couldn't Mikey come home?

Madge liked Janet. She was young and vivacious and fun and she loved Stinky. They were good together. Stinky had been so happy. Stinky wasn't happy now. He'd been downright surly since coming back to Seattle, but he was talking to her. That was something, after not speaking for a year.

He needed some fun in his life. He needed a girlfriend. He needed a wife. Because he was going downhill fast.

Something was happening to Stinky. He didn't see it. He didn't know.

Someone was killing his patients. It was glaringly obvious to Madge.

# Chapter 31

The day seemed endless. Michael spoke to Hunter Stark again as soon as he finished in the OR, meeting the man in the ICU and explaining as best he could. Mrs. Stark was there, and that certainly helped. Hunter didn't scream, but he didn't meet Michael's eyes, either. When Michael stuck out his hand at the end, Hunter Stark turned away without shaking.

Michael started his evening rounds, climbing stairs to the highest floor. His orthopedics cases were scattered around the hospital, no longer confined just to Level 10 like when he started at Cascadia. A new administrator's cost cutting verve closed whole wards to save money, housing all types of patients together wherever there was an empty bed rather than by specialty. That's how his mother ended up in the same room as Chrissie. Efficient for room use, not efficient for doctors and staff who now traveled up and down the stairs instead of up and down the floor.

Michael's pager sounded. "Need to talk. I'll be in my office another twenty minutes, then have board meeting. Phil."

Oh, boy.

He would tell Phil his theory about the antibiotic order. He forgot to log off and someone else wrote an order on the wrong patient. If nothing else, the doctors could all learn from this cascade of mistakes to prevent it happening again.

Something to discuss at the next M & M.

Michael reversed course and headed all the way back down the stairs and toward the clinic building. The surgery clinic lobby was empty this time of day. The front desk, too. He flinched when he saw the bare counter, remembering the note he'd found. He paused to verify there was no note today.

He walked toward Phil's office, slower and slower with each step. Did he really want to know what Phil had to say? He pictured the man's pen clicking, his grave expression.

Brent Williams' door was open. Brent sat at his desk staring at a white envelope in his hand. His expression was so intense, Michael stopped abruptly.

Was this another note? Had Brent received a note? Was it about Brent? Was it about Michael?

Did Brent write the note?

Michael must have made a sound, because Brent looked up, startled. He stared just as intensely at Michael. He dropped the envelope and covered it with his hands.

"Everything all right, Brent?" Michael held his breath. He had to see what was in the envelope. Was Brent ready to hand it to Phil? Plant it on the front desk? Was he the guilty party?

Brent's face did not look guilty. He looked sick. Maybe the note was about Brent. Maybe Phil had received it and handed it over. If the note was about Brent, then Michael and his abilities weren't being singled out at all. He felt a flash of hope.

"Saw your mother's still in the hospital," Brent said dully.

"What? Yes." How did Brent know?

"This is how it starts. Something simple at first, then a complication, then a longer stay, then a rehab facility, then back in the hospital, then back to rehab, then you linger, then you die. That's what happened to my mom."

Brent's voice rose. "You know exactly what I'm talking about. Don't you?"

Was Brent accusing Michael of something? Was it all laid out in the note in his hand? "Uh...yes. Unfortunately we see this sort of thing often."

"Cherish your mother while you can." Brent's voice was a whisper now. He lifted the envelope and opened it. A pink card fluttered out and landed face up, the swirly writing clearly visible. Happy Mother's Day.

Michael leaned back against the door frame. This was not a threatening letter. Not a complaint about a second surgeon, so Phil could excuse it as the work of a crank.

A simple Mother's Day card.

"Got this downstairs for my wife. Ben's two, so I buy the cards." Brent picked up the card and fiddled with it. "My own mom's dead. Last fall. That's when you find out how close your family really is. Not. The squabbles. The bickering. My mom didn't have much, but man, everyone wants a piece of it. My sister took care of her and wants a larger share, which is fair, but how much larger? My brother needs money and won't let anything go without a fight. I'm in the middle and I just want out."

"I'm sorry, man." This poor guy. They'd run together a few times, meeting up on the lake or running into each other spontaneously. This was the first Michael had learned anything about his family.

Brent nodded. He tucked the card back in the envelope and said softly, "Plus, I miss Mom."

Brent ducked out. Michael's chest squeezed, a forgotten heaviness he remembered from seeing friends with their mothers, witnessing natural easiness and love and all the normal family interactions that settled in his chest and made the whole topic so difficult.

Michael's own mother, whom he did not miss in the slightest, was upstairs waiting for his nightly visit. She'd have to wait longer because he still had rounds to make.

And he had to talk to Phil. Oh, my God, he'd forgotten about Phil.

Michael rushed from Brent's office and down the hall. Phil was locking his door, briefcase in hand.

"Baker. I'm late for my meeting. But we need to talk. Tomorrow." Phil strode off, his pen clicking away.

# Chapter 32

Stinky was late. He usually came twice a day, not like clock-work, but good enough. She tried to concentrate on his patients and what had happened to them. Instead, she spent the afternoon getting another painful NG tube. And thinking about Stinky's drinking—worrying, frankly. She always came back to his lost love. That's the only other time in his life he drank. Madge never knew the whole story about Janet. She tried not to pry, but it was hard for a mother. Stinky evaded her innocent questions. Even her more pointed ones. But enough was enough. If Stinky was heartbroken, he needed to mend. Maybe she could help.

As soon as he showed up, late in the day, she blurted, "You're drinking again." Best to get it right out there. No secrets. "Is it Janet?"

"Janet?" He apparently had not spent his afternoon reminiscing as Madge had. He sounded perplexed.

"Yes, Janet, the love of your life. There's unfinished business there, I know."

"There's no unfinished business, Mom."

"Then why are you drinking?"

She maybe should have begun with a softer start-up, but this got his attention. His fingertips were back on his temple. He knew better than to deny it. To an expert.

"Why am I... Look, Mom, this is not about Janet. A lot is

going on right now. Plus, Janet and I are done. It wasn't going to work."

"Nothing's ever done. Tell me what happened."

Miraculously, Stinky started talking. Madge lay back on her two pillows and listened.

"She told me she was studying for a special nurses' certification. Then she tells me she was really studying for the MCAT, and she took it, and she was going to apply to medical school. She wanted to surprise me. She was worried she wouldn't do well, so she did it in secret."

"Secrets. There should be no secrets."

"Well, I tend to agree with you there. I was ready to propose. That was my secret. I thought we were about to get married, maybe even start a family."

Marriage! Babies! How Madge wanted grandchildren! But wait, if Janet went to medical school, who would take care of the babies? Mikey? Why not?

"And Janet's secret was that she was about to embark on a whole new career in the field of medicine." Mikey slumped against the wall.

"She must have been thrilled! Do you remember when you got your MCAT score back? You were so excited, Mikey. You called me all a dither. You couldn't wait to send those applications out."

"I know. I remember. Janet and I... We weren't in the same place in our lives. She would move away for medical school, then move again for internship, then residency, then another move if she did a fellowship, then move again for a job."

Hmm. Madge saw the problem. Mikey himself had made four moves in a little over ten years. It did sound difficult. But not impossible.

"For love, Mikey. You can do anything for love."

"Mom, come on. It wouldn't be feasible for me to move that many times. My job..."

Hmm. Mikey wouldn't be moving. He and Janet would be separated all that time.

"Mikey, a job isn't everything." She well knew. Look what she'd done for love.

She'd never told Mikey all her sacrifices. They'd been her choices, and she didn't want to burden his childhood with anything more. He'd had it hard enough as it was. But now, as grownups talking about adult problems and adult decisions... Maybe her experiences could help.

"But my particular job—"

"Your job. Your job. What about Janet? What is her job? Second clarinet?"

"Second fiddle, Mom. No, nothing like that. I just figured our lives would be one way and she had an entirely different plan."

"You aren't the center of the world. I know your job is important, but Janet is important, too."

"We didn't think we could maintain our relationship long distance."

He wasn't listening. This long-distance idea was hooey. She opened her mouth to tell him so, then snapped it shut. Stinky had a red spot on his cheek. Stinky was lying.

# Chapter 33

Michael left his mother's room. Slunk was a better word. He didn't need to be thinking of Janet. What he needed was a drink.

He started down the stairs toward his office and home. Should he stop at the store for more liquor? He only had the remnants of his mother's alcohol, and there wasn't a lot left.

Janet was on his mind, there was no denying it. Even his mother was bringing her up. After he and Janet broke up, they still worked together every one of his operating days, so three days a week. It was too hard, and they both knew it. She loved her job and he loved his, and neither wanted to leave. She was angry when he suggested it had to be her. He'd worked there far longer, and he was on the fast track, heading up, up, up in that prestigious hospital system. She'd be leaving in a year and a half, going off to medical school, so it wasn't her forever career. Somehow, at the time, he couldn't fathom why she might even consider that he should be the one to go. How much of an arrogant jerk could he be?

Finally, after three months of seeing each other three times a week in the OR, of disappointed looks and bruising words, Janet moved on. She started a new job. She blocked him on social media, and he'd done the same. A clean start, they agreed. They hadn't been in contact since.

That was the day of his last drink. Until now.

Janet would have spent this last year filling out her medical school applications for next fall. She might know already if she'd been accepted. It wasn't easy to get into med school, but if he were choosing, with her nursing background and her way with patients, she'd be a shoo-in. She'd make a great doctor.

But after three months of torment, she'd made it very clear she did not want to be his wife.

She'd told him she wanted to be a doctor and she knew they could work it out. He told her it would be impossible, that their relationship would not survive being apart. He could still picture the shocked and stricken look on her face.

That's what he'd told her, but it wasn't true.

He could hardly admit the truth to himself.

He drifted back to his office, remembering how his day began, with Matilda and Katherine meeting in Phil's office, then getting accosted by Hunter Stark in the lobby during lunch. Then Brent with his forthright and unabashed love for his mother. Then barely missing Phil. Michael grabbed his coat, glanced disgustedly around the tiny, dark room, and slammed the door as he left.

"Michael?" Katherine poked her head around the door to her office. "I was hoping to see you."

Michael pictured his short glass and the sound of clinking ice. "What?" he said.

"Did Phil speak with you?"

"Not yet. Tomorrow."

"Oh. Okay, then." Katherine took a step back into her office.

"Katherine." Michael held her eyes. "Tell me."

Katherine nodded. "Phil is going to make a formal announcement at the end of this week. I wanted to talk with you myself as well, but I was going to wait until he spoke to you first. Phil asked me to be chair, and I accepted."

Michael didn't reply. He concentrated on Katherine's name tag, which drooped straight down so you had to turn your head sideways to read it. Had the pin come undone?

"Michael?"

"Your name tag is loose," he said.

"Did you hear what I said? Matilda made it clear the position could not come to you. I'm sorry."

He nodded and left her in her doorway, adjusting her name tag as he walked away.



Michael drove home without stopping and sang to the lizard as he opened his crate. Frank predictably followed him to the living room and soon Michael was seated on the couch with the lizard resting his front legs against it so they were face to face. The three liquor bottles sat on the coffee table along with the glass from last night. Michael picked up the vodka and poured an inch into the glass.

Did he have any juice for this stuff? He edged around the lizard and headed to the kitchen. He found orange juice, carried the carton back, and started to pour. Frank had not moved.

"You're a good companion, you know that?" How had he lived alone here for so long with nobody to talk to? Frank might not respond, but he was there. He could listen. "Let me make my drink, then we can talk. You're not going to believe what happened today. I still can't believe it myself."

Michael's pager blared and he jumped, spilling the juice. Frank's tongue flicked in and out but didn't touch the liquid.

"Excuse me for a moment, will you, Frank?" He dialed the hospital operator. "Dr. Baker, answering a page."

"It's the Emergency Department, Doctor. I'll put you through."

"Hi, Michael, it's Mark. Got a compound fracture for you, college kid on a scooter."

"Sorry, Mark, I'm not on call. Let me check the roster and tell you who is."

"Thanks. Sorry to bother you."

Michael flipped screens on his phone. Oh, no. This couldn't be right. But there it was. He was on call. It came back to him now, the last-minute switch in the schedule. He'd completely forgotten. Usually it would make no difference. He would not have plans beyond his mother.

Today, he'd almost had a drink.

"Mark, turns out you're right. It's me. I'm on my way."

Michael eyed the lizard. "I'll be a while. We'll have to shelve our discussion. And you'd better eat without me." Frank blinked his bright eyes as if he were just as disappointed. Michael leaned forward to rub his belly, but Frank skittered away, leaving Michael grasping at his tail.

Frank pivoted in a flash and sank his claws into Michael's arm right next to the healing welt from before.

"Ow!"

Two red beady eyes of blood shimmered on his forearm, then swelled until red tears ran down and dripped on the couch.

Frank regarded him with his own round eyes, now wary. Michael's arm throbbed.

"Just when I thought you could do no wrong. Those claws of yours are sharp."

"I'm a lizard," Frank's expression said. "What did you expect?"

Michael washed and bandaged the wound and hoped the pain would ease before the surgery. He left the lizard in his crate enjoying his banana and ground turkey. He pinched a second banana off the bunch for himself.

He peeled the banana and ate half while waiting for the

building garage door to rise. The thing was excruciatingly slow. He glimpsed the lower half of a blue car driving by, but when the door lifted fully, the car was gone. Was it the blue car he'd seen that morning? He eased into the street. The other vehicle was nowhere in sight.

Was someone following him? Hunter Stark? Did he go in for vintage cars? Did people really go around blaming doctors and terrorizing them? Possibly. Hunter Stark was furious, and understandably so.

This was ridiculous. The blue car guy probably lived nearby, and their paths crossed. Seeing the same car twice, maybe three times now, meant nothing. He probably passed the same cars every day, but they all looked alike, blue or gray all-wheel drive SUVs or station wagons. They were ubiquitous in Seattle, so they were invisible.

This was an old-fashioned car, all edges and no curves, which made it distinctive. Not ominous.

Still, once Michael pulled into the hospital garage, he felt his fingers relax on the steering wheel and his shoulders unhunch. The toll booth wasn't manned at this hour, and he used his card key to open the gate. Anyone else would need a card key, too. He drove through, and the gate clanked reassuringly behind him.

The parking garage was empty. His quick footsteps reverberated off the concrete as he crossed to the stairway. He glanced over his shoulder. He was alone. He caught himself checking again and forced his head forward. No one was going to attack him in a hospital parking garage.

The college kid's tibia was shattered, and he'd broken his arm, too. The surgeries took all evening, but Michael didn't mind. The anesthesiologist smiled at him, and Michael realized he was humming. Even in the middle of the night, he loved surgery and the thrill of the final x-rays confirming perfect alignment.

Afterward, he went over his orders three times to make sure the antibiotics were in place and nothing was wrong. He double-checked that he logged off the computer. No one was around when he wrote the orders, but he scanned the hallway anyway for a skulking evildoer. The last thing he needed was a problem with a kid. He'd be in that room several times a day to make sure all was well.

He didn't get home until after midnight. He heard Frank rouse in his cage, but he was burrowed again when Michael looked in. Michael tumbled into bed, praying that would be the only call of the night.

He didn't get called again, but he may as well have. He didn't sleep. Another lost night. He lay there tossing and thinking about Katherine Pierce snaring his chairmanship and about Janet becoming a doctor and all the things he never told her. He finally fell asleep only to have his alarm sound soon after.

He took a blessed shower, cold and bracing. At the hospital, he avoided his office and anything to do with Phil Perkins and Katherine Pierce. He'd have to meet with Phil at some point, but not now.

Michael proceeded straight to the college student's room, and he was fine, feeling well.

"Doc! Picture?" He grinned and waved his phone with his good arm. Michael crouched next to him and smiled, feeling the unnatural stretch of his lips. How long since he'd smiled?

"I'll post it now. No one believes I'm here. I need proof," the kid said.

Michael left him and steeled himself for the ICU.

Reginald Stark's wife sat at his bedside holding his grotesquely swollen hand. She looked tiny sitting next to the large man.

"Good morning, Mrs. Stark." He pulled up a chair and sat by her side.

"Oh, Dr. Baker. Good morning. They want to start dialysis," she said.

He knew this from reading the chart. "Yes, to help his kidneys."

"Will it hurt?"

"No. They do it with a tube in his arm, here in the ICU."

She turned her gray eyes on him. "Hunter was pretty harsh when he spoke with you. I don't feel the same way he does. I don't blame you, you know. You've kept me informed, you've been here every day. I don't blame anyone. You're all trying so hard. I just want him to live."

He reached for her free hand and squeezed it gently. She might not blame him, but he was to blame.

He was drained after the visit, but he had a harder visit to follow. To his mother, with her prying eyes and her piercing questions.

He missed Boston, where he'd practiced forever, where they knew him and wanted him to be chair. Where they trusted him, and he trusted in himself. He was here for his mother. But he missed Boston.

She was part of the reason he was unfocused and distracted and making mistakes. Reginald Start was in the ICU because of his mistake. But it was *his* mistake, not his mother's.

Her room was empty. "A volunteer took her for spin in a wheelchair to get some fresh air," Mildred said. "I'll tell her you stopped by."

Hallelujah.

He returned that afternoon after rounds, earlier than usual thanks to an OR cancellation. He bent to kiss her cheek. The feeding tube was thankfully still in place and taped to the other cheek. Her skin was papery and cool, but her room was sweltering. Or was he just hot and bothered? He wiped his forehead and took off his white coat, draping it over the back of the chair.

"Stinky, what's up? Something's up."

How did she always know? "They gave the chair to someone else."

"Oh, Stinky, no! You're supposed to be the chairman." Her words sounded nasal from the tube in her nose, but the vehemence was obvious.

"Four months I've prepared, meeting and planning."

"How could they? Who could possibly be better than you?"

"Katherine Pierce." He could barely say her name without fury. If you'd asked him yesterday how he felt about Katherine, he would have said she was an excellent general surgeon, an excellent colleague. He'd referred many patients to her. That was how he felt yesterday. Before his job was hers. Before she was shooting to the top and he was sinking into the abyss.

"I know her! I have to say, I did like her, Stinky."

"It's my job, not hers. And why Katherine Pierce all of a sudden? The department is full of competent and capable surgeons, including me."

"Name one. Besides you."

"Brent Williams."

"Isn't he a little young? I remember when he couldn't so much as give me a few ice chips without talking to an older resident. Anyway, the nurses say he's grumpy. Insufferable since his mother died. Angry phone calls with his siblings. Snappish with the nurses. Grumbling about his intern who's on restricted hours because she's eight months pregnant. Let him carry around an extra thirty pounds of delicate life and let's see who's grumpy. Next?"

Who told her these things? Michael certainly didn't know this story about the intern. It wasn't the sort of thing Brent might volunteer while running. And he'd only heard about Brent's mother yesterday. She'd died long before Michael moved to Seattle, so that wasn't unusual. "Okay, Jennifer Gorst."

"Jennifer Gorst? She consulted on me last year. Her bedside manner is potatoes. She can't look you in the eye, and she mumbles."

Oh, for heaven's sake. "Neil Partridge."

"Neil Partridge? Come on. That doctor who slept with the resident?"

"Ten years ago? How do you know about that? I just found out that's how they met. They ended up married. Two kids. But okay, not Neil. Me, then. That job should have gone to me."

"I thought your whole mantra was about the patient, put the patient first, improve the patient experience. Are you forgetting about that? Don't you think Dr. Katherine cares about the patient?"

That stopped him. Because he knew Katherine cared. But had she spent the time he had analyzing every patient interaction, from the call center to the techs to the MAs to the nurses to the doctors? Did she have his ideas, his ingenuity, his creativity, his skills?

Did he?

Suddenly he was tired. He'd come to Seattle for this second-best chairmanship, and he couldn't even hold onto that. "I've worked toward this for years," he said. "And they've just handed it to Katherine. As if she deserved it. I'm the one who deserved it."

His mother hesitated. Then she unleashed her bit, words nasal but clear. "There you go, thinking you're the center of the universe again. That you are the only one. Just like with Janet. Mikey, I'm sorry the chairmanship isn't going to you. But if it can't be you, then Katherine Pierce sounds like a fine choice. Better than all of those other surgeons. And if you can't see it, maybe it's just as well you're not going to be the leader."

# Chapter 34

How did Stinky turn out the way he did?

Madge remembered Katherine Pierce, and she doubted Dr. Katherine was given anything without deserving it. She had been the surgeon on call for one of Madge's pancreatitis admissions. Dr. Katherine had taken the time to explain things and drew Madge a very detailed picture of her pancreas in distress. She even took extra time to discuss Madge's drinking. Not that it helped.

But Katherine Pierce was a surgeon. Usually this talk came from her primary care doctor—though Madge never saw her because Madge was always in the hospital—or the hospitalists like Dr. Francine or Dr. Hal. Maybe the GI doc. Madge was touched that the surgeon would try as well. None of the other surgeons ever had.

Dr. Katherine was given the chair job because she was the best, after Stinky, of course. Caring. Thoughtful. Concerned. Skilled. Good with people.

Her Stinky was all of these things, when he was thinking straight.

When someone wasn't out to get him.

He'd lost the chairmanship because his patients were dying. Couldn't they see it wasn't Stinky?

Still, that didn't give him the right to denigrate Katherine Pierce.

Stinky was dedicated to his job, it was true. He put his patients first, he put his hospital first, he thought of the team before he thought of himself, he practically lived in the operating room. But he wasn't the only one.

Katherine Pierce's little chat had been at nine at night because she had a late surgery that day.

Plenty of people worked hard.

She, Madge, had worked hard. She had to. Stinky's father could never hold down a job, never supported them, always flitted from one thing to the next best thing, the next big thing. It was never the right thing. For him.

Madge was on her own.

She had sacrificed her dreams, her life. She was in law school when she became pregnant. A city hall wedding, bed rest, and an early delivery to a colicky baby scuttled any thoughts of going right back. Plus, they needed the money from two of them working, and she returned to her pre-law-school job as a paralegal. Then the drinking began, the two of them exhausted at the end of the day, relaxing with a cocktail, then a few, then calling in sick one time too many and no longer working as a paralegal. And so they went.

Stinky never knew what she gave up.

When he'd stormed out, he had left his white doctor coat on the chair. She gazed at it, that symbol of Stinky and all he'd accomplished. What could she have been if given the chance? Not a doctor. She'd leave that to Janet. But definitely a lawyer. Where would she be today if she'd continued her studies? If she hadn't had to feed the three of them?

Yes, Stinky wasn't the only one to work hard.

What made him think he was God's gift to all?

Was she to blame?

She never made him do chores, the dishes, vacuuming, garbage, laundry, cooking. She figured he did enough of that on his own during her bad weeks. The house held together when she was out of it, so she did absolutely everything when she was with it.

She'd tried. Lord knows she tried. Maybe she pampered him too much, spoiled him. Her little prince.

It was true. When she wasn't drinking... When she wasn't drinking she attempted, as much as was possible, to make it up to him. It wasn't possible, of course. He'd seen her passed out in the front yard. He and the neighbors. He said they telephoned all night to make sure she was all right, to make sure *he* was all right. How many times had they had to call? To check on him? He told her he couldn't walk down the street without shame because everybody knew.

*I know you and you know me. You know my secrets.* Isn't that how his song went?

He knew her secrets, all right. He'd seen her covered in vomit and undressed and unable to stand on her own. He seen her threaten his teacher when the man suggested they contact his father, that a father figure would be good in Mikey's life.

So when she was sober, she smothered her boy in kindness, in goods, in praise. Hell, all the parents spoiled their kids in those days. Medals all around. Participation is everything, everyone's a winner here. She just went more overboard than the rest.

She remembered giving him a standing ovation after his saxophone solo with the jazz band in high school. She was the only parent standing, applauding wildly. She may have even whistled. The other parents sat quietly when their children soloed, perhaps gave a smattering of polite applause, but she wanted Mikey to know she was there, that she thought he was the cow's meow. And that she hadn't been escorted out, like she once had when security caused an embarrassing brouhaha that stopped the show.

Mikey made sure she remembered that episode. "Just take your seat and don't worry where it is or what other people are doing," he scolded her before each performance. No matter that that other mom blocked her view taking a video with an enormous video camera.

Mikey had to grow up fast because of her. Well, because of his father, really. Because of that night. Mikey was never the same carefree little boy after that.

Alcohol was to blame, all around.

How many times had she been to rehab? How many meetings had she attended, promising herself to just get through that one day, one single day, without the booze?

Yet here she was. And here he was.

He was not the center of the universe, for all that she'd made him the center of hers.

They both worked hard. And they both lost.

She was not going to let her son lose.

And she was not going to lose her son. Not again. She would do whatever it took to keep him in her life.

# Chapter 35

Michael ripped off the bandage and held out his arm to the lizard. Two angry red marks in swollen tissue. "See what you did? Hurts like hell. It better not get infected."

Frank flicked his tongue, oblivious.

The lizard was ignoring Michael because he'd yelled. In the time it took to scramble them both some eggs, Frank had scavenged several shirts from the dirty bin plus ties from the rack and gathered them into a burrowing pile that now spread shredded in the living room.

Janet's picture was part of the pile, scattered in pieces across the floor. Her smile, her eyes. Michael couldn't find much more.

Then the tegu streaked away, tripping Michael. His sore arm cracked against the coffee table. The bottle of vodka teetered and the alcohol spilled everywhere.

"I should have left you to rot in Chrissie's apartment! I don't want you, I don't need you." The words flew out before he realized what he was saying. Including, inexplicably, "I don't love you."

He'd calmed down now. It was his own fault, not Frank's. Frank was a lizard, doing what lizards do. Michael should have been more careful.

"I'm sorry, Frank. I would never have left you. I do want you. I'm happy you're here."

Frank didn't know the photo was Michael's only tangible reminder of Janet. Which is what must have prompted his words.

Michael dropped to the couch, the air flowing out of him. He'd said those very words to Janet. "I don't need you, I don't love you." How could he?

He never said what he truly felt, the words he couldn't bring himself to speak. "I do love you. I need you. I see you. I want what you want. Your dream is my dream."

Coward.

Janet had known him for years. She knew him better than anybody. They were meant to be together forever.

She'd seen his mother at her worst, spewing vitriol and vomit, and she was still willing to make a life with him. "I don't like it, but I love you, and she is part of the package. Thank God she lives in Seattle." That pretty much summed it up for Michael as well, and the reason he stayed on the East Coast all these years.

Janet was waiting when he came home that day. She said she had a surprise. She had dinner and candles and flowers.

He racked his brain to remember if he'd forgotten an anniversary. Nope. He was clear on all their anniversaries. And there were a lot. The day they met. Their first date, their first kiss. The day they first told people at the hospital. The day she moved in with him. None of these momentous occasions was that day.

Was she pregnant? His heart skipped, and he prayed this was going to be her news. A baby.

He was ready for a family, for the two of them to start the next chapter. They'd talked about children. Her exact words were, "Promise if we ever have kids, we'll never leave them alone with your mother."

Of course this was her news. A baby. Look at her. She was glowing.

He'd been planning to propose for some time. They'd dated over two years, they'd known each other much longer. They had a weekend on Cape Cod at the end of the month, and he was going to ask her then. But today would work just as well. Better, even, what with her news. He formed his words. "I love you. Let's be a family. Let's get married." He never said them aloud.

She spoke first. "I took the MCAT. Michael, I did really well."

The words she said were so unexpected, so different from what he imagined. His face wasn't right, he knew. Her look of horror likely reflected his own expression. He stuttered and stammered and made it clear that her being a doctor was not what he had in mind.

She listened to his reasons. She'd been in a difficult long-distance relationship before. She said she understood.

She believed him. She should have known him better.

He should have known himself.

It was time to be truthful. With himself. With Janet. He'd lost her anyway. Why not let her know the real reason why.

They met on her very first day in the OR. A complicated case made more complicated by an arterial bleed. "That was amazing," she said after. "You found the bleeder in all that blood. I was so scared." She hadn't looked scared. She opened the suture he asked for with quick and steady hands.

The next day she dropped a bone saw on the floor, and they had to send for a new sterile one. Momentary fear flicked across in her eyes, waiting for his reaction. He laughed, a genuine "welcome to the team and what a great first week" laugh.

"I love the tone you set in the OR," she said, regaling him with horror stories of other ORs she'd dealt with, the hierarchy, the condescension.

She thought he was unique.

"I can't believe how well you laid out the options," she gushed when he helped a diabetic patient make a difficult decision about amputation.

"Aw, shucks," he demurred. But his insides were singing.

"That poor family. Thank God they have you for their doctor," she whispered when he explained a complex procedure to the parents of a trauma patient.

He was a doctor. That was who he was. Was that how she saw him? Was that the allure? Was that what she loved?

If she were a doctor, too, would the magic vanish?

The lizard ambled over and lay at Michael's feet. Michael leaned over to stroke his head.

Frank's mouth twisted, as if to say, "That's stupid."

Michael gently scooped him up, minding the tail, and set him on the couch. "You're right. I don't know what I was thinking."

He had envisioned her working hard over the decade of medical school and residency and fellowship, growing more and more distant from him, metamorphosing with each year into a better and better version of herself, more knowledgeable, more compassionate, more caring, more able. While he stagnated with no new tricks to entice her and no ability to match her change. She was off to the races, starting out on an exciting new path. He was plodding through a pasture like a draft horse, on track for promotion, sure, but basically the same workhorse. Not a stallion.

And it was true he didn't want to move. It wasn't the real reason, just a convenient excuse. He didn't want to leave his job and his rising career.

As if he hadn't just moved across the entire country for his mother.

What *had* he been thinking?

Janet made him feel he was the most special person in the world.

He'd thrown his life into medicine, with a single-minded belief that his value came from this caring of others, from the measures of success of healthy patients and awards and promotions. His achievements. He thought Janet valued him for all those things as well.

And that she was about to see he was nothing special.

He lay his hand on Frank's smooth back. "She loved *me.*"

Frank flipped over so Michael's hand lay on his soft underbelly. He cocked his head, black eyes on Michael's.

"Of course she loved *you.* You are good at your job. But that's not all you are."

The lizard hadn't said a word. But the lizard was right.

# Chapter 36

Madge might not have the full picture of what happened between Mikey and Janet, but babies were at stake. Her son's future happiness was at stake.

Mikey still loved Janet. Okay, then. With Madge's help, he could win her back.

"Time for a walk."

Drat. Tony the Torturer. What was he doing here so late? She let him hoist her and fasten her into the safety belt. All the while her mind was on Mikey. Step one, fall on his knees and promise eternal love and half the housework. Step two, get to work on grandchildren. She would be happy to move to Boston to watch them while the two of them were out administering to the sick every day. Maybe she could even live with them. That would be nice.

First and foremost, though, clear Mikey's name. She would keep her eyes and ears open in the hall.

Tony paused in the doorway and adjusted her strap. She studied her bright yellow socks, incongruous against her white crepe paper shins. The socks had sticky grips on the bottom, but why couldn't she just wear actual shoes? Mikey had taken her shoes home along with all her other personal property. If she wanted to break out of here, she would have to do it in these telltale yellow socks and backless hospital gown. As obvious as an orange prison jumpsuit.

Though she would never dream of going on the lam. She didn't mind the hospital one bit.

Unless the murderer came after her.

If her legs were stronger, she'd have a better chance.

Tony was taking forever. Madge's backside was cold. She should have worn her pink nightgown today. These gowns were worthless.

A moan escaped from the room next door. Hmm. Madge perused the hallway with its glossy linoleum floor and its multiple doors, some shut, some ajar. Behind each door was a story, and none of those stories were happy. This wasn't the baby ward. People arrived here suddenly and by accident, like Chrissie, or over and over with a chronic illness that took its toll. Or, like her, with a preventable problem she couldn't control. Anyway, this place was full of fear and disease and heartbreak. How did Stinky stand it?

Well, the same way she did. For Stinky, this was his workplace, shared with colleagues as dedicated as he was, toiling away to save lives. For her, this was a haven of familiar faces and caring souls who, even if they didn't cater to her every whim, at least saw to her comfort and her health. They didn't chastise her for her multiple readmissions. They didn't roll their eyes and close their doors and say never darken our doorstep again. They opened their arms and told her they'd help and that getting her well was all that mattered. And if she wasn't allowed to eat, they brought her those swishy sticks with the green sponge tip to moisten her lips, and sometimes even a cup of ice water to re-dip them herself and surreptitiously sip if no one was looking. They let her wear her own nightie and didn't confiscate her lipstick or her perfume. The staff indulged her. She knew that.

Except Tony. He went above and beyond in his quest to improve her well-being, no indulgence at all. Tony needed to get with the program.

He gave her a nudge that undeniably said, "Get moving." He marched her down the hall, slow step by slow step. Excruciating, bone grinding on bone, flaccid muscles straining to support her.

"You're favoring one side. Does that right knee give you trouble?"

She swiveled around as best she could, dangling from his strap. She eyed him, tall and muscular, probably not an arthritic joint in his body.

"What do you think, Bub?"

"I think we need to build up your quadriceps. I have a pamphlet I'll bring you."

Geez.

Finally he was finished, and she tottered next to her bed while he wrote his note, one eye on the portable computer he'd pushed in from the hall, one eye on her.

"Three minutes," he said. "Try to stand on your own without my support for three minutes."

As if.

The computer wasn't working. He couldn't log in.

"Don't think I'm standing here any longer, just because you forgot your password," she said.

"Three minutes. I'm watching the clock."

He wasn't watching the clock at all. He was fishing around in his shirt pocket. He brought out a card.

"Mikey does that, too."

"Who?"

"Mikey. My son. Michael Baker, the surgeon." She indicated the white coat on the chair as if Mikey were sitting there himself.

"I didn't know Dr. Baker was your son."

Madge could hear the obvious respect in his voice. Maybe he wouldn't torture her now. She should have mentioned Mikey earlier.

"Yes. He has his passwords on a card, too. He makes them ridiculously complicated, then he has to write them down. Mine is easy. Mikey1. Oops. Guess I'll have to change it now."

This whole password thing was silly. She used Mikey1 for every account, but only used one website regularly, and that was her hospital chart. The hospital put her whole medical record on the computer now, and she could read every word. She couldn't fathom why they would do that, but she gobbled it up. Although she did get tired of reading how her pancreatitis was due to alcohol, her subdural was due to a fall from alcohol, she'd been offered alcohol rehab and had refused it, etcetera, etcetera.

Anyway, whenever a site needed a password, she used Mikey1. She'd gone her entire life with this one password, and she wasn't going to add to her collection now.

"Three minutes is up," she said.

"It's not, but you can sit down. Before you fall down." He eased her onto the bed and positioned her pillows and finished his note. He was back in no time with a green pamphlet of knee exercises that could be performed lying in bed and a promise to add more at their next PT session.

"Goody," she said to his retreating back.

Madge glanced at the pamphlet. Since these were exercises meant to keep her from hobbling, she wasn't reassured by the crutch decorating the cover. She tossed it aside and counted the many hours until she'd see Stinky again.

# Chapter 37

Michael's hand moved back and forth across Frank's belly. Janet loved *him*. The whole of him, not just the strong persona he showed the world. His breath caught. Maybe, if he were being entirely truthful with Janet, maybe he could tell her why he woke up in sweats in the night. Why he didn't eat fried chicken. Could he be this honest with her?

She might know him better than anybody, but she didn't know everything. He had not told her everything.

One thing at a time.

Frank tilted his head. Michael's phone was on the table.

"Frank, it's midnight there."

The next morning, early, after very little sleep, Michael sat in the same spot. He saw his life with a new lens now. His condo, too, with his sleek couch, his stark painting, his stream-lined glass tables. They were so spartan, so cold. so empty. Janet brought color and flowers and light to his condo in Boston. He had forgotten how bleak it looked when she left. How bleak the same furniture looked here in Seattle. But not for long.

He breathed deeply, free and light. Whatever it took, he would win her back.

He could stay at Cascadia and clear his name, maybe even gain some sort of promotion. But what was a promotion compared to Janet? Even the chairmanship in Boston, really. There was more to life than his job.

If Janet was starting medical school in the fall, he'd go with her. Wherever it was, he'd follow.

He punched in the familiar number on his phone. Not for Janet, she'd blocked that, but for his old hospital. He'd already double-checked her social media accounts but came up with nothing. He was blocked on everything. They'd both agreed it was for the best. After all the angry words.

"Barbara, it's Michael Baker again. I'm trying to locate Janet. I never knew where she went after she left. You gave her a reference, right? Do you know where she is?"

Barbara gave him the name of the hospital without hesitation. "I miss you both. I hope you work things out."

He dialed the hospital and waited while he was transferred from line to line and finally to the OR front desk. "My name is Dr. Michael Baker and I used to work with Janet Smalls and I'm trying to find her."

"Oh, Dr. Baker, she doesn't work here anymore. I think she moved to Philadelphia."

"Philadelphia?"

"Yes, I'm pretty sure. Sorry I can't help you more."

He pulled out his computer and placed it on the coffee table, pushing aside the dirty glass from his birthday. He would look up all the hospitals in Philadelphia. He'd call them one by one.

He'd find her. He'd talk to her. He'd fly out there if he had to. He loved her and always would and he was half of a whole without her.

He typed in "hospitals" and "Philadelphia."

He sucked in his breath and gaped at the screen. Somehow Janet was smiling back at him from the computer. Her blue eyes twinkled, and her light blonde hair framed her heart-shaped face with her ever-present grin.

In a daze, he clicked on the picture. The words made no sense. The caption might well have been written in Latin, it was so utterly incomprehensible. It was so unthinkable that he covered it with his hand to block the words.

Frank nudged his way under his arm on the coffee table. Michael forced himself to again face the screen. He breathed deeply and slowly raised his hand.

"Philadelphia nurse murdered, found strangled behind hospital."

# Chapter 38

Michael sat without moving. Janet smiled at him from the screen on the coffee table. She whispered to him that she hoped their children would have his height not hers, his easy-going nature, his brains. She laughed and said they were sure to be towheads, with two blond parents.

His pager bleated, and he grabbed at his belt to shut it off. "First clinic patient is in the room. Haven't seen you yet." His medical office assistant, Robin, tactful as always. He snatched up his phone and called her back.

"I'm not coming in today. Is Dr. Partridge in clinic this morning? I'll talk to him. He may be able to add my patients."

"What?"

"I'll miss clinic today. I'm...sick."

Robin lowered her voice. "I guess you heard they're making the announcement today. About the new chair. I heard a rumor—"

"No! That has nothing to do with it. I just... I'm not feeling well."

"Oh. Of course. Sorry. I shouldn't have mentioned it. Look, Dr. Partridge has a light schedule. I see him just down the hall. I'll ask him about your clinic, and he can call you back if there's any problem."

"Thank you. Thank you. That would be great."

"Don't worry about clinic. You just take care of yourself."

Michael sank back. He'd have to go into the hospital eventually, to see his inpatients and to see his mother. Neil couldn't do everything. But Michael wasn't going now. Not yet.

He'd stared at this picture of Janet long enough. He leaned forward and placed his finger on the screen, on Janet's lips. He closed his eyes. He remembered how her true lips felt, soft and playful, and her mouth, ready to laugh at any moment, tilting toward his for a kiss. He shook his head, opened his eyes, and scrolled down.

The black and white words blurred. Only snippets registered. "Late shift." "Strangled with her lanyard." "Police seek public's help."

The whole story was too much for him to read right now. Too much for forever.

Time moved on, but he sat without moving. The light shifted, golden then bright then shadows. His pager blared. He hit the button to silence the cacophony. Frank grew restless and crawled away.

Janet was dead.

How had he let her go? Why hadn't he been there with her?

Had she been afraid?

He closed the computer gently, as if this picture of her were real. Two bottles stood behind the closed computer, the empty whisky bottle and the gin. The vodka bottle lay on its side on the floor. He hated gin but raised the bottle in the air in a salute to Janet and downed a swig.

His pager wailed again. Hal. Oh, Lord. This was the second time. Michael dialed and Hal picked right up.

"Your mom has a fever. I'm sending her to CT. I think her pancreatic necrosis is infected. I left a message with your MA earlier." Hal was polite and didn't mention the unanswered page. "Your mom looked fine then, just a slight fever, but now it's higher. Don't want her to get septic. Keeping you in the loop in case you want to come up."

Hal assumed he was in the hospital. "I'll be there in twenty minutes."

"If she's not here, look for her in CT."

Frank eyed him gravely. Michael patted his head, steering clear of the tail. He looked for his white coat, but it wasn't in the living room or the bedroom. He tried to picture the day before, but his mind was full of Janet. Then he remembered his mother and her probing and how quickly he'd fled after that. He was never without his coat. It was a part of him. Could he have left it behind?

He drove out of his garage thinking not of his mom but of Janet. She was with him when he chose this car, and the midnight blue color was thanks to her.

"I'm not riding in a red car," she said.

"That's quite a declaration, don't you think?" he said. "The red is pretty."

"It's not pretty. It's orange. And if you have a red car, you'll drive too fast. It's a known fact." Then she burst out laughing. "I'm teasing," she said. "I just don't like orange."

"It's red," he said.

"Get the blue," she said.

And he did.

At the corner, he spotted another blue car. The old blue car was parked just past the intersection. The street was tree-lined and leafy, but he could see it clearly. He was pretty certain there was a man in the driver's seat. What was going on? This was getting out of hand. He slowed as he turned and glued his eyes to the rearview mirror, but the blue car never materialized. Had someone really been in it? Did the guy live there? That would explain why Michael saw the car so often.

He didn't have time today to find out. He forced his eyes back to the road but couldn't keep them there. He was lucky the drive to the hospital was short and traffic was sparse because he drove with one eye on the mirror the whole way.

Michael found his mother in the Radiology Department, her heavy perfume filling the hall. Even if he hadn't known she was there, that cloying scent would have given her away. She was finished with CT and lying on a gurney in the hall awaiting transport back. Her damp hair clung to her forehead, and up close he smelled the fever's sweat mingled with the nauseating perfume.

Her flushed face reminded him of all the days of his childhood, her face flushed with alcohol and shame.

"How are you feeling, Mom?"

"I'm missing *Creature Friday*."

He was in no mood for her flippancy. "I guess you're feeling all right, then."

"You didn't come today. Are you still being pig-headed about Janet?"

A punch hit Michael in the abdomen, and he shot against the wall. He pressed both hands against the thickly painted cool concrete blocks for balance.

"Stinky! Are you okay? I'm the one who's sick here."

"Janet," he managed.

"Yes, Janet. I can see you still care. Get over yourself. Go after her. You love her. And I want those grandbabies."

Tears filled his eyes. His throat tightened and his jaw ached. He leaned against the wall in the Radiology hallway, taking shallow breaths to keep from breaking down.

"Stinky, Stinky. What?"

"Janet's dead. She was strangled. Two months ago. I just found out."

"Janet? No!"

He couldn't speak but nodded. His mother adored Janet. She never knew how Janet felt about her. At first Janet said, "She's full of spit and fire." Then she had to deal with that spit and fire herself, and she changed her view. But she remained polite and engaging when they visited. "I love you, and she is part of the package." That's what Janet said.

Had said. Before she was dead.

His mother sat bolt upright in the middle of the bed. "Not another bad thing! Chrissie. Dead. Me. Almost dead. Antibiotic Man. Soon to be dead. Hopes of the chairmanship. Dead. Janet. Dead. Stinky, why are all the people around you dying? What is going on with you?"

Her words jarred Michael back to reality. His voice was harsher than he intended. He was angry, at himself, at his mother. He was sick of her games, sick of her questions, sick of her.

The ugly words spilled out before he could stop them. "Chrissie died of a fat embolism. I didn't see her that afternoon because I didn't want to see *you*. Mr. Stark is in the ICU because I didn't log off the computer because I was distracted by *you*. You're sick because you have pancreatitis because *you* drank even though you know how dangerous it is. I lost my chairmanship because I was forced to leave Boston to take care of *you*, because *you* are an alcoholic."

His mother sat perfectly still, back straight, eyes forward. "Stinky, I think you've been drinking." She said it quietly, a contrast to his shouts.

"Don't turn this on me," he growled. "You can smell it a mile away, can't you? One sip. That's all I had."

A soft bell chimed in the hallway. The baby bell. He and his mother both turned their faces up toward its beautiful sound.

Janet was dead. The baby bell would not ring for them.

His mother's voice remained soft. "And Janet? I suppose I strangled Janet, too?"

He was spent. He was done. "Janet is on me," he said. "I wasn't there for her. I wasn't there."

# Chapter 39

Michael walked the six flights from Radiology to the tenth floor to see his first inpatient. The college student was going home today. He'd mastered maneuvering with one leg and one arm. Michael composed himself on the way, clasping his hands together to keep them from shaking, sucking in the dank stairwell air to expunge his mother's perfume from nose and mouth. By the time he reached the floor, he was outwardly calm.

The kid was on the phone and grinned as he hung up. "That was your assistant, making my follow up appointment. I'll see you again in two weeks."

Michael made a mental note to tell Robin thanks. She was a marked improvement on Katherine's MA, whom they'd shared until Robin was hired. That woman never got the hang of scheduling the postop follow ups proactively, leaving Michael to cram patients into the lunch hour or at the end of the day when they called needing to be seen.

Robin probably wouldn't be his medical assistant for long. Her duties now included greeting patients, taking basic histories and blood pressures, answering phone calls, and scheduling, but she was a quick learner. Embarrassingly, she once mentioned her sister was a doctor, and Michael asked if she'd ever considered medical school. He'd meant it as a compliment. Robin was smart. Her expression told him she did not see it this way. "What's wrong with being an MA?" she'd said.

MA or not, Robin would soon be recognized and promoted to bigger things that did not involve him. Because she'd thought she was signing on to be the assistant to the chairman of the Department of Surgery. But that was not him.

He went from the college student and his smiles to Reginald Stark and his ventilator in the ICU. Mr. Stark's son sat by his bed. Michael hadn't seen Hunter Stark yesterday. When they'd talked the day before yesterday with Mrs. Stark in the room, the man had at least been civil. He didn't look civil now.

Hunter crossed his arms and scowled. The guy was a chip off the old block. Did he drive a retro blue car?

"What are you doing here? Haven't you done enough?" It was clear by Hunter's acerbic tone what he meant.

"I come by every day. The ICU docs are taking good care of him, but I still like to visit."

"He wouldn't be here if it weren't for you. This is your fault." Hunter spit the words out, and Michael saw heads spin in the hallway outside.

"I'm sorry." What more could he say to this angry man? Nothing.

"Have you been drinking?" Mr. Stark's son stepped closer, and Michael involuntarily stepped back. "Is that it? Are you a closet alcoholic?"

"What? No." Michael was aware of absolute silence in the hallway now. The hallway would normally buzz with motion and noise.

Hunter Stark gestured at the door. "Please leave. And don't come back."

Michael stepped out of the room and caught several eyes on him. He walked calmly through the ICU, head up, eyes forward. It wasn't until he was off the floor and headed down the stairs that he stopped. He gripped the banister and closed his eyes and stood for a moment until his mind cleared.

He left the staircase and gritted his teeth as he paused in his mother's doorway. She'd be back from radiology by now. He did not want to see her again. The room was dark as always, and he heard a snore and a snort. He crept forward. Her eyes were blessedly closed, but that didn't mean she was asleep. He lifted his white coat quietly off the chair and slipped back into the stairway.

He had a few more patients. Thanks to his mother and Mr. Stark's son, he now knew he'd better stand a good distance away. His one slug of gin was surprisingly noticeable.

Maybe he could find a breath mint. Although his lifelong experience smelling his mother's minty but alcoholy breath told him that would not work.

He visited his next patient, loitering at the foot of the bed and calling out his questions as if this were normal. What was wrong with him? Two nurses called "good afternoon" as he passed, and he navigated around them with a wave but no words. Good Lord, was the hospital always this crowded?

Francine greeted him at the computer station, a smile lighting her face. He chose a spot safely away from her. Was it time for the night shift already?

"Michael. Hi. Haven't seen you in a while. Since..." She stopped. The smile disappeared.

He knew exactly when they'd last seen each other. At the code when Chrissie Johnson died and the next morning. Francine must have realized this, too, because she changed the subject. "Saw your mother's CT. Her necrosis is infected. Hal started antibiotics earlier, and she's already turned the corner."

She hesitated. "And... Mike?"

"Yes?"

"When she goes home, she'll be on antibiotics. They don't mix with alcohol."

He kept his mouth shut lest his own little alcohol sip seep out. He understood what Francine was saying. He would need to watch his mother closer.

How much closer? He wasn't moving in with her, that was for sure.

Francine's eyes held his gaze. He nodded. She twisted her short hair between two fingers. He should have said, "Thanks. Gotta run." He wasn't fast enough, and Francine continued talking.

"I read your department's email announcement today." Michael willed her to stop, but she didn't. "Sorry about the chairmanship. I understood that was to be your position."

He was stuck now. How could he respond to that? The entire hospital staff knew he'd been hired to take over for Phil Perkins. Now the job was Katherine's.

He nodded again, but he couldn't speak. He hoped she'd take it as a thanks. Plus, he certainly didn't want Francine to smell his breath. Mercifully, she took the hint and left him to write his notes in peace.

He should have expected some sort of fallout after such a crazy week. He should have planned for trouble.

Phil Perkins was waiting the next morning when he arrived. They'd spoken last night on the phone. Since Michael hadn't been at work, Phil called him to formally announce the decision to give the chairmanship to Katherine. "I'm certain you will support her in every way," Phil had said.

Today he stood in his doorway and waved Michael in.

"Michael. Perfect. Good to catch you."

How could Phil not catch him? Three secretaries and medical assistants had stopped Michael on his way in to tell him Phil was looking for him. His own MA warned him,

"Dr. Perkins wants to see you and he doesn't look happy. He's clicking that pen. Best to be prepared."

"Thanks."

"By the way, Dr. Dexter called here asking for you yesterday. I didn't know your mother was in the hospital. I'm so sorry to hear it. Did he get hold of you?"

"Yes, thank you." Great. Now Robin would find out why his mom was an inpatient, and then the whole clinic would know.

He'd recently come across a bunch of medical assistants in a lively conversation, and Robin later told him Trudi's mother was moving to a retirement community. "Why doesn't Trudi take her in?"

Michael thought a retirement community sounded like an excellent idea himself. Robin continued. "My mother sacrificed everything for us. She even took an extra job when my sister decided she wanted to go to medical school. She never complained. I'd never let my mother go into a home."

"Yes, well..." was how he'd replied. Now that Robin knew about his mother, he could say good-bye to the clinic as the last work bastion where his life's embarrassment wasn't known.

This meeting with Phil Perkins had better not be about his mother. That's the last thing Phil wanted to deal with in the waning days of his career.

Especially if... No. This past week his mother had been furious, but she still held her tongue on what mattered to him most.

Phil probably wanted to speak to him in person about the chairmanship. That was all.

Michael stepped into the office and took his usual seat in the tall wing chair. It wasn't until then that he saw the other wing chair was occupied. Katherine Pierce smiled weakly.

"Hello, Michael," she said.

Lord, what now? Not another anonymous note?

"Michael, I asked Katherine to be here, since she will soon be in charge." Click, click.

Each of Phil's words hit Michael like a dart, flying from Phil's desk to Michael and landing on the bull's eye of his chest, punctuated by two piercing clicks of the pen. Michael's breath was sharp and ragged. He looked anywhere but at Katherine, who sat rigidly next to him. Outside Phil's window the clouds sat heavy and low, with gray Puget Sound waters and no ships today.

"One of the nurses from the ICU wrote me an email. She said she heard a patient's relative ask if you'd been drinking. Were you drinking?"

Jesus.

"I want to emphasize that what you say to me will become part of the record on this matter."

What in the world? Part of the record? He heard Katherine shift in her chair.

"I also want to let you know that we have support for physicians with impairments. Confidential. A program with an excellent success rate. If you feel you need it. Or if we feel."

Rain started to fall outside, with a slight darkening of the lighting and a soft patter on the windows.

"I didn't work yesterday," Michael said.

"Yes. Dr. Partridge took your clinic." Phil missed nothing.

"Yes. Dr. Partridge kindly took my clinic. I had had some bad news. In the afternoon, I had one sip of a drink, but my pager went off and..." Did he want to discuss his mother with Phil?

"One sip?" Phil asked.

"Yes. One sip. Then I had to come into the hospital, and I saw my inpatients while I was here."

Katherine spoke for the first time. "It is unfortunate that the patient in question is Reginald Stark, that this relative is a relative of Reginald Stark's."

Michael let out a short breath. "Yes. His son. He was quite angry already."

"One sip of alcohol is certainly acceptable. But I'm afraid this will open a case for you, and new measures will be in place. This may not be the end." Phil looked ready to finish the meeting. Michael surely was. He stood to leave.

"One more thing," Katherine said. Michael reluctantly turned to her. "It's best if you don't visit Reginald Stark again. If there are ongoing orthopedic needs, we can have someone else see him. If there are not, then there is no further reason to round on him. The ICU team has it from here."

The rain slammed hard against the window, adding an exclamation point to her message.

# Chapter 40

Michael sat in his tiny office and glared at the four blank walls, devoid of decoration except for one empty bookcase. He hadn't even hung his photo of Mount Rainier. He hadn't planned on staying long. Now he'd be lucky to hold onto this miserable office, this job. With Katherine at the helm, who knew how long he'd last at Cascadia?

Taking him off the Reginald Stark case! Next they'd suggest a leave of absence, take some time for himself. He knew what that meant. Get it together or get out.

A cup of cold coffee sat on his desk, God knew how old. After three nights with little sleep, his eyes were gritty and his head was splitting. He took a long sip. It was disgusting. He slammed it back on his desk, spilling coffee everywhere.

Pain seared his arm. The coffee wasn't hot. What in the world?

He shoved his sleeve up and assessed his arm. The forearm was swollen and the skin around Frank's puncture was purple. That lizard!

Michael's arm was infected and suddenly throbbing, the boom, boom, boom of his arm matching the boom, boom, boom in his head.

What was happening to him? He felt things spinning completely out of control. When he was little and his mother was drinking, he used to spin in circles until he was dizzy, until he couldn't see the world around him, and his life and his mother were a blur. Now his world was spinning, and his mother was still at the center, the fulcrum on the spinning top that was his screwed up, topsy-turvy life right now.

His pager blared. The seventh-floor nurses' station.

"Dr. Baker? This is Evan. Your mom's nurse today."

The man paused and Michael pictured him shifting from one foot to another gathering up the courage to talk. Michael wasn't scary. What if the guy were calling Brent Williams? Even Michael's mother called him grumpy. Brent once snapped at a nursing student who interrupted his clinic and they all endured a Phil Perkins pen-clicking discussion about respect for all, treat everyone as if they were a member of your family.

Evan finally got to the point. Michael's mother wanted to talk to him and was standing right there at the nurses' station on her morning PT walk.

"Put her on," Michael barked. He saw Evan flinch as if he were standing right in front of him.

"Stinky!"

"Mom, I've got clinic now."

"You're busy. I know. I know."

He waited. His watch told him clinic was about to start. "Mom, what is it?"

"Oh. I wanted to say good morning. You were so pissy yesterday." She lowered her voice, but Michael knew Evan and others at the nurses' station could hear every word. "I wanted to check on you. Because...you know. What with Janet, and your drinking—"

"Mom! Shut up about that! Just shut up!" He didn't need more complaints filtering down to Phil. The phone clicked in his ear, and he slammed his down, too. Pain shot up his arm from the infected scratch.

It served him right. He'd screamed at his mother. So much for respect for all, treat others as if they were a family member.

A rustling from the doorway gave away Robin, papers in hand, eyes wide and mouth agape.

For Christ's sake. "Ah...that was...my mother called."

"Oh."

"She and I had an argument."

"Oh."

Now he was irritated. With his mother. With himself for losing control. With Robin for witnessing it. Mostly, though, with himself.

"What can I do for you?"

"Right." Her shocked face shifted immediately to a professional calm. "Your first patient canceled, so you have a little time." She handed him a short stack of papers. "These need signing."

She usually left the papers on the desk and returned later to pick them up. She lingered in the doorway. She must have something more to say. He was definitely not in the mood. Especially if it involved his mother.

It was not his mother. "Remember your meeting with the clinic staff at noon."

His head pounded harder. He'd started the clinic staff meetings to get to know the staff and for them to get to know him, since he was going to be chair. So they'd feel comfortable coming to him with little problems before they escalated. Also, because the clinic staff didn't go to the hospital or the OR, he showed them pictures and discussed the different surgeries and the postoperative courses so the staff would know what the patients went through in the hospital.

What was the point? He wasn't going to be chair.

Robin read his mind. "We all really enjoy the meetings. I hope you continue them. We learn so much."

"I'll be there." Today, maybe. Today might be the last.

She remained in the doorway. He shifted his eyes to his computer to signal he was finished.

"I'm really sorry you're not going to be the chairman." He faced her again but couldn't hold her gaze. At least he had one person in his court. Of course, she didn't know all the facts.

She was still there. Why didn't she leave, leave him in peace?

"Dr. Baker?"

"What?" He didn't mean to sound so brusque. She'd just heard him yell at his mother, and now her? But the alternative was worse. He was worried his voice might break. She took a step back and he immediately felt awful.

She pointed at his coat. "Your coat's a mess. Let me change it out for you before clinic."

He frowned down at his coat, brown coffee stains on the front. A mess was right. Everything was a mess.

# Chapter 41

Mikey's Janet was dead. That lovely woman who suited her picky son so, who evened out his seriousness, who had brains and pep and adored Madge as well. Mikey's Janet was dead, and he would have no interest in Madge's theories now. He had too much on his mind. And he thought he was distracted before.

It was up to Madge. She alone would uncover the truth about what was happening to his patients at Cascadia Medical Center. She alone would save her son.

Then he would see her with new eyes.

Madge fished her clear liquids menu out from under the magazine on her bed table. Fat lot of good this menu had done her. She had one clear liquid meal, then it was back to NPO and a tube in the nose for her. She flipped the menu over and considered the blank side of the paper. Perfect for a list of suspects.

She still didn't have a pencil. No point ringing the nurses. They'd take forever. There must be something to write with in this room. She peered around. The second bed remained empty. Nurse Mildred mentioned that they'd had a lot of discharges, and not many admissions, and Madge wouldn't get a roommate if patient counts remained below a certain level. Madge would prefer a roomie, someone to talk to, someone to commiserate with. But right now, she just wanted a pencil.

Madge spied the whiteboard with its black marker stuck to the corner. That would do. She shifted around until she was sideways and lowered her legs over the edge of the bed. *Okay, now just push off the bedrail.* As if she had the strength. She fell right back onto the bed. She leaned forward and gripped the bedrail again and pushed. She rose to her feet and stood holding the rail. Ta-da!

She had not been out of bed on her own in forever, not since being admitted. The whiteboard was tantalizingly close, but the six steps in between her and the marker may as well be six miles. She couldn't let go of the bedrail.

"Hey, hey, hey! What are we doing?" Nurse Evan was in the room and standing beside her before she could register that help had arrived. He guided her to a sitting position. "We can't get out of bed without one of us being here. What is it we need?"

" 'We' don't need anything. 'I' need a marker." Madge did not think she'd said this aloud, but apparently she had, because Evan retrieved the marker for her. Oops.

Her slip of the tongue had not improved his pronoun usage, because he immediately said, "Do we need something to write with? I'll find us a pen. Better than this big marker. And paper."

She clamped her lips together to make sure no words passed from her brain to her mouth. As soon as he was out of the room, she used the thick marker on her paper to make columns. Suspects, opportunity, motive. Three columns at the top. Along the left side she made wide rows, with one name on each. Chrissie. Antibiotic Man. Madge. Now it was just a matter of seeing whose name was in each of the rows.

"Here we go." Evan was back, a veritable school supply bundle of paper and colored markers in his hand. "Do we want the light on?" He switched it on before she could answer.

"Eek! That light hurts my eyes!"

Evan leaned over. "What are we making?"

Madge covered the menu with her arm, trying to be casual. "Christmas list," she said, though it was May.

"Never too early for Christmas," Evan agreed. He placed the paper and markers on her table, clicked off the light, and left with a hearty "Merry Christmas."

Nurse Evan would make the perfect killer. Like a *Creature Friday* she'd seen where the mild-mannered neighbor turned out to be collecting women with red hair. It ended with him inviting the new redhead on the street over for crumpets. Crumpets, my patootie. The woman would end up with the rest of them, glassy-eyed heads with their shiny red hair combed out and beautiful.

That had been a particularly disturbing episode as Madge herself had gone through a redhead stage. No longer. Mother Nature took her gray-as-Seattle-skies course, and it was too hard to fight.

In any case, Nurse Evan seemed pleasant enough, but what did anyone really know about him since he was new? Did he have all his marbles? Did he have it in for Mikey? Did he like redheads?

Madge wrote Evan's name in the suspect column in each of the rows. Opportunity, too. A nurse would definitely have the opportunity to do whatever with whomever. Chrissie, Antibiotic Man, Madge. His name went in each box.

She wrote Nurse Bob in dark red letters under Evan's name in each row. Bob was definitely a suspect. What about Tony the Torturer? She didn't like the man and neither did Chrissie. She added his name. Then she wrote Mildred's name in small letters, more to be complete than because she thought Mildred was behind the killings.

Now motive. Maybe this wasn't about Mikey. Maybe Chrissie and Antibiotic Man both witnessed the same thing and were killed to keep silent. A nurse pocketing the extra morphine? Money changing hands in the elevator? An over-heard conversation about organ harvesting? A doctor shooting up in the supply closet? Maybe Mikey was an innocent by-stander in all this.

"Margaret McGillicuddy?"

Madge didn't recognize this officious tone. In the dim light she made out a tall woman with a clipboard, but she didn't know her.

"That's me."

"I'm Carol Layney. Head nurse."

Ah. The one who had the affair with the director of Central Services. Madge searched the hands cradling the clip-board for a wedding ring. Hmm. Were they both unmarried? No scandal there. Central Services meant hospital supplies. Good thinking to get in cahoots with someone who could keep her nurses supplied and her storeroom stocked. More power to her.

She didn't look like a nurse. She didn't wear the obligatory blue scrubs. The woman wore a brown suit and high heels that pitched her forward from the waist. Maybe a head nurse could wear whatever she pleased. But why did she feel the need to wear such unnatural shoes? Wearing them for the Central Services' guy, most likely. Madge was glad those days were over for her. She hadn't dressed up for anyone since Stinky's father.

"I am in charge of this floor and several more. I'm here to discuss the nursing situation. The nurses have kept me apprised of your dissatisfaction. I have tried to accommodate your wishes as best I can. But tomorrow Nurse Bob will be your nurse. I wanted to tell you personally. We need to get back to scheduling as usual."

Nurse Bob? "No, no, no. He's dangerous. See?" Madge waved her menu in the air.

"Dangerous?" The woman took a step closer.

Madge was not yet ready to show her chart. All in good

time. Once she had some evidence. Then they'd see Nurse Bob behind bars and Stinky returned to his rightful position.

"I'm not saying more," Madge said coyly. "Keep your eye on that man."

"If you have a concern, I'd like to hear it."

Hmm. The woman wanted specifics. "He sneaks in and watches me while I sleep."

"All nurses check in on their patients while they sleep."

"This is more than that. I mean *watching* watching."

"I'm not sure I understand." Ms. Layney cocked her head and lowered her voice. "Do you feel unsafe?"

"I'm not saying more," Madge repeated. "But I do not want Nurse Bob in this room."

Ms. Layney stepped right up to Madge and her bed table. Madge slammed her hand on her chart. The woman was not taking it.

Ms. Layney slowly extended her arm and placed a card on the table. "That is my number. I am ready to listen when you are ready to talk." She retreated on her heels, the clickity, clickity fading as she walked down the hall.

Well, I'll be. Someone who would take Madge seriously when she accumulated her evidence about Nurse Bob. Back to work, then. Motive? Why would Nurse Bob, or anyone for that matter, want Chrissie dead?

"Hey."

She was concentrating so hard, she didn't hear Mikey come in. She instinctively covered the paper again. Better wait until she solved the case to show Mikey. He had enough on his plate.

"Hey, yourself." He was quiet, and she added, "I'm so sorry about Janet."

"Janet." His voice drifted off. He nodded, and she studied his face, drawn and pale. His hair was combed, and his shirt was pressed, but he didn't look good. The last time she'd seen him, he'd been shouting, but he wasn't shouting now. She could barely hear him. "Is there something more? What's wrong, Mikey?"

"Nothing. Everything's fine." A red spot appeared on his pale right cheek. Mikey's tell.

"I know that's not true. A mother always knows. You might as well out with it. Save me badgering you."

He dropped into the chair by her bed. "They think I was drinking." Before she could open her mouth, he said, "Okay, you were right, but one sip, I told you. Now there's a file on it. On top of everything else that's happened."

"Oh, no, Stinky! That's awful!" Every ounce of maternal protection burst forth. She was ready to spring from the bed, if only she could stand.

"Katherine Pierce is way worse than Perkins. She's going to be hell as chair."

"Stinky! Enough about Katherine Pierce. Have some respect." Why did he talk like this? Had she failed him as a mother? Again?

"It's enough to drive a person to suicide like poor David Eaves. Maybe he had a chair like Katherine Pierce."

"Suicide? Stinky, are you being serious or joking? Because suicide is nothing to joke about."

Stinky sobered up. "You're right. That was uncalled for. I don't mean to joke about David Eaves."

"Who's David Eaves?"

"He's an anesthesiologist I knew. In Boston. He jumped off his apartment building. He's dead."

# Chapter 42

Michael watched his mother's face change in the darkened room. One minute she was chastising him like he was a three-year-old, and the next she was gawking with her eyes as wide as her open mouth.

"Stinky, don't you see?" she cried. He almost didn't hear the rest because he bristled every time she called him Stinky.

"Don't you see?" she repeated. "Chrissie. Antibiotic Man. Me. Janet. Anesthesiologist in Boston. That's too many people. Plus, young people didn't go around dying. They must all be connected."

What was she saying? His arm burned. He was having trouble concentrating. She didn't have her facts straight. "I didn't really know the anesthesiologist. We worked together on a few cases, that's all."

"That's enough," his mother said. "I'm adding him to the list. It's a clue."

"What list? What clue?" What was she talking about?

She tilted her head and blinked her eyes. She was always going on about his tell. She had a tell, too. She was hiding something. He saw this head tilt innocent look whenever he found a bottle in her house.

Her eyes twitched to the paper on her bed table. He could see a graph under her arm. He gently pushed her arm to one side. "What's this?" he asked.

She pouted now and swiveled her face away. "You're going to say it's all in my head," she said. "Well, it's not. It's all right here in black and white."

Michael picked up the paper, the back of a menu. He held it close to his face so he could read it with the lights out. Names ran down the side. Chrissie. Antibiotic Man. Evan the nurse's name was on the paper next to them, and Bob's.

"Mom, what do you have here?"

She snatched the paper from him. She scribbled "Janet" and "Anesthesia Man" at the bottom. "Look. It's all right here. All these people. I didn't add Janet before because she seemed like an outlier, but now... Coincidences don't occur in real life. We just need to figure out who is behind it. Because it's not you, Stinky."

He still didn't get it. "Behind what?"

"Murder, Stinky! Murder."

He closed his eyes and counted to ten. "I don't think so, Mom."

"Just wait. You'll see."

He almost wished it were true. That this weight of responsibility was on someone else.

He kissed her cheek and left her with her graph. With her nonsensical thoughts.

He ran into Hal at the nurses' station. "Where were you, Mike?"

"Where was I?"

"Two weeks in a row, man."

"Basketball. Right." Basketball was the farthest thing from his mind. The last time he'd played, he'd been on top of the world. A mere two weeks ago. These days, he'd completely forgotten about basketball.

"You gotta get back at it. Get out of this place."

*Before you lose it.* That's what Michael imagined Hal was about to say.

"Maybe we could catch some jazz one night. You said you had that club in Boston, right? There's a place I go in Belltown. Might not compare to what you saw in New York, but I like it. Man, I'd love to check out that jazz scene. I've never even been to New York." Hal sounded wistful. Maybe slightly bitter.

Hal's life would have been so much different if he'd won the scholarship and not Michael. Did Hal ever think about that? Well, Michael's life would have been different, too. It would have been hell.

"We can count on you for hoops next Thursday?"

"Not sure." Michael pushed up his sleeve and exposed his angry wound. "I'm out of commission for a while."

"Yikes, Mike, what happened?"

"Bad scratch. Would you write me for antibiotics?"

"Sure. Of course. Wow, that's deep. Watch it close to make sure it improves. Tetanus up to date?"

"Yes. Up to date."

That should have been that. Hal expressing concern for his well-being. Hal doing him a doctorly favor, glad to help. Michael thanking him and saying "see you on the court next week."

But Michael didn't leave it at that. He sat there waiting for Hal to finish the prescription on the computer, his arm aching and his head pounding. He dreaded the thought of another sleepless night.

"Could you write me something for pain, too?" The instant the words were out of his mouth, he was sorry. This was a no-no, a definite hard line a doctor could not cross. Fifteen years ago, maybe, but not now.

What was he doing? The pain clouded his judgement. His mother clouded his thoughts. He'd made a huge mistake. He saw it in Hal's face immediately.

"No, sorry, man. You know I can't do that."

"Yes. No, I'm sorry. I shouldn't have asked. No problem."

It *was* a problem. Hal's eyes told him so.

Hal hadn't actually said it, but his friend was right. Michael was losing it.

# Chapter 43

Michael rounded on one more patient before going home, eight-two-year-old Evelyn West. She'd been his first case of the afternoon, hours earlier in this interminable day. Her knee replacement had gone smoothly, something he never would have doubted in the past. When he saw her, smiling as usual, her eyes crinkly and joyous, he felt his shoulder muscles ease. She sat forward in bed, a pencil poised over a book.

"Math puzzles," she said. "I was an accountant and had the good sense to retire before I started making mistakes, but I do love a math puzzle."

Math puzzles. Amazing. She'd only just had surgery.

"That's great," Michael said. "Has the physical therapist been by?"

"Yes, and I've already stood on this new knee. Very exciting, I must say. But I'm glad I live at Mountains View. I don't know if I could manage on my own alone."

"Don't you worry, we won't send you home until you're ready," Michael said. "Plus, Mountains View has an excellent physical therapy program. You'll be in good hands there."

"As I'm in good hands here." Her smile widened and for an instant he forgot everything else about his afternoon, until she said, "I'm hoping to go home without any pain medicine. Do you think that's wise?"

His whole interaction with Hal flooded back, and his face

flushed. Michael walked her through the benefits and risks of the pain medication, all the while reproaching himself for asking Hal.

He left her smiles and her confidence and headed for his office to get his briefcase, sneaking in the back way and practically tiptoeing so he could slip in and out without seeing anyone.

Thankfully, the garage was empty as well. Each echoing footstep bounced off the walls back at him, screaming his troubles. Chrissie. Stark. Katherine. Phil. Hal. It was so loud, the names were all he could hear.

What a mess. He halted. The shouting ceased. But the footsteps continued.

They were slow and soft, but footsteps nonetheless. The echo made their location hard to pinpoint.

Michael took a slow, silent breath, inhaling motor oil and dust. The bright red exit sign at the far end of the garage encouraged him to find a way out.

He whipped around. He was alone in the open space. The footsteps grew louder. He scanned the parked cars. Was the blue car there? Did this have to do with the blue car?

A shadow sprang out from behind a concrete pillar. A man appeared, a large man rushing toward him.

What options did Michael have in a parking garage? The stairwell? His car? Should he tackle the guy?

He might as well face it, whatever it was. He stood his ground.

The man came into the light.

"Bob?"

The nurse stopped just in front of him. He was bigger than Michael, taller and broader. He stood there, breathing hard, his lips pursed and his face red and tight.

"Tell her to back off," he snarled.

"Excuse me?"

"Your mother. Her complaints will get me fired."

Michael was being accosted in the parking garage, and somehow it was because of his mother. He almost burst into laughter in his relief, but Bob's livid face cut him short.

"What complaints?" As if he didn't know. His mother thought Bob tried to smother her. And was a vampire. Michael was still hearing the fallout from this, how if all the patients could choose their nurse, they wouldn't be able to run a hospital, and if patients could choose their nurses, then the nurses might want to choose their patients, and did he think anyone would volunteer to take care of his mother? Etcetera.

Bob's face was furrowed and purple, so Michael added, "I don't think they take her complaints very seriously."

"They talked to me about it. That's serious enough. Twice now. She has some new vague accusation. I make her feel uncomfortable when she's asleep. Load of bull."

Bob was right. Would she never stop?

Bob stepped closer. His voice was gruff. "I've got a family. I've got a mother myself to support. I'm not losing this job because of baseless lies."

Michael stared him straight in the eye. "What do you think I can do about it?"

"She's *your* mother. Get her to stop. You can control your own mother, can't you?" Bob sneered.

The sneer said it all. No one could control Michael's mother.

# Chapter 44

How had Michael come to this? Patients in jeopardy. Acting out at M & M. Chairmanship lost. Accused of drinking. In trouble with Hal. Cornered in the parking lot.

Michael's mother had some wild ideas about what was going on. And right now, late at night, curled up on the couch with Frank beside him, her ideas didn't seem so outlandish. He rubbed Frank's scaly neck.

"Why should two people from the hospital in Boston die within a few months of each other? One a suicide, one a murder."

Frank wasn't buying it. He kept his eyes shut.

"I know. You think her theory is bizarro. But listen, it's not implausible. Until last week, I had never had a complication like Chrissie's. It's not a complication I could have prevented. It's just bad luck. But I'd never had anything remotely like that. And that note? Someone telling Phil outright I'm a bad doctor. Then Reginald Stark. Someone wrote the order. Not me. And...what if it wasn't an accident?"

Frank did look up now. His skeptical expression made it clear he thought Michael was dreaming. Grasping at his mother's theory because it would conveniently absolve him of neglecting to sign off the computer.

"I think you're hungry, Frank. You'll see things better after you eat." Michael moved slowly toward the kitchen, and

Frank followed. He placed a kale leaf in Frank's bowl and retrieved a hard-boiled egg from the pot on the stove. Shelling the egg was awkward with his injured arm, and he gave up.

He thrust his arm toward the lizard. "This is thanks to you. Good thing it's Friday night and I'm not on call for surgeries this weekend. This arm is killing me. You are a menace, you know that?"

The lizard ate his kale.

"I'm in trouble with Hal because of you." What had he been thinking?

"Because of me, too." The lizard didn't acknowledge him but flitted his tongue in and out. Michael pulled an onion and a chicken breast from the refrigerator and started on his own dinner, his arm smarting with every slice.

He and Janet cooked together every night. The memory of Janet hurt as much as his arm. They were a team. In the kitchen, in the OR, in life.

Now Janet was gone.

Had Janet known David Eaves?

She had to know the guy. She was an OR nurse. But she and Michael worked together most of the time, and Michael rarely worked with David. A few cases only. Including the one two years ago with the terrible complication, with the incorrect medication.

Of course. That's how Janet would know David Eaves. She was the nurse in the room.

The woman was Michael's patient, but he wasn't even in the room. While Anesthesia set up, he was scrubbing in the hallway. He didn't know there was anything wrong until the code team poured into the room from all directions. When he arrived, David Eaves had already resuscitated her. She never had her hip replaced. Michael made a brief appearance at the Anesthesiology Department's M & M. The medication error caused the patient's heart to stop, the anesthesiologist ran the code almost by himself and brought her back to life. Unfortunately, the patient had a stroke. Michael was never mentioned. It wasn't his M & M.

What was the woman's name? Michael couldn't believe he'd forgotten. All his patients blended together over the years, and sometimes he only met them once before surgery, but this patient was engraved in his brain. An elegant woman who loved dancing. Which is why she wanted the new hip. So she could get back to her ballroom dance classes. He'd visited her in the ICU, but he had no actual care of her. Just like he visited Reginald Stark.

He and Janet talked about how devastating it was. The case haunted Janet because she saw the whole thing play out, though she was halfway across the room readying the instruments when the woman coded. The case haunted Michael because this was his patient, though he'd never actually performed any surgery. She'd had a rocky course in the ICU and finally was discharged. If they were haunted like this, imagine how David Eaves must have felt.

If they'd known what the man was going through, could they have helped him? They had each other to confide in, to comfort. They needed to talk about the case, and they hadn't been the one responsible. Who did David Eaves have to talk to?

They should have reached out. They should have offered support. If they had, would David Eaves be dead?

# Chapter 45

Michael dumped the chicken and onions into the pan and stirred. In his mind he stirred the names, around and around.

Chrissie Johnson. Reginald Stark. David Eaves. Now Janet.

What if they were connected? Could someone have deliberately changed an order on a sick man? Could someone have done something to Chrissie?

Because...David Eaves was dead. A fall. Janet was dead. Strangled. Deliberately.

"What do you think, Frank?"

Frank whisked through his legs and out of the kitchen. An acrid smell filled the room. The chicken was charred in the pan. Michael set it in the sink and opened the window before the smoke alarm went off.

Frank inched back in, nose lifted to the window. Michael gently picked him up, and together they inhaled the fresh, cool air.

His mother had made an actual list of suspects. Evan and Bob and even Mildred. His mother did not like Nurse Bob. Bob had all but threatened Michael. Was Bob the connection?

Frank's forked tongue darted in and out, left and right. "I know, I know. I'm grasping. But do these people have anything in common, Frank?"

Michael breathed in the crisp air and his head cleared.

Of course.

Two in Seattle, two from Boston. All connected to *him*.

What had his mother said? They must all be connected. But *what* connected him to them?

David Eaves and Janet didn't know each other. They were tied to him and he was tied to them through only one case.

There was more to that case than the basic facts. And Janet knew it.

Though she wasn't certain about what she knew. She told Michael in confidence, and she only told him part of the story, but she told him enough.

David Eaves had given the wrong medication because the boxes looked too much alike. Similar size, similar color. Once he made the mistake, the entire system changed. All the anesthesiologists in the department were cautioned, warning labels were added, and the hospital contacted the manufacturer.

But he wasn't the first one to make that mistake. At least Janet didn't think so.

She hadn't thought anything of it at the time, only in retrospect. She thought she'd seen another anesthesiologist draw up medication into a syringe, study the box, and chuck the full syringe into the sharps container before starting over again.

As if they had almost made exactly the same mistake. One week earlier.

One week before Michael's patient. Plenty of time to alert the other anesthesiologists, contact the pharmacy, add warning labels. Plenty of time to have saved Michael's patient.

Janet wouldn't tell him who the anesthesiologist was. She wasn't one hundred percent certain of what she'd seen. She was across the room and not paying attention. She could think of several plausible explanations. Maybe they had contaminated the syringe with their hand and needed to discard it for that reason. Etcetera. Janet didn't want to tarnish a prominent reputation if she'd gotten it wrong. She said it didn't matter anyway.

Janet didn't want to talk about it further, said she was sorry she'd told him. Michael encouraged her to at least talk to the chair of the department. Let them investigate. Let them deal with it.

And who, exactly, had been the chair of the anesthesiology department in Boston two years ago? Who was now the current chief of staff at Cascadia Medical Center? Who had helped usher Michael's application to the top of the recruitment list?

Matilda Walters.

# Chapter 46

Michael's head whirled as if he'd been drinking. He gulped in the clean air.

"Frank..."

Had Janet spoken with Matilda about her suspicions? And had Matilda swept it under the rug, leaving poor David Eaves to think he was solely responsible, the only one to have made such a mistake?

Or... Michael shifted Frank to one arm and gripped the windowsill. Had Janet told him it didn't matter because the chair of the department she would go to with her information was the very person she had seen?

Had Matilda almost mixed up the drugs herself and never told? And then the tragic case with Michael's patient followed, and the stakes increased immensely? So she just kept quiet? Then David Eaves killed himself, and the tragedies piled higher? And Janet knew Matilda could have stopped the whole cascade of events?

Michael sucked in more clean air.

He had not stopped the antibiotics. He had not forgotten to log off the computer. He was not complicit in Reginald Stark's deterioration. He thought he had believed this, but the relief of knowing for certain was immense.

His head whirled again. He stared into Frank's shimmering eyes. Frank held his gaze, but Michael couldn't focus.

If it wasn't him, then someone, namely Matilda, had intentionally and methodically set out to cause harm, and Reginald Stark was the victim. And Chrissie. And Michael himself.

Matilda had written the anonymous note. Matilda had changed the antibiotic order. He was being set up.

His mother had been way ahead of him. She had known something was wrong from the beginning.

Matilda certainly had the opportunity and the means. She could go anywhere in the hospital, do whatever she wanted, and no one would question her. As for motive...

If she had come forward with her near miss with the medications, she could have stopped it all, right from the beginning. Stopped a huge hospital payout. More importantly, stopped a patient suffering a terrible fate.

Even if she waited, and came forward *after* Michael's case, she could have eased David Eaves' guilty mind. Stopped him from taking his own life.

Could she have stopped Janet's murder?

Or was she the murderer herself?

"Whoa, whoa. Frank, I sound like my mother. That's ridiculous." But was it?

Matilda knew Janet knew. Had Matilda hunted Janet down in Philadelphia and arranged a final meeting? And, in case she'd told Michael, she seduced him into taking the job at Cascadia only to tear him to pieces so no one would believe a word he said.

Frank's nose nudged his arm, and Michael set him down.

"What's that, Frank? Preposterous? You think I'll start accusing everyone now? Is Bob getting even with my mother by sabotaging me, her only son? Ha! Even better, it's Katherine Pierce, making me look bad so she can have my job."

Preposterous or not, Bob and Katherine were not from Boston.

Matilda Walters was.

# Chapter 47

Madge lay still and tried not to breathe. The pain was bad. Her fever was back, too, starting that morning just before rounds. Mildred said Madge wasn't thinking straight, that her brain was muddled by infection and they might need to change the antibiotics, and that they'd called Mikey and he should be there soon. Dr. Hal said she was confused and might need a drain in the infected gunk of the pancreatic necrosis. Madge didn't care what she needed, she just needed it now.

And then two little bottles appeared, the airlines kind, one whiskey, one rum, waiting for her when she opened the drawer in her overbed table. At first she didn't see them in the dark, but they clunked together when she closed the drawer, and she knew that noise like she knew Mikey's tiny voice in the night when he was little. She didn't like rum neat, but she wasn't choosy. From where they appeared, she didn't care. They were there and she was hurting, and this was exactly what she needed.

Getting the screw cap open was another matter. Her hands weren't working very well. They were shaking and her eyes were blurring, but she finally cracked one open. How long had it been since she'd had a drink? Almost three weeks. She was drinking right up until Mikey found her at home, doubled over in pain from the pancreatitis and drinking whiskey to make the pain go away. Whiskey was good that way.

She pressed the miniature bottle to her lips, the plastic cool and inviting. She tilted her head back, setting off a ripple of agony shooting through her stomach and a wave of dizziness. A drink would fix that. A drink would fix everything.

Peace flowed through her as she tasted the whiskey on her tongue. She held it there for a moment before she swallowed. Yes. Exactly what she needed.

She took a bigger sip, savoring the fluid in her mouth.

"What are you doing?!"

She sat upright and sputtered, spewing whiskey everywhere. Mikey? What was he doing here, her baby, all grown up and standing over her? Whiskey hit him in the face. He grabbed the bottle from her hand, sloshing alcohol on both of them. He fumbled to screw on the cap. He whisked away the other bottle, too, and pocketed them.

Her alcohol. He took her alcohol.

She snarled and flailed, trying to wrest it back from his pocket. She had no strength and couldn't sit forward. She collapsed back, exhausted.

"Where did you get this?! What are you doing?!" Mikey was angry, angry, angry. Why was Mikey so angry?

"They're mine. I need them."

"You're in the *hospital*. You can't drink in the *hospital*. More importantly, you can't procure alcohol in a hospital. So where did this come from?"

"Beats me." Why was Mikey so upset? He shouldn't talk to her like this. He needed a time out. Maybe she'd send him to bed without dinner. That would teach him.

"Mom, you're sweating. Are you feeling all right? Mom? Mom?"

Right now, though, she just wanted to sleep. She would deal with Mikey in the morning before school. She would deal with everything tomorrow.

# Chapter 48

Michael raced down to the nurses' station. "Page Dr. Dexter. My mom lost consciousness. Her pulse is weak. Looks like septic shock."

Mildred was in the room with him in no time, fastening a blood pressure cuff to his mother's arm and hooking her up to a cardiac monitor.

"Eighty over forty. She's hypotensive all right. I'll open up the fluids."

His mother lay flat on the bed, unresponsive and diaphoretic. The heart monitor showed her racing heart, one hundred twenty beats a minute. This was septic shock, all right. Michael didn't think the alcohol could be involved. The one open bottle was almost full when he grabbed it from her. She hadn't had much. He didn't feel the need to mention the alcohol to anyone else.

Hal arrived, breathless.

"Blood pressure's ninety now. Getting better," said Mildred.

"That's better?" Hal glanced at Michael. His tone was all business. "Mike. Looks like sepsis. She needs a drain. I'll get it arranged." He nodded to Mildred. "Keep the fluids going full bore. If things don't improve, we might need the unit."

The intensive care unit. With Reginald Stark.

"She's still on antibiotics, right?" Michael's tone must

have sounded tense, because Mildred turned the portable computer monitor toward him and pointed.

"Yes, Dr. Baker."

"I'll broaden them. But we need the drain now," Hal added.

Michael had seen his mother's CT scan. This septic turn was common, almost expected. She'd done it so many times before. There was nothing sinister. This was normal medical stuff. Even as he thought it, he wondered where Matilda was. It was Saturday, but she was always at the hospital, day in, day out. Had she visited his mother?

As soon as his mom was stable, he intended to find out.

His mother twitched in the bed, first an imperceptible flit of the head, then a fluttering of the eyes.

"Mom. You're here with us. You'll be all right." Michael took her hand. It was cold, clamped down. He enveloped it in his.

"George?"

George? George was Michael's father. Michael remembered bits and pieces, the best and worst times, shadows on the edge of his mind. Not a fully formed man and certainly not a father. Clear in his head was the last fateful night. That, he would never forget.

His mother rarely mentioned his father, and when she did it was to shoot him down, carve him up, and scream how much better off they were without him.

"It's me, mom. Michael. Your son."

"Is George here?"

"Interventional Radiology's ready for her." Hal was back. "They have an opening right now, if we can get her down there quickly."

Michael stepped back as they moved his mother to the transport gurney and off to Radiology.

"I'll page you as soon as she's out," Hal said.

Michael started slowly down the stairs. Until he returned to Seattle, his father was an image tucked away years ago, a topic best left unexplored. He hadn't seen him since the day he left, his dad crouching to Michael's ten-year-old eye level. His dad tousled his hair and laid a hand on his shoulder. "It's for the best," he said. And he was gone.

At least that's how Michael liked to remember it. How he'd re-written the scene in his head.

His mother mistook him for his father. They looked alike, Michael knew, from an old photo he'd found when he was hunting around for hidden bottles of alcohol. But like Michael, his mother hadn't seen his father since that disastrous day thirty-five years before. She was septic and hallucinating.

She'd been this sick before, but it had been a while. Wasn't that why Michael had given up his life in Boston? He was in Seattle to prevent all this, prevent her drinking, prevent her getting sick, prevent her getting sicker. Now here she was, in the hospital, drinking and sicker. He'd prevented nothing.

He took the two bottles of alcohol from his coat pocket. One was nearly empty. His mother hadn't drunk that much. Most of it was on Michael's white coat. How had she gotten alcohol in a hospital?

He'd seen all his patients early, before his mother. If he'd seen her first, would he have caught someone in the act, placing alcohol in her drawer? Matilda?

He paused on the stairs. It was alcohol, wasn't it? Not poison, as his mother would say? He unscrewed the cap and brought the bottle to his nose.

It smelled like whiskey, nothing more.

Would he know poison if he smelled it?

"Michael?"

Directly below him, one short stair landing down, was Katherine Pierce.

Christ. What were the chances? She had the Saturday

morning clinic duty and must be rounding on her inpatients during the spot they kept free for emergency add-ons. He shook his head in disbelief.

Or...what if Katherine planted the bottles in his mother's room? What if she was the one behind all this? She could easily have placed the bottles, confident that at some point Michael would find them and confiscate them. For Katherine to discover.

He'd done her one better. He'd spilled alcohol over himself and had the bottles on full display when she came upon him.

That was ridiculous. She couldn't count on any of it happening the way she planned. Plus, this was Katherine. She wasn't evil. And no one was this good an actor.

Katherine's open mouth gaped, and her eyes bulged. She sniffed, at first a slight sniff she tried to hide, then frank sniffing, as she walked up the stairs, her shoes loudly tapping on each step like the slow beat of his death sentence.

She held out her hand, palm up. "I'll take those."

"They're not mine," Michael said.

She stood one step below him, her face even with his coat. She curled her lip and wrinkled her nose and gave a final, huge inhalation.

"Save it," she said.

# Chapter 49

Michael sat in the interventional radiology waiting room and tried to concentrate on Larry's words. "Pus poured out when I put in the drain. She should do fine now. Blood pressure's already back to normal. She's just gotten to recovery, we'll have her up to the floor by late morning, but the sedation will have her pretty groggy."

"Thanks, Larry. I'll peek in on her now, if that's all right, then see her upstairs."

A clear case of an infected phlegmon. Standard pancreatic complication despite being on appropriate antibiotics. No one could have done this to her. That, at least, was a relief.

And he'd discovered where Matilda was, safely ensconced in the auditorium presiding over a two-day conference on the future of medicine and Cascadia's role. She had a midday break and then an evening reception starting at five and slated to end at eleven, then back at it in the morning at eight. She was in charge, and she would be busy. She was not a threat right now.

However, the alcohol was a problem.

Katherine would turn him in. She had no choice. He'd do the same if he were her. She had overwhelming proof that he was drinking on the job.

Could he possibly convince her otherwise? Should he even bother? Katherine knew about his mother and her drinking, but any denial from him would look as bad as his denial about the antibiotics. He couldn't begin to tell her his fantastical idea about Boston and Matilda. Or Bob. Or her, for that matter. Her trust in him was shattered.

Where had his mother gotten the alcohol?

Why was his mother talking about his dad?

Michael found his mother in the recovery room and searched her face. She was sound asleep. She had spider webs of broken capillaries on her nose and cheeks from drinking. Her lips parted with every exhalation, sputtering out each harsh breath. A tiny globule of saliva pooled in one corner of her mouth.

How many times in his childhood life had he seen her this way, passed out, saliva or vomit crusting her lips? How many times had he crouched beside her, watching for her chest to rise, praying she wasn't dead? Turned her on her side so she wouldn't choke? Counted her breaths to make sure they weren't slowing?

She would sleep for a while now. She wouldn't know he was there any more than she knew he was there when he was young.

Michael gathered his things and left the hospital. He used the clinic back door to avoid Katherine's office. Was she in there even now making the call?

Michael didn't understand where he was headed until he made the turn toward his mother's house. He sat with the car idling for a moment, then finally turned off the engine.

The house was unassuming enough, a typical Seattle red brick Tudor, three bedrooms with slanted walls under its pointed roof. His childhood bed lay directly under one slope. He used to lie there and stare up.

His heartbeat quickened, thinking about it even now.

Day after day, staring up, or squeezing his eyes shut against it. When he was a kid, that slanted wall bore down on him with the weight of all he'd done.

He slammed the car door, strode along the walkway, and climbed the front steps. Then he hesitated, like he had hesitated each and every time before he entered the house since he was little. What would he find?

A smaller pointed roof mirrored the main roof and covered the porch and deep green door. What was behind that door? What catastrophe awaited inside? He'd been in this house just after his mother was hospitalized. He'd left it empty and neat, but his stomach was queasy, and he felt like he was a child again.

He pushed open the door and stepped into the front hall.

He knew what was there, hidden in and behind the tree-like coat rack. When his dad lived there, they never had a coat rack. The day after his dad left, the coat rack appeared, and it had stood sentry in the hall ever since.

Michael reached in through the coats and grasped the pole. He coughed as the coats shed years of dust. He lifted the rack, surprisingly heavy with all the winter coats, and set it down in the middle of the hall. He knew what he would find, but he recoiled anyway. He hadn't seen it since he was ten.

A ragged hole leered at him from the wall. His mother left it just the way it was.

She and he had cowered there, against that wall. His father aimed his fist at his mother's head, but he missed. In the moment it took to disentangle his hand from the plaster, Michael's mother sprinted to the kitchen, dragging Michael behind. She grabbed the enormous chef's knife from the stand and waited, Michael shoved behind.

"Keep quiet," she said. "If anything happens to me, run as fast as you can."

Michael's lip trembled. His legs trembled. He was small

for his age, but his mother seemed larger that night, completely shielding him from the threat in the other room.

His father cussed, his voice low. It grew louder as he neared the kitchen. Then he was there, towering in the doorway, quiet now. The kitchen was silent. Michael peeked out to see if he was still there.

His father's face was twisted. He studied them. Michael's mother stood tall with the knife held high. Michael slid his body further behind her.

His father didn't move, didn't say a word. He just stood there. Then he pivoted and left, his gait slow. He paused at the front door.

Michael crept forward. His body kept moving until he stood at the front door himself. He held his breath. His dad bent down to his level. Michael flinched as his dad touched his shoulder. His husky voice said, "It's for the best." Michael knew he was right.

That's how he liked to remember that night. It wasn't the truth, but it was the story ten-year-old Michael told himself.

Now Michael was back in his childhood house, back among these memories he'd rather forget. He faced the coat rack and fumbled between the coats, feeling for the center pole. He slid his hand down to the metal circles and flat disc meant to hold umbrellas. His fingers brushed against wood. It was still there.

Michael gripped the handle tightly and pulled it out. The old chef's knife, as large and menacing as he remembered, though he had been ten. The blade glinted in the morning light from the slim window next to the door. That window they peeked through every time the doorbell rang.

His father never came back.

The knife was there for self-protection. Though what good would it be in an emergency, hiding among the winter coats? Somehow it made them feel better, knowing.

Michael turned the knife this way and that so it flashed in the light. The blade was shiny and clean. Because they had scrubbed it. In the real story of what happened that night.

Michael replaced the knife and hoisted the coat rack back to its spot in front of the hole in the wall. He involuntarily glanced through the skinny window before opening the door. Once outside he breathed deeply, letting the moist air and the mossy scent cleanse away the dusty memories.

# Chapter 50

Michael drove back to the hospital, not bothering to look for the blue car, his mind on his past, his mind on his mother. He'd been gone less than an hour, but it seemed like thirty-five years.

Why had his mother called him George?

He pulled into the parking garage and waited for Raymond, the attendant, to raise the gate.

"Back so soon?" Raymond's wife had broken her arm and Michael had been the one to set it. Raymond always gave him a hearty welcome in the morning.

"Forgot something," Michael said.

In the surgery clinic, he involuntarily glanced at the front desk. He couldn't pass it now without searching for another note. He headed for his office but stopped short.

"I like him. You do, too, that's the problem." Katherine was on the phone, and her voice carried clearly in the quiet clinic.

"He's like a whirlwind. Look how much he's done already. Updated the standard operating procedures, revamped our call schedule—it's so much better now. How had we not done that? That committee of patients to show the patient experience? Brilliant. We've simplified scheduling, streamlined appointments so patients don't have to run all over the hospital, improved our instruction sheets, brought the pre-op clearance clinic to us—these were all his ideas from that patient committee. You know he meets with the medical assistants, the techs, the nurses, even the call center? They feel like he listens to them. Not that you didn't, Phil. But he's new. Four months. Just today, Michael's medical assistant was the Saturday MA, and she helped me with a dressing change. That's way outside the abilities of an MA, but she did great, said he showed her how."

Michael couldn't believe Katherine was saying all this. That she'd noticed. However, he sensed she was about to turn the conversation. He didn't want to hear anymore, but he had to hear more. His job was on the line.

He breathed as shallowly as he could. He switched his pager to silent mode. Her voice was softer now and he crept a few steps closer.

"I know all that, Phil. I was on the recruiting committee. He had it all. Surgical expertise, research, people skills, stellar references, glowing patient testimonies. Matilda vouched for him, but his application was a standout even without her. We thought we lucked out. Now I'm not so sure."

There was silence while Katherine listened. What was Phil saying?

"He's decompensating in front of our very eyes. First, his two patients. He still hasn't admitted he's to blame, let alone learn from his mistakes. Then, the alcohol. We have two separate incidents. We gave him a warning, and he showed up drinking again. We can't ignore it."

Phil must be talking again. Michael held his breath.

"I know. I've thought about that. But a leave of absence won't help if he can't stop on his own. His mother, you know. It must run in the family. There was no hint of this in any of the references. I combed through them again today."

More silence.

"I think you might have blinders on, Phil. There are patients to consider. We can't put any more patients at risk.

You've called in an impaired physician before. Douglas Knight, remember? He thanked you after. Right before he retired, as I recall. The licensing board is set up for this. The state can decide. They'll do their assessment. If they agree he's impaired, he'll go through their treatment program, then they'll reinstate his license, and he'll be back in practice again. Just not here."

Michael's chest clamped tighter and tighter. Katherine was going to turn him in.

# Chapter 51

Where was she? What was this tube in her nose? What was this tube in her side?

Madge peered around the darkened room. A curtain on rings. Ah. The cozy, comfortable hospital. Her home away from home.

She shook her head to clear it and was immediately sorry. The feeding tube jerked and made her gag. She hated these things. She usually pulled them out. But if she couldn't convince them to leave it out, they'd replace it, and she had learned the painful way that having them jam it in her nose again was far worse than just living with it.

Why was she even in the hospital? She hadn't been here in so long. Since before Stinky came home. Why was she back?

She'd tempered her drinking when Stinky returned. Didn't give it up. She could never do that. She'd tried and failed, tried and failed, so no point in trying further. In any case, she had it down to a science, she was sure of it, enough alcohol to satisfy, not enough to trigger another bout of pancreatitis. Or, God forbid, a fall. So why was she here?

She lay back on her pillows and contemplated the curtain.

Oh, yeah.

George.

The love of her life. Her first love. Her only love. She'd given up everything for him.

They'd been so happy. Cuddling in bed when she was pregnant, newlyweds dreaming of the baby. She was on bed rest and wasn't allowed up. George brought her tea and cocoa and kisses. He was between jobs, and she should have been concerned, but she was high on hormones.

Mikey came early and they almost lost him. He was blue, so blue, when they pulled him out, and she only had a glimpse before they whisked him away for resuscitation and the NICU. She and George huddled together, waiting, waiting, until finally the nurse returned and said things looked good and they could see him now.

Mikey was wrinkly and red and his head was pointy, but her heart heaved, and from then on it was Mikey first for everything. She didn't have a choice, really. He demanded attention thirty hours a day. Crying and fussing and writhing around.

George started drinking, and she joined right in once she stopped breast feeding, which was almost immediately in the hopes of finding a new diet to calm the tyrant child. Mikey didn't take to the breast anyway. He never latched on properly and feeding him took forever and still he didn't gain weight. Formula was better. For all concerned.

In the rare bliss of Mikey's afternoon nap, she and George sat on the porch steps with their Manhattans and pretended they were sophisticated grownups, not thirty-year-olds with a finicky baby and no jobs. Then Mikey would scream out, and she would go to him, and then she'd find George on the porch with the whisky bottle drinking it straight.

They had some fun times, their little family. But Mikey grew older, her little prince, her angel, her reason for being, and George grew distant. It took a lot of alcohol to get him shouting, but his words could slice, especially through Mikey.

Then George lost control. And that was that.

Until three weeks ago.

When George showed up.

There he was, standing on the porch like he'd never left. Same blue eyes, older and paler, but unmistakably George. Mikey had his eyes. Same messy hair, blond and too long, as thick as when he was thirty, the gray blending with blond. Same rumpled plaid shirt. In fact, it may have been the same shirt, for all she could tell.

He didn't say a word. He searched her eyes, and he pivoted to go. She almost cried out, but then he sat, stiffly, like the old man he was, on the top step. Like all those years ago. He patted the concrete beside him. She wasn't about to sit. It was too far down. She leaned against the railing and listened to what he had to say.

When he left, she fished a whiskey bottle out of the clothes in the dryer and sat with a glass and an ice bucket and the whiskey. The next day she was here. Back in the hospital.

# Chapter 52

Trumpets blared and Michael jumped. What was that? He had to keep quiet or Katherine would hear him, sneaking around, loitering outside her door.

"Hi, hon." This was Katherine talking on the phone again. Her ringtone must be this trumpet onslaught.

"I know, I thought so, too. I got delayed, and I'm not done yet. I won't be home in time. I'm sorry. Could you take her without me? Put her on?"

Katherine's voice changed to a softer, higher voice. "Hi, Ellie. Daddy's going to take you to the zoo, and we can all meet up after. Say hi to the monkeys for me."

Michael pictured adorable three-year-old Ellie, blonde like Katherine, but curly-headed like Paul. He could hear her loud giggle over the line.

"Cheesy toast? Your favorite. Save some for me... You're making me a card with flowers? It's a secret? Okay, I'll pretend you didn't tell me."

Another Mother's Day card.

"Oh, hi, Paul... I know, I know. This is just the beginning. Welcome to chairmanship. At least today I could still run things by Phil."

A pager shrilled. Michael clamped his hand to his belt. Katherine would hear it, she'd know he was there, listening to all this.

No, his was off, already turned to silent mode. This was Katherine's.

"Great," he heard her mutter. "He wants to meet... No, Paul, your job is important to me, too... Now, don't be like that. We can work this out... But not today. I might be later still."

Michael didn't want to hear this private conversation. He tiptoed back down the hall.

Katherine and Phil were going to meet. They were going to decide his fate, and there was nothing he could do about it, no way to explain until he had proof. Matilda was still at her conference across the street. Today's morning session would be over at one.

He'd be waiting for her. He'd confront her there, quietly, but in the crowd of doctors and administrators in case things got ugly.

His pager vibrated on his hip and he leaped in the air in surprise. Tap, tap, tap. Katherine's heels in her office. She was leaving. Michael raced around the corner to the clinic lobby. Her door shut. Had she seen him? He fled into the staircase and down one flight.

He waited in the stuffy staircase, waited for the door to open and for her to call out to him. What could he say? I heard everything you said, I stood there and listened to it all?

Thankfully, he heard the elevator ding. She hadn't seen him.

He unclamped his hand from the stairway railing. He closed his eyes. Soon he would meet Matilda. Confront Matilda.

His pager vibrated again, almost sending him down the stairs. He wasn't used to the vibrating. It would do this every minute until he looked at the page. He pulled the pager off his belt and held it near his face to see the message in the dim stairway light.

"Be there in 10 min, Mike. Almost forgot we had a roof garden."

This was from Katherine Pierce. What was she talking about? Did she think he'd paged her?

Oh, my God. His pager had first gone off while he was in the hallway and she was in her office. She had sent this page from her computer.

After she received a page she thought was from him.

He couldn't call her from the stairwell with its dead zone. He started up the stairs two at a time.

His heart raced and his lungs screamed. He had not paged Katherine.

But someone had.

His mother had told him about the roof garden. He had never seen it. She knew all about it, like she knew about everything, this secret roof garden, designed for patients but banned once the administrators realized it had become a smokers' haven. It wasn't locked. It just wasn't advertised. That was five years ago, but his mother remembered. She once tried to coax him into wheeling her there, but in the end she couldn't find the right door. It was the eleventh floor, though. She was clear on that.

He sprang out of the stairway into the desolate eleventh floor hallway. No patients, no nurses. The floor was for patients staying overnight after procedures, but they had all been sent home that morning. The floor was completely shut down until Monday.

"Katherine!" he shouted. He was met with creepy utter silence.

Where was the roof garden? He dashed down the hall, fumbling for Katherine's number on his phone. It would be no use, here in the old hospital with its thick concrete walls.

The hallways in this part of the hospital branched several times to meet up with the new hospital. Michael veered along one only to find a bank of elevators. The next led to a storage room. Each wrong turn added time. He had to find her.

"Katherine!" His voice echoed in the empty halls.

He sprinted around the next corner. He was completely out of breath from all the flights of stairs and the running around. He braced against the wall and gulped in air. Two sets of doors lay ahead in the hall, and he glimpsed light shining through at the end.

# Chapter 53

Michael burst through the door to the roof garden, the light blinding him for an instant after the dark hall.

He cast around to get his bearings. Plants overflowing their containers, trees in giant pots, winding wooden plank paths, and a spectacular view of Puget Sound. But no person.

"Katherine!" he shouted.

A crash sounded from the side. Michael ran toward the noise. He rounded the corner and spotted a crumpled heap at the far edge of the deck. Katherine!

A shadow darted, behind the trees and barely a blur. Michael halted. He whirled around, ready to chase, but the door to the hallway banged shut in the distance, and Katherine lay right in front of him.

A long gash split the side of her head, oozing a startling amount of blood. She must have hit the planter. Her eyes were closed. She didn't move.

"Katherine!" His voice seemed muffled, his heartbeat was so loud.

His fingers searched her neck for a pulse. She was alive, her artery throbbing against his fingertips. She was breathing. She just wasn't awake.

His pushed one hand against her bleeding wound and used the other to try to dial the hospital operator. It was impossible with one hand. He shed his white coat, took off his shirt, and fashioned a pressure dressing, tying it tightly around her head.

Trumpets blared and Michael jumped. The trumpets continued, harsh and demanding. It was Katherine's phone. He hunted around and found her purse partially under her, but not her phone. The trumpets shrilled again. He fumbled in the large ceramic planter and found the phone among the shrubbery.

He swiped it open and the trumpets ceased.

"Katherine?" said the man on the other end of the phone.

"No. Is this Paul?"

"Yes. Is that Michael? Katherine said she was meeting you. Is she there?"

Michael breathed deeply. Katherine stirred, her head scraping on the deck. Michael cupped his hand under to cradle it off the bloody wood.

"Paul, she's hurt. She hit her head. She lost consciousness. She's coming to now. I'm taking her to the ED. I'll meet you there."

"Oh, my God. I'm on my way."

Paul hadn't asked what happened, but as soon as someone did, it would be all over for Michael. Katherine had seen him drinking. She planned to turn him in. She got a page to meet him on the roof. Her husband knew. Now she was a bloody mess in Michael's arms. If he hadn't arrived when he did, would she have been a bloody mess eleven floors down?

Like David Eaves, the anesthesiologist in Boston?

# Chapter 54

Madge pushed herself up. Judging from the light outside, it was afternoon. She'd lost a good part of the day. Was *Creature Friday* over? Where was her clicker?

The tube in her nose tugged and the tape pulled. Drat. Darn thing was still there.

Colored markers and papers covered the bed table. She shoved them aside. Where was that remote?

Wait a minute. There was a reason for these papers, these markers. She'd made a list. The suspects. On the menu.

Maybe she should add a column for weapon. One person died after eating one bite of a Reuben sandwich. One tumbled off a roof. One was strangled. One was near death through some shenanigans with the antibiotic order.

She might see the pattern if she could get it down on paper.

Where was her list? She lifted the papers and fanned them out and rifled through them. The menu was gone.

She leaned forward to hit her nurses' alarm. She was immediately sorry. Who would come? Nurse Evan, who tried so hard to peek at what she was doing? Nurse Bob, who was Suspect Number One? She'd better be careful.

"Good to see you coming around. You gave us a scare this morning." Mildred materialized from behind the doorway curtain.

Thank heavens. Still, Madge wouldn't mention the missing list. She'd make up something else.

"Scare? I don't remember. When can I get this tube out? Can you ask Dr. Hal?"

"Now, now, you've had a big day. Let's see how you do. Anyway, Dr. Dexter left early. Headache. Dr. Mead came in to cover for him, and she's swamped. If you don't need anything, I'm off for my break. It's my birthday, and the guys said take my time, so I will."

"Good for you. Happy Birthday, Mildred."

"Thank you."

Hmph. Headache. When did a doctor ever get to leave early because of a headache? Although maybe he tended toward migraines. Because she remembered him having a headache as a boy. He'd delivered the large box of jazz band fundraiser grapefruit, and he carried it into the kitchen for her. He politely relocated her alcohol to one corner to make room on the counter. "These will make great Greyhounds," she said, and because he looked puzzled, she added, "Grapefruit and vodka. Shall I make us one?" He seemed so old, with his afro and his moustache.

"No, thank you, Ms. McGillicuddy. I have a bad headache, and I have to get home," he'd said.

She'd enjoyed that grapefruit. The band switched to holiday wreaths for Mikey's last two years, and she hadn't care for those.

Hmm. That meant that when Hal carried in the grapefruit, he must have been sixteen, seventeen at most. Oh, boy. A little too young for that drink.

Mikey never brought his teen friends home. Maybe this was why. Hal didn't really have a headache then. Maybe he didn't really have a headache today. Maybe it was his go-to excuse when he needed out.

Did Mikey ever need out?

# Chapter 55

Madge sank back on the pillows, eyes closed. What would she do differently if she had to do it all again? Everything.

"You're awake."

She leaped in the air, and both drains tugged painfully.

"What in the world? Mikey. Scare a person to death."

"What in the world, Mom? You'd think I was a ghost."

His flowing white doctor coat was in his hand, but he might still be a ghost, so closely did he resemble his father. That man was gone. Only a ghost of a memory remained.

"A little on edge, dear."

"Your procedure went well. You're on new antibiotics. I double-checked with the nurses."

"Yes, yes." He thought she was worried about a little infected necrosis.

"You called me 'George' this morning. Why?"

Had she? Maybe. Mikey was so direct. He'd always been that way. Asking for what he wanted and most of the time getting it. Her fault.

"Your dad's been on my mind."

"Dad's been on your mind? Since when?"

"Since now." Was Mikey ever impertinent. She didn't care to explain every private thought to him.

"I haven't heard you talk about him in thirty years. Now he's on your mind?"

"He came to see me." Mikey stopped his pestering questions then. His face froze, his eyes open wide.

She might as well tell him. He'd find out soon enough anyway.

Mikey closed his eyes and placed both hands on the bed table to steady himself.

"So he's not dead."

He put into words the answer to the question they'd secretly wondered—no, feared—for decades, ever since the man walked out the door. They had never stated it out loud, not to each other.

"No. He's not dead."

It gave her such relief to say it. George wasn't dead. She hesitated, then told him the rest. "But he's dying. He has liver cancer."

Mikey's expression gave him away. His mouth fell open and his eyes scrunched up and he dropped his head into his hands.

She closed her own eyes to hide the sight, but she had seen.

Michael was devastated. This father he'd barely known, this man who threatened their lives on a violent night and then abandoned them forever, was somehow still loved by his precious son.

Michael showed more emotion in that one expression than he'd ever shown for her.

One thing. She'd only ever wanted one thing.

It wasn't enough to give up everything for your child. It wasn't enough to wipe his nose and tie his laces and make him oatmeal with raisins. Bandage his knee and unscrew the training wheels and scream he had to wear a helmet. She was a mom and a dad. But Mikey's expression told her he wanted a real dad. That she fell short.

It wasn't enough to cover up his mistakes. Wash away the blood. It wasn't enough to lie.

Two could play this game. She took the knife, that chef's knife that hid for so many years among the old coats, and rammed it in, metaphorically speaking. "He moved out of state." Mikey lifted his head, and she saw tears. Actual tears. She continued, slicing away. "He has a new family. New wife. New kid."

She watched Mikey's face fall in, as hers had fallen three weeks ago. She wrenched the knife blade deeper. "He sobered up. Years ago. He said he wanted to come back. But he was ashamed. He knew we'd always remember, know what he'd done. He left that night because he was afraid it might happen again. Now he was sober, and he knew it never would. But he didn't want the reminder there, day after day, that it had. The scar was reminder enough."

Mikey's face paled further.

"He didn't want to come back *that* much." Madge gagged, her feeding tube pushing against her throat again and again.

When the retching finally eased, she spit out the word. "Coward."

"He's dying of cancer." Mikey's voice was flat.

Her mouth was full of sour stomach juice. She swallowed, but the bitter taste was still there. "He wanted to make amends. Finish the story. Let me know what happened." She let all the bitterness seep into the words.

"New family," Mikey said.

"Kid's twenty-five. So not terribly new. He didn't come back to us. He forgot all about us."

Mikey turned his back. He was leaving already? No. He stood away from the bed, his broad back still, his head bent.

Something was wrong. It took her a moment to figure it out. Then she blurted, "Stinky, why are you in your undershirt?"

# Chapter 56

When Michael carried Katherine to the emergency department, she had been fully conscious. They put her in a room, and he told them what he knew, that it looked like she'd fallen and hit her head on the edge of the planter. He left out the shadow running from the roof. He was well aware that her pager and her husband put only him at the scene.

Katherine herself was in no condition to disagree. She'd lost an entire day. The last thing she said she remembered was putting her daughter to bed the night before and kissing her husband good night.

Which meant she didn't remember catching him in the stairs with the alcohol. Or heading off to see him at the roof garden. Or what happened when she arrived.

"Concussion this bad, she may never get this day back. Amnesia is very common." Michael sat with a frazzled Paul as the ED doc explained.

Katherine's daughter, Ellie, sat next to Paul and kicked her legs against the chair. "Where's mommy? I want to go to her office and see her. I don't like this place."

Paul scooped her into his lap. "Mommy's not in her office. She had an accident and has an owie on her head. We'll take her home and you can cuddle with her."

"Right?" Paul asked the doctor. "She'll be all right?"

"Yes, yes. Good thing Michael was there to stop the

bleeding. She lost some blood, and she'll have a whopping headache, but she'll be fine. CT doesn't show any brain bleed or swelling or fracture. You can take her home. I'll give you instructions for what to watch for. We'll see how she does. She will be off work several days, then probably return on a reduced schedule. She can follow up with her primary before coming back."

"Yippee!" said Ellie. "Mommy's staying home with me."

So Michael was in the clear. For now.

He stood in his undershirt in his mother's room and thought about his father and thought about Katherine.

He had no defense. No proof of anything. "It's not me" was not going to fly with police.

Matilda was long gone. He'd missed the end of her conference, didn't know if she was still there when Katherine was on the roof or if it had already concluded. He had nothing.

If Katherine's memory came back, he knew what she would think. That Michael had tried to kill her.

That was exactly what he and his mother thought about his father.

It hadn't stopped Michael running from his bedroom to the top of the stairs as a kid every time there was a knock at the front door. He wasn't afraid. He was longing to see his dad.

Katherine would not be longing to see Michael, he was certain. He would lose his job. He would be arrested. It was only a matter of time.

How many times had Michael watched other boys with their dads, throwing the pigskin around, shooting hoops? Shaking their hands at graduation and clapping their backs?

Michael's father taught him baseball, the rules, the teams. He bought him a mitt and softened it up.

Those memories were strong. There were other memories. The shouts, the threats, the fear. The always present potential for anger just below the smiling surface, a drink away.

Which is why he'd known his father would never come back. Not after what Michael had done.

His father hadn't turned and left. His father hadn't tousled his hair or told him "It was for the best." Michael liked to remember it that way. But that's not what happened.

His father had stood in the doorway of the kitchen. Michael had cowered behind his mother.

"Keep quiet," his mother said. "If anything happens to me, run as fast as you can."

She held the knife high. She would protect him.

Standing in his mother's hospital room now, Michael shook his head. There were current threats to worry about. His father was the past.

But he was back. He'd come back. Michael had to face what his ten-year-old self had done.

Michael hid behind his mother. The knife looked huge, high above his head.

Should he step out? Throw himself between them? Would that make it better or worse?

She must have read his mind. "Stay put. Don't antagonize him."

His father loomed in the kitchen door. He didn't turn and go. Michael willed him to, but he didn't.

His father stepped toward them, slow step by slow step. Michael's heart pounded. He wanted to close his eyes, but he forced himself to see. His father was right in front of them, much bigger than Michael, a head taller than his mother, so close his chest touched hers.

His mother stood frozen. Then she took one step back, pushing Michael back, too. Her hand with the knife quivered, then dropped to her side.

His father scoffed. "You're useless, even at this." He reached for the knife, the only thing standing between Michael and his mother and the great beyond.

Michael was quicker than his father. He grabbed the knife from his mother's limp hand. He jumped forward and plunged it in. His father yelped. He spun and ran. From their lives.

His family could have recovered from his father's anger. But not from Michael's deed.

Especially if he was dead.

Even in this version of the story, still not the truth but the version Michael could live with, his father's blood was on his hands.

How could he live with what really happened?

That was for another day.

When he was a teenager, Michael searched for his father, slowly, meticulously, contacting every George Baker he could find. He couldn't be dead. He was alive. He had to be. Michael had not killed him. He was alive and he would have changed. Michael would apologize. His father would understand. His father would rescue him from the chaos that was Michael's daily existence.

George Baker was a common name and after multiple dead ends spanning years, Michael gave up.

Because, in all likelihood, he had killed the man.

He was ten. Old enough to know what he was doing.

He buried his father and all the false stories he told himself in the deepest pit of his mind and went on with his life.

Now his father was back. He was not dead.

The relief was so great, Michael's knees trembled, and he had to brace to keep standing.

His ten-year-old self was not a killer.

His father *had* changed, exactly as Michael always hoped and dreamed. He'd pulled his life together. But he had not come back for Michael. Michael understood why. The knife. His own son had stabbed him.

Michael had escaped on his own. He left Seattle and his

alcoholic mother and any hope of reuniting with his father far behind.

Now Michael was back and so was his father.

And Michael's life was falling to pieces.

# Chapter 57

Madge lay on her pillows and stared up.

What was it for? Why had Madge dropped out of law school? Lain flat in bed for months? Birthed him and soothed him and put up with his colic? Protected him with her life? Let the one man she ever loved slip away without a whimper of protest. Worked two jobs so Stinky could have sailing lessons and a saxophone. Taught him to read when he fell behind in first grade. Hired a tutor when he did poorly in physics. Pushed him and encouraged him and comforted him. Saw him through the stress and excitement of college applications and medical school applications. Cheered from afar at every publication and research grant. Delighted in his girlfriend and regaled her with Stinky stories. Welcomed him home with open arms and an offer to move right back into his same old room.

All so he could tell her now that he would have rather had a dad.

Even a dad who tried to punch their heads in. Even that, apparently, was better than a mom, better than her.

She'd only ever wanted one thing. The love and respect of her son.

Was this the lot of a mother? They said you were only ever as happy as your least happy child. But were you also only ever as much of a person as how your least grateful child saw you?

That was ridiculous. A child shouldn't hold so much sway, so much power. Where was her backbone?

When it came to Stinky, her backbone was malleable. A sodden noodle.

She would just wallow here today. Dig out every wrong and examine it and soak up unhappiness.

When Mikey left for college, he'd traveled to New York on his own. He flew across country with his suitcases and one box he mailed himself. He didn't leave the box for her to send. He didn't give a reason, but she knew why. She might have forgotten. He hadn't trusted her with this simple task. It still stung.

A few months later, she saw another mother in the grocery store. Her son went to the same college.

"We thought for sure we'd run into you, on the plane or at the welcome brunch," she said.

"What?" Madge said.

Then the whole story came out. Parents weekend. Somehow Stinky had kept this from her. He didn't want her there. He didn't want to introduce her to his friends and his friends' parents. She called him on the telephone and cornered him. He hemmed and hawed and said something about a wine and cheese party. As if she couldn't handle a wine and cheese party. These things weren't always a disaster. She might have been able to hold it together for a weekend. She wanted desperately to show him that she could. She never had the chance.

The ingrate. She could have had a life. Now *he* had a life, and she had him.

There was no medal for being a mom.

Moms did things more incredible than any of Stinky's superheroes. When did she get to be the hero?

She'd always been proud of him. But the feeling wasn't mutual.

"Miss McGillicuddy?"

Tony the Torturer.

"I'm not here."

"You *are* here, finally. I came by earlier, but you were out. Walking the halls?" Tony smiled at his joke.

"No. For your information, I was down in Radiology having a life-saving procedure and right now I need to rest. No PT today." That should do it. The guy should take the hint.

"Yes, PT today. PT every day or your muscles will atrophy."

Oh, for Pete's sake. "Can't I get a little peace around here? No wonder Chrissie called you Tony the Terrible."

"Chrissie? That young woman who died?" He glanced toward the empty bed.

"Yes, that young woman who died, and your PT likely sent her to an early grave."

She didn't mean it. He must know she was kidding. But his face changed from normal, hardy Tony the Torturer to the pasty face of Chrissie before she died or Stinky when he told a lie.

"She was fine after PT. I never saw her again." He hefted his big body first on one foot, then the other. His eyes shifted back to the empty bed with the pristine sheet and precise hospital corners.

Madge felt she had to say something. He was taking this way too hard. She'd been right to add his name to the suspect list. The *missing* suspect list.

"I agree. I was making a joke," she soothed. "After physical therapy, she was fine. I saw her. It wasn't you, okay? It was a glob of fat, broke off and blocked her lungs and killed her."

Tony nodded, satisfied with this official answer.

Madge clenched her teeth to hold in the rest of her thought. *That, or a poisoned sandwich.*

# Chapter 58

Michael headed to the exit through the clinic lobby, empty on a Saturday afternoon because the clinic was now closed. The hospital lobby might be empty, too, but he didn't want to risk seeing anyone. He wanted to be alone.

The lobby gift shop was dark, but its door sported a fat pink ribbon proclaiming "Show your mother some love." The window was stuffed with said love, though the papier-mâché bouquet and most of the crystal hearts were missing.

Tomorrow was Mother's Day. Good grief.

Michael's eyes involuntarily flicked to his own picture on the wall. His mother loved it. Doctor of the Quarter. What a joke. Since then one of his patients was dead, one was in the ICU, his career had tanked, and his new boss thought he wanted to throw her off the roof.

All these innocent people. All connected to him.

Someone was out to destroy his reputation, to destroy *him*. The human cost be damned.

When Matilda Walters, in her chief of staff role, told him he was Doctor of the Quarter, voted on by doctors and nurses and support staff and every other member in the hospital community, he had been honored. He had been honored like this in Boston, too, and, frankly, had never doubted he would end up on that lobby wall here in Seattle.

Such conceit he had.

Now he understood what a truly incredible honor it was. To be recognized by your peers and the people around you as special, caring, dependable, capable. He felt none of those things now. He doubted anyone in this hospital would ever think these things about him again. Katherine had made that clear in her phone call with Phil.

Matilda had absolutely glowed as she shook his hand and they posed for pictures. "I'm so happy we're working together again," she said. She seemed so sincere. How could she be the one?

The picture was hung a mere six weeks before. In six weeks, his life had cratered lower than even when Janet left.

He was outmaneuvered, behind at every step, too late to catch the shadow on the roof, but at least in time to save Katherine.

Was it Matilda? Had she tried to kill Katherine or just scare her? Either way, the result was the same for Michael. When Katherine's memory returned, she would believe the threat had come from him.

If he couldn't figure this out, his days at Cascadia were at an end.

He could barely look at the picture.

Wait a minute. His mouth went dry. He inched closer to the picture. His larger-than-life-sized face smiled at him, a confident, friendly looking doctor. With red capital letters scrawled across his shoulders.

KILLER.

He reeled back. Killer! Who knew, besides him and his mother?

All his life, he'd waited for this, for someone to discover his secret, the secret he and his mother held onto since that night when he was ten. A siren blaring in the middle of the night. A knock on the classroom door when he was little. A whispered conversation among administrators in high school.

A summons to the dean's office in college. Year by year the threat decreased, but apprehension was always there, waiting for the veneer to crack, ready to erupt.

Now here it was, in large red letters, out in the open. Not a secret anymore.

KILLER.

Wait.

He was not a killer. His father was alive. He had not killed his father.

He had carried this with him for so long that he almost couldn't believe it wasn't true, especially with this word glaring in front of him.

His father was alive. This word was not about his father.

Was this about Chrissie? Like the note? Of course he'd jump to her, but he hadn't killed Chrissie. His logical mind knew this.

Was it about Reginald Stark, then? Had Reginald Stark died? Oh, no.

Michael hadn't seen him since before the meeting with Katherine and Phil. No, no, no. He couldn't have died.

Though odds were, he could, he would. He was so sick, on a ventilator, bad lungs, organs shutting down. He could easily have died.

Michael fumbled with his phone. He dialed the hospital operator and asked for the ICU. The operator typed and connected, each click excruciating while he waited. The ICU phone rang and rang.

*Pick up. Pick up. Don't be dead.*

"ICU, Glenda speaking." Finally.

"I'd like to speak to the nurse taking care of Reginald Stark. It's Dr. Baker."

"Dr. Baker, she's in with him now, giving him a bath. She'll be a while. Can I help you?"

Michael's whole body relaxed in a sudden ooze, and he

almost dropped the phone. "No, no, that's fine. I'll call back later. Thank you."

The man wasn't dead. Michael stood a moment as his heartbeat slowed, then he glimpsed the photo and it quickened again.

KILLER.

If this wasn't about Chrissie and it wasn't about Reginald Stark, what was this about?

Was someone trying to pin Katherine on him? Someone who didn't know she survived?

Matilda?

He searched frantically around. No one was there.

Two security cameras faced the entrance. Neither was trained on this wall, and unless the person left the building, they would not be captured on film. Anyone could see the cameras, could write this word and then return up into the clinic area without notice. Then back into the hospital area or any other area. Anyone who knew Cascadia could do this. Because the person was surely from Cascadia.

He would solve this. Until he did, no one would see the picture.

The word was written on the photo's glass. He lifted his undershirt and scrubbed at the red letters until the picture was restored and his white undershirt was as blood red as the white shirt he'd wrapped around Katherine's head.

# Chapter 59

Madge couldn't believe it. Tony wanted her to walk the entire length of the hall to the far staircase, prove she could descend two stairs, and walk back again. He seemed to have forgotten that just that morning she was at death's door, fading fast, one step from St. Peter's gates. Shouldn't she be allowed a pass for today? This Tony had a one-track mind.

She only agreed because it was Nurse Mildred's birthday. If she timed it right, she could be near the nurses' desk for the big celebration. Inhale cake smell. Examine the treats. She couldn't eat them since she was still NPO, and she'd never expect to since it wasn't like she worked at the hospital, though sometimes the nurses offered if you looked longingly enough. Today she could at least peruse the selection. She did enjoy a birthday, despite all the trouble with Stinky.

More to the point, it was one thing to see a nurse in a patient room, fulfilling duties, professional and following protocol. It was quite another to see them in party mode, albeit work party mode. If Madge walked slowly enough, she might overhear a useful tidbit. She was furious with Stinky, but that didn't mean they didn't have a case to solve. And Stinky sure wasn't solving it.

Madge gripped the stairway railing and limped down two steps, one leg at a time, Tony's belt holding her weak frame. What in the world was she going to do when she got home?

Her house had stairs. Her muscles had definitely turned to jelly during this hospital stay. Use it or lose it, they said. Tony might be onto something, with all this forced exercise.

Once they were back in the hallway, the singing started. Was there cake? Madge had been so good at cakes, twelfth birthday notwithstanding. That one had looked good, at least, albeit a little flat. A perfect likeness of the superhero. Like her train cake with individual cars. And a snake cake slithering across the table. A bear with a marshmallow egg nose. Didn't this prove she'd been a good mom? Did she get any credit for cakes?

Had anyone made a special cake for Mildred?

She slowed her step to maneuver around an abandoned wheelchair. She would like to sit in that abandoned wheelchair. Maybe Tony would let her rest there. Maybe Tony would push her back.

She paused and gazed at it hopefully.

"Don't you even think it," Tony said.

Torturer. She resumed her slow, painful crawl. Maybe she should do those knee exercises Tony gave her. At this pace, though, she'd be able to dawdle unsuspiciously near the party.

Conversation drifted her way. Her keen ears soaked it in.

"What was she doing in there?" This was Nurse Evan.

"I don't know, but she wasn't the only one in there. The Central Services guy came out right after." Mildred said this, but Madge wasn't interested in this old news. Get to the good stuff.

"He's a far improvement on her ex-husband. Remember him?" Mildred again.

"How many times did I want to punch that guy? No respect. The way he talked to her." This was Nurse Bob, of all people.

"You'd never treat a woman like that," Mildred said.

"Certainly not."

"You know who treated his wife badly?" Nurse Evan again. "That guy with the knee who went to the ICU. Did you ever hear him go at her?"

Madge stopped abruptly. This was more like it. Tony, trailing behind with her safety belt, almost ran into her.

"What the—?" he said. "No stopping. You're just creeping along anyway. You have to pick up the pace or you'll never improve."

"Can't I rest here for a moment?" She strained to talk and listen at the same time. Tony was yabbering again and she could only hear him.

"We have to keep going. I have more patients to see today. They all need their walks." He made a flicking motion with the belt as if she were a horse and he held the reins.

"...wanted to punch him, too. Good thing he went to the ICU or I..."

"You have to pick your feet up. No shuffling." Tony's voice drowned out Bob's. This was scary Bob, threatening Stinky's patient in no uncertain terms.

"Have some cake, Bob," Mildred said.

"Don't mind if I do. What kind is it?"

Evan mumbled something. Bob bellowed now, catching Madge off guard since the yell was directed at them.

"Tony! You're from Boston, right? It's Boston cream pie. We'll save you a piece."

Jackpot! Tony was from Boston. Stinky came from Boston. Anesthesia Man and Janet were from Boston.

"Evan made it," Mildred said. "His cakes are delicious."

Evan could cook? Mr. "Do We Need To Go Wee Wee" did baked goods?

"Maybe you can give me the recipe," Tony said. "My mom used to make it, but I never thought to ask her for the recipe."

Tony the Torturer was going to bake? Would wonders never cease?

"Easiest cake going." Evan blushed. "Since I use a box mix for the cake and a box mix for the pudding."

"I'm touched," said Mildred.

"Probably don't need the recipe, then," said Tony. "Times like these, I miss my mom."

This giant man said that? Madge could hug him. Tears stung her eyes and she swiped them away. No point getting all sentimental. Tears got you nowhere.

Would Stinky ever say anything as beautiful as that?

# Chapter 60

Michael unlocked his door, finally home, and his sore arm exploded with a pulsating pain that buckled his knees.

"Could use those narcotics, Hal," he muttered.

All day he'd popped anti-inflammatory medicine. Now it was time for the good stuff.

So much had happened. Too much.

He'd called the Security Office on his way home and made up a story about finding a pair of glasses in the clinic lobby. He'd bring them in tomorrow, but could they review the camera film to see if it was someone on staff who might have left them? And, just as he thought, they confirmed that no one had been in or out of that door for hours until he himself left the building.

His brain needed a break. From his past and his dad, from the present and his job.

"Frank?" The lizard crept silently in.

Michael's arm screamed as he twisted the top off the bottle of gin. He filled his glass and drained it. He filled it again and left the top off the bottle for easy access.

He sprawled on the couch in his dirty undershirt, his dirtier white dress shirt and his doctor coat on the floor beside him. He had one leg on the coffee table, one dangling over the couch arm, a drink in his hand, and his aching arm propped on a pillow. He was punch-drunk, giddy with alcohol. He wanted to talk, but not about the day. He wasn't yet ready to process all that had happened.

"What's up, Frank?"

Frank eyed him from the coffee table. He crouched and looked ready to pounce.

"Touch my arm and you'll be in your crate." He motioned with his drink. Frank settled back with a clear look of disdain.

"Don't give me that high and mighty crap," Michael said. "And, yes, I know I'm mixing antibiotics and alcohol. I'm the doctor here. You're a lizard. Who sounds like Francine."

Frank lifted his nose and sniffed.

"Francine's a doctor friend."

Michael laid his head back and inspected the ceiling. "We dated, okay? One date. Well, two."

The date was fun, actually. It wasn't really a date, more like leaving the hospital together and Francine asking what he was doing that night, because it was the First Thursday Art Walk, a monthly night when the galleries in Pioneer Square stayed open late.

"Quick dinner first?" Francine said.

"Sure," he said.

"There's a new fried chicken place just around the corner," she said.

"I don't like fried chicken." No one ever cared why.

"Thai?" she asked.

"Perfect."

Francine ordered a dish so spicy it made her sweat. She ended up eating his pad thai, and he ate her curry. Then they wandered the art galleries, which were crowded and lively and packed with paintings and sculptures. Francine was taking an art class and wanted inspiration.

"I traded a shift with Hal to come to this tonight," she said. "He's working the night. Good thing we both have tomorrow off."

They nibbled on tiny cookies and chatted with artists. They ogled the price of a painting they both admired of colorful abstract flowers in a mountain valley.

"Looks like Mount Rainier," Francine said. "I think I've seen this very view." She fiddled with her phone and produced a photo that looked remarkably similar to the painting in front of them. "This was last summer. I try to go for a few days every July. Sometimes I'm too early for the wildflowers, if you can believe it. Sometimes there's still snow."

"I haven't been to Mount Rainier since I was a kid." Michael didn't tell her it was only once, on a school field trip. Less than three hours from Seattle, most of his friends went every summer, for a day hike or camping. He and his mother never went anywhere.

They finished the night with gelato, and they walked back up the hill to the hospital parking garage. He reached his arm around to hug her as she stuck out her hand for a shake. So he shook, and they went their separate ways.

So that night had been fine.

Then the spring party the following week. What had he been thinking? They ended the evening together at her place, which was lovely at the time, until it wasn't.

Her apartment was tiny and smelled of oil paint and lemons. So did she, it turned out, not of hand sanitizer or latex. She made breakfast the next morning, bagels and eggs and huckleberries.

That's when she returned to the topic of Mount Rainier. "I once stumbled on a huge crop of ripe huckleberries. They were delicious, warm from the sun. I would have eaten more, but I was hiking alone. I was worried a bear would come along any minute."

"A bear!"

"They're all over. I've only seen them from far away, like down in the valley. As far as I know, at least. Maybe one was closer when I was eating those huckleberries. Haven't you ever seen one?"

"I've only been there once." He didn't mean to say it, because he imagined that no one in Seattle had only been to Mount Rainier once.

"Only once?" Her shocked expression told him he should have kept quiet. "You grew up here. You don't like to hike?"

"No, I love to hike." He'd hiked all over the Berkshires, the Green Mountains, the Catskills. Christ. "Just...busy, you know?"

"I know." She smiled, a big smile that showed a dimple in one cheek. "You know what? We should go for a hike this summer."

That's when he realized what he was doing. Setting himself up for a relationship with someone in the hospital.

Her statement hung there like the final blare of horns in his favorite jazz piece.

He didn't try to cover the silence. She twisted the end of her short hair and buttered her bagel and changed the subject to a tricky patient they both shared.

He and Francine never talked about that night again.

The lizard's shiny eyes bored into him.

"I'm not doing that," he told Frank. "I know what you're thinking. With my life, my hours, where else will I meet someone? But I'm not doing that."

Michael was never again going to stand next to someone after a breakup, day after day, often with an audience of other nurses or techs and the anesthesiologist, angry and heartbroken and seething inside. For years he and Janet were a team, joking, teasing, laughing, even planning a surprise going away party for an anesthesiologist who'd worked there forty years. The guy had tears in his eyes, and Michael imagined himself in the same situation years later, retiring after a distinguished career, adored by staff and colleagues.

In Michael's retirement vision, Janet was by his side, as she always was. Standing so close their legs touched and handing him tools before he asked because they'd done it so many times. Surgery was easily the best part of his day. Then it was ruined. The OR was silent, stiff, tense. Words were terse, to the point, and always on the edge of explosive.

Janet knew he had a past. She'd bided her time, waiting for him to explain. He never had. How could he tell the woman who wouldn't so much as crush a spider that he'd killed his father? When he couldn't even admit it to himself?

She threw it back at him. "I feel I don't know you. Maybe I never did." It hurt because it was true.

"You've never let me all the way in. You've never been completely honest." She was right. He had not been honest about the two things that mattered most. His father and his love for her. It was far too late by then.

They endured every day in the OR for three months. They had no escape.

It was all sour.

He tried to explain it to Frank. The tegu stared back, unblinking.

"I'm not doing that again," Michael repeated. "Look where that got me."

Frank leaped gracefully from the coffee table to the couch. He crawled onto Michael's chest and positioned his broad face above Michael's.

Michael tilted his head back and closed his eyes. "It got me years of happiness, didn't it? I was happy. Then I was a jerk."

# Chapter 61

Michael's hand shook as he lifted his glass. Alcohol splashed on his chin. Frank jerked away and climbed up on the back of the couch.

"You'd drink, too, if you had the day I had." Michael's head swam in a woozy daze remembering everything. He couldn't believe it himself. "Mom hallucinating, getting alcohol from God knows where, Katherine accused me of drinking on the job, then she almost dies, and she thinks it was me. Matilda was in a conference all morning, but I don't know..."

Frank wasn't listening. Michael continued anyway. "My photo was defaced. Plus, my father is back." Saying it out loud made his whole body shake. Good thing he was lying down. "I didn't kill him."

Frank's head bobbed up.

"Oh, now you're interested? I thought I killed my father. It was a long time ago. But I didn't kill him." If Michael said it enough times, it might finally sink in.

Michael was not a killer.

"You probably want to meet him, Frank. I want to meet him." Michael shook his head. "He has a new family. He's... He's dying."

Frank looked sorry, with his head down and his big eyes closed.

"He's dying like Katherine almost died." Michael took a swig, sending the gin down the wrong pipe in his reclining position. He choked and gasped and sat straight up, and Frank slipped onto the floor. "I'm done for," Michael said.

Frank rose on his hind legs and stared with his unblinking black eyes. "What, Frank, you think I've had enough? Because I'm not finished yet."

The tegu dropped down and scurried from the room. Michael called after him, "What do you know? You drink milk."

He raised the glass and threw back the rest.

Maybe Katherine would never get her memory back. Maybe she got a look at her assailant and knew it wasn't Michael. Or had she been surprised from behind?

Michael pictured the scene, Katherine in all the blood, the whoosh of the shadow behind the planters, the door slamming shut.

Wait, wait, wait. Step back and think. Katherine had received a page supposedly from him telling her to go to the roof garden.

This person was in the paging system. In Michael's own account on the computer. Again.

Michael had written his notes early today. Hadn't touched a computer since before his mother was sick, long before the page to Katherine. No one could have piggybacked on his forgotten log off.

Anyone could page a doctor to a phone number using a phone. But the sender's name only showed up if you used the computer system, and the computer system was also the only way to send a text message. The password protected computer system.

Michael's passwords were hackproof, chains of nonsense characters, numbers and letters. He'd thought this through and had been quizzed by IT after the antibiotic order, and he'd changed his already complex hospital password then. He leaned over and patted his white coat pocket that held the card.

Yet someone had gotten into Michael's account. Twice. How?

His mother had used one password her entire life. He used a different one for every account. His complicated passwords, so complicated he had to write them down, were foolproof.

Frank was back. His cold eyes held Michael's.

"I'm the fool," Michael said.

Michael gripped his glass so hard he thought it would shatter. He set it carefully on the floor next to the lizard.

The passwords were written down. Kept secure in a card in his pocket. Michael was never without his doctor coat. It was a second skin. Except once.

He'd left his coat in his mother's room the day she yelled that he was not the center of the universe. She was right, as usual. But he'd left his coat behind.

Michael sat absolutely still, not even breathing. The alcohol made it hard for his tired brain to keep its train of thought.

Before anything else, he had to change his password. Again. He logged on to the hospital system, opened his account, and made the change, this time not so complicated but hopefully complicated enough. JS for Janet Smalls, the date they'd broken up, and an exclamation point. He'd never forget that.

He knew the "how." Someone had seen his hospital password written on the card in his pocket when his coat was in his mother's room. Now the "who."

The "who" was someone with access to his mother's room.

Matilda could pull it off. So could any of the other doctors. Or the nurses. Or any of the staff that were in and out of his mother's room all the time.

His mother had a list of victims and suspects. Chrissie Johnson, Reginald Stark, Janet, David Eaves. Now Katherine Pierce. Too many people, as his mother said.

Michael's head cleared as if the alcohol were back in the bottle.

Seattle. Boston. Philadelphia. Chrissie, Reginald Stark, Katherine Pierce. David Eaves. Janet. Michael was the common denominator. He had to be. And only one thing tied Michael, David Eaves, and Janet together. It all still came back to the case in Boston, the patient with the stroke.

He couldn't even remember her name, the woman with dreams of dancing who had suffered a grave medical error.

*She* was the true connection. Who was she?

# Chapter 62

Michael lifted Frank onto the couch and concentrated on the lizard's steady breathing.

Was it Matilda? Hiding her error, compounding the pain?

The woman was in the hospital day in, day out. She'd won an award they created just for her. How far would she go if her career was in jeopardy?

Matilda lived for her job. Was she willing to kill for it?

Who would be next? Was his mother at risk?

Information about Matilda's conference was in the weekly newsletter. He called the restaurant. "I'm running late for the Cascadia function," he lied. "Have I missed the speeches?"

"Oh, no, sir. We were late starting our dinner service, so Dr. Walters said she would delay her remarks until we can get the dessert out. That should be around nine-thirty. She said an hour for remarks. Then we have coffee bar and digestifs. Should I hold a plate for you?"

"No, thank you. I won't be eating."

"Very good, sir."

Matilda was busy. She couldn't hurt anyone tonight. But Matilda could not be the only one to worry about. Who else? Who else would cause all this pain?

Someone in pain themselves. Because the pain was real.

His patient, the woman with the stroke, had suffered a

terrible fate. She was in pain. She had loved ones. They were in pain. Was a loved one behind this?

What was her name? It wasn't Johnson or Stark. He would have known that. Besides, if his theory was correct, Chrissie Johnson and Reginald Stark were unfortunate pawns in the killer's game. A killer related to the woman from Boston.

Michael hunched over his computer and typed in his old hospital and "settlement" and "medical error" and any other phrase he could think of. Nothing came up. The settlement had been quick. Publicity was negligible. The hospital had been happy about that.

He knew how to find her name. But he'd have to wait until morning. Or even Monday. He would call the Anesthesia Department and speak to the current chair, or the head of Anesthesia M & M, or anyone at all he knew. If they didn't remember, they could easily look up the case for him.

Monday was too far. He drummed his fingers on the computer. Who? Who? Had someone followed Janet to Philadelphia, him to Seattle? He punched in the Cascadia staff directory. He found Evan's and Bob's last names, but neither seemed familiar. Bob had been at the hospital a year. Relatively new, but he would have had no idea Michael would move to Seattle. A year ago, Michael hadn't known himself, would have scoffed at anyone who suggested it. Probably could cross Bob off. Michael's mother would not be pleased.

Evan was hired only two months ago. He fit the timeline. He was a likeable guy, in an overly earnest sort of way. Didn't mean he couldn't be a killer.

Michael whipped out his phone.

"It's Michael Baker. Could you please page Carol Layney. The head nurse on seven. I'll hold."

"Dr. Baker."

"Ms. Layney. Sorry to call so late. I have an unusual request, and I know it might be difficult because of all my mother's staffing preferences, but is it possible to have a nurse other than Evan to care for her?"

There was silence, then Carol Laney cleared her throat. "You do not wish Evan to be your mother's nurse?"

"Correct. Just for the time being."

"And I take it the ban on Nurse Bob is still in place."

"Well, I know my mother prefers that, so yes."

"Let me get this straight. Of our three regular nurses, you wish only one be available to take care of your mother. Is that correct, Dr. Baker?"

He sighed. "Yes."

"I'm going to say this, and then you and I will never speak of it again." Did he hear a smile in her voice? "I assume you have your reasons. Just like your mother. I will honor your request. And you will be pleased to know that Evan is away for three days. He left work early tonight to fly home and be with his family for Mother's Day."

Michael phoned the floor first thing Sunday morning to check on his mother, and Mildred assured him she had just left the room and all was well. "So much better than yesterday. Good thing you were there when she turned septic."

Was that only yesterday? Before Katherine and the alcohol and the roof and finding out his father was alive and the picture with "KILLER" blazoned across it. Jesus.

At least he didn't have to worry about Evan. And according to Matilda's conference schedule, she was in a breakfast meeting and would moderate a lengthy panel at eight. He had some time.

He called the Anesthesia Department in Boston. The phone in the department rang and rang and went to voicemail. It was Sunday. He left a general message to telephone him back. He was able to reach the anesthesiologist on call, but the guy didn't know Michael and didn't remember the case.

He'd have to wait until tomorrow to find the woman's name. Unless Katherine's memory came back, and he was arrested for attempted murder first.

Phil knew about the alcohol, too, of course. If he talked to Katherine's husband and learned why she was on the roof, he'd also have reason to involve the police.

Michael was on borrowed time. He needed the name to pop into his head.

Maybe he'd go for a run.

Sometimes when running, with his mind blank except the rhythm of his feet, he'd get an epiphany. He'd be enjoying the trees, and he'd suddenly remember that the reason he couldn't find his leather coat was that he'd left it on the bleachers at the gym after basketball. Sure enough, the coat was waiting in the Lost and Found. Another time it suddenly occurred to him to look for his mother's hidden alcohol in the toy chest in his room. He'd searched everywhere else, but he hadn't thought to look in his own childhood bedroom. And there it was, a brand-new bottle of whiskey, cradled in the soft arms of Charles the Bear.

A little time out in nature, and the woman's name would surely surface.

He tucked Frank into his cage and set out, down the hill to the lake. The day was sunny and crisp. He turned onto the lake path, where a runner stretched against a tree.

"Michael!" Brent Williams, whom his mother called grumpy. Who wanted Michael's job. He pushed a jogger stroller, and a toddler slept inside. "Giving my wife the morning off," he said. He sprinted off, motioning for Michael to come, too. There were plenty of people around. The lake felt safe. The jogger stroller felt safe. What could Brent do to him here?

Brent was one of these ultramarathoners. He was from Colorado and returned every year for a marathon thirteen miles straight up Pikes Peak and then down again. He was not the casual runner Michael was. Plus he must be ten years younger. His pace was fast despite the stroller.

"Beautiful day," Michael said. He ran with one eye on the view and one eye on Brent. They headed south, with Mount Rainier around each curve, peeking through the leaves of a willow tree or rising above the masts at the marina. If they ran far enough, they'd reach the boathouse where Michael took sailing lessons as a kid.

"Talked to my brother today," Brent said.

"Oh?" A one-word response was easier at this speed.

"Somehow each discussion devolves into 'Mom loved you more.' How does my brother jump from the fact that he got in trouble and I didn't when we crashed into the plate glass window to 'Mom loved you more?' He was chasing me, by the way. I cut my arm. Blood everywhere. Of course he got in more trouble. Anyway, you'd think he was five, not thirty-five."

"I don't have any siblings."

"Be glad," Brent said. "I always thought my brother liked me. I didn't know he resented me."

They ran in silence for a while, then Brent started talking again. Michael huffed and puffed. It was all he could do to keep up. He felt old, lumbering along next to Brent.

"One day he said he didn't think we were full brothers. He insinuated I had a different father, said Dad mentioned something once. My dad had dementia. Who knew what he was saying? My sister didn't know anything. Plus, she's angry at me because I recommended we give more money to my brother and because I dated her roommate years ago and apparently their relationship was never the same."

They passed a man walking a dog and Brent was quiet for a moment. He picked up again a few strides further.

"It's probably not even true. About my dad."

"Right," said Michael.

"Even if it is true, I didn't want to know this secret of my mom's."

Michael understood that. The poor guy. No wonder he was grumpy.

"I thought we all loved each other. Heck, I thought we all liked each other."

Brent slowed. Thank God. "I thought we were a family. No one is speaking to anyone. My mom would be so sad. Today's Mother's Day, you know?"

Brent stopped suddenly and Michael stopped, too. He leaned forward against a tree sucking in air.

"Mother's Day," Brent repeated. He grabbed Michael's arm. Michael pulled back instinctively. Brent's bright eyes bored in to his.

Michael glanced around, wary. A large group of walkers approached, and Michael relaxed against the tree. He was still breathing heavily. Brent was, too.

He leaned on the stroller and his shoulders trembled. Brent was crying.

Michael pushed off the tree and stood next to him. The lake was calm, the surface like glass, with the sun and one lone cloud reflected perfectly in the middle. A single sculler rowed silently past.

"I'm sorry," Michael said. "Families are hard." As he well knew.

Brent nodded. He stretched his legs one at a time behind him. "Ready?"

It was Mother's Day. "I'm heading back. Going to see my mom," Michael said.

"You do that," Brent said. "While you still have a mother."

Before Michael could respond, he turned the stroller and raced away.

Was this a sinister warning? Or just another pessimistic allusion to Michael's mom's downward trajectory? Could the killer be Brent?

His mother had recently died. What if his mother was the woman in Boston with the stroke? A doctor had access and abilities like no one else. Had he visited Michael's mother and found the computer password? Had Brent done all this for revenge for his own mother? What about his brother and his sister? Who were they? Did they live in Seattle? Work at the hospital?

It couldn't be Brent. Brent was from Colorado. How much of a coincidence would it take for Brent's mother to now live in Boston and have her doctor there, supposedly Michael, move across country to work at Brent's hospital in Seattle? Far too much of a coincidence.

What about Brent's ambitions? Right now both Michael and Katherine were out of the way. Did Brent trash Michael's career and lure Katherine to the roof? Because of aspirations to be chief?

That was ridiculous. No one would harm patients and staff just to be chief. Would they?

Michael's mind swirled and names popped in and out, but the only real thing he accomplished from his run was putting off going into the hospital and seeing his mother on Mother's Day.

His mother. That was it.

She was his epiphany. She held the answer. Whoever found the password, they found it in her room.

# Chapter 63

Was Stinky coming this morning? It was Mother's Day. He had to come.

Madge waited and waited. Tony the Torturer might love his mother, and he was probably thinking about her on Mother's Day even now, but he was from Boston and Stinky's anesthesia friend died in Boston. And Tony was mighty cagey about Chrissie.

So he might be a murderer. Murderers could love their mothers. There was a *Creature Friday* like this, a deranged man who was nice to his mother and no one else.

Where was Stinky? Was he angry with her? He was always angry with her.

Like George, toward the end. Angry and finding fault at every little thing. Angry at himself, really. She understood that. He left one job thinking he could do better, then lost that one after sharp words with the boss. He came up short in his hunt, week after week, and by the end had been out of work for months, and the sharp words were for Madge and Mikey.

She allowed him his shouting, his threats. Empty, she thought. Until they weren't. It was the alcohol. It wasn't George.

George was loving and caring and full of joy. He had been, anyway.

They met on her first day of law school. She arrived ten

minutes late to orientation and missed the introductions but was in time for socializing on the lawn. They clumped by a round fountain with an expanse of green sliding down to a view of Mount Rainier in the distance. A gaggle of students chattered away. They were a lot younger than Madge, who was twenty-nine and felt ancient in her paralegal skirt and blazer she'd thought suitable for this first day.

Off to the side stood a man about her age in a shirt and tie. He was tall and blond, and when he turned he had the bluest eyes she'd ever seen. His name tag said George.

"Hi, George," she said.

"Hi, Margaret," he read from her own name tag.

"Madge," she said. "I go by Madge."

"I've never known a Madge, but I had a great-aunt Margaret. She taught me to tell time when I missed that week in school. She taught me piano and her favorite song, 'Greensleeves.' She lived two blocks over and was like a second mom to me. A better mom in many ways. When she died, I played 'Greensleeves' at her funeral. I missed her so much I named my pet mouse after her. Margaret the Magnificent Mouse."

With that outpouring of nervous chit chat, Madge was smitten.

Her first day of law school and she'd met a dreamy fellow law student as well.

She eagerly accepted his invitation to dinner that night. She was enthralled by the picnic he proposed in the arboretum, complete with a wicker basket and red checked blanket. He unpacked French bread and cheese and strawberries and chocolate. He was such a romantic. If he hadn't already won her heart, the chocolate would have been the clincher.

She ran into him at the law library the next day. She sat at a long study table struggling to unload thick books from her satchel. He walked by and stacked them tidily for her as if they were featherweight and not tomes that took two hands for her to lift. She indicated the empty chair next to her.

"Can't today," he said. "How about a trip to Pike Place Market this weekend? You can show me that bakery."

They ate their way through the market. Handmade fish chowder, doughnuts, honey sticks, and five kinds of apples they sampled from a farmer. George bought her an enormous bouquet of dried flowers he said would keep forever, "as a memory of this day."

It was too hard to say goodbye, so they meandered back to her house. The next morning they finished the doughnuts in bed.

Madge had never done anything like that before, slept with a man so soon. But she'd never felt as wiggly kneed about any man before. George was the one. Why wait?

Monday afternoon brought her back to the library. And to George. He was behind the desk, checking out books for a long-legged redhead who always sat in the front row. Darlene.

Madge waited behind her and when George saw her his face lit up and she knew he didn't care about long legs or redheads.

"What are you doing here?" he said.

"What are you doing here?" she said.

"Working," he said. "Of course."

"You work here? How can you manage that? What with classes..."

George's beautiful face changed. Madge had once seen the huge balloon floats at the parade downtown on the day after Thanksgiving. Afterward her parents took her to view them up close in a big parking lot at the end of the parade route. The handlers deflated the balloons, and one by one the giant bears and tin soldiers and puppy dogs caved in, scrunching inward on themselves.

George's face did the same. It was obvious to Madge that

it was obvious to George that she was just this moment realizing he worked in the law library and was not, in fact, a law student.

She racked her brain to think how she had been so certain. He'd been at the orientation, that's how. He had not said one word since that indicated he was a law student. She'd missed the introductory comments. Had an introduction to him, a helpful face in the library, been part of those missed remarks?

She had made an assumption. Now she realized her mistake.

He was a hopeless romantic and he cared what people thought about him, and he especially cared what *she* thought about him. His devastated face told it all. He thought she'd fallen for him knowing what he was, and now he knew she fell for him thinking he was something else.

What did it matter anyway?

She hastened to assure him. "So I thought you were a law student and not a law library assistant. Who cares? Not me."

She hastened to assure herself. She liked this boy. She'd *slept* with him, for God's sake.

And he liked her. Before long, it was love.

They spent a blissful year canoodling and exploring. He greeted her in the predawn hours with coffee and a scone to see the sunrise from the beach in Madison Park on the east side of the city. He took her to the beach at Golden Gardens Park on the far western edge and they snuggled under a blanket to watch the sunset. They spent two days cuddling inside by the fire while a rare blizzard raged outside. They walked the trails in Lincoln Park, and they hiked at Mount Rainier. He never arrived without a flower in his hand, and he never left without a sweet nothing in her ear.

She hadn't made many friends in law school because she was always busy with him. She was utterly, unequivocally, euphorically in love.

There were signs all along that George might not be the economically sound man a girl dreams of when she's twenty. He'd been only too happy to move out of his shared apartment and into the home Madge had inherited from her parents. He'd been overly excited about her summer internship that paid almost more than he'd made that whole year. He'd been more keen than she to hear the projected salaries of lawyers who were invited back to work at that firm.

These warning signs hadn't mattered to Madge, pushing thirty and soon to be a well-compensated lawyer. She would work hard, and she would have a supportive partner beside her.

Even when they found out she was pregnant, early in her second year, life seemed grand. A slight pause in her law school education, and they'd be back on track in no time. It wasn't until several years passed by that they realized this was it and made adjustments.

She'd loved him so much. It scared her to think what might have happened if she'd arrived in time for the intro-ductory remarks, for the introduction of George, the law library assistant.

She'd loved him so much she would have been willing to take him back all these years later. When she opened the door and found him on the porch three weeks ago, her knees went as wiggly as the day they met. If he'd come asking to be let in, to join forces with her once more, to spend their golden years together, she would have him back in her life already.

Instead, she fetched the dried flowers from her bedroom dresser and pitched them into the trash. They shattered into tiny pieces, like the love she'd held onto for forever. Dried up and gone.

But all that time ago, if she had known right from the beginning that he wasn't a law student, would she have fallen so hard, so fast?

She was embarrassed and terrified to know the answer was

no. His being a fellow student was part of the allure, part of the magic. If she'd been on time, she'd be standing in the middle of the crowd. She never would have noticed George standing to the side.

She never would have known George's love. And she would never have had Stinky.

# Chapter 64

Could his mother figure this out? Remember who had been in her room while his coat was on the chair?

Because of the run and a stop for flowers, calla lilies, her favorite, it was already midmorning when Michael arrived at the hospital. He checked on his mother, but she was sleeping, and he ducked out quickly. He peeked into the auditorium and confirmed that Matilda was on stage at the end of a long table. Then he rounded on his other patients. Sundays were quieter than weekdays, but the floors were still plenty busy.

Striding down the hall toward his last patient, he almost bowled over Matilda Walters. She jumped out of his way, her straight black hair swinging.

"What are you doing here?" Why wasn't she moderating her panel? What time was it? Was his mother all right?

"I'm here all weekend," she said. "The Future of Medicine conference." Was her expression surprise? Guilt? The confidence of a cool killer?

"I know," he stammered. "Why aren't you there now?" He should leave right now and check on his mom.

"We're on break," she said. Did she sound nervous?

His pager blared and he took his eyes off Matilda to glance down. "Your mother wonders when you'll be in." Thank God. Bless Mildred for this page that normally would only irritate him. His mother was fine.

"Michael, if you'll excuse me..."

He was in her way, and he didn't move. She was trapped.

*Did you kill Janet?* He wanted to shout at her, but he couldn't show his hand. Not yet.

"Michael, as long as you're here, we should talk." She definitely looked cagey as she gave him the side-eye.

Killer cagey? Or boss cagey?

Oh, no. He'd forgotten about the alcohol. She'd demoted him, and now she was going to fire him. But she wasn't stepping close to smell his breath, so Phil may not have mentioned anything about the complaint from Hunter Stark or Katherine finding the little alcohol bottles.

"I heard about Katherine Pierce," she said.

Maybe she did know.

Matilda continued, "What a miracle you were there to help her."

Thank the Lord. She didn't know.

Time for him to talk now. "Janet Smalls is dead."

"Janet Smalls? The OR nurse in Boston? Your old girlfriend? Oh, my, I'm so sorry. What happened?"

"Did you see her? Were you in Philadelphia?" He restrained himself from his real question. *Did you kill her?*

"Philadelphia? What? Why?" Matilda's expression was cautious.

She didn't ask him "when," probably because she already knew. "Two months ago. Were you in Philadelphia two months ago?"

"I'm sorry about Janet, but why are you asking me this?"

"Were you?" he persisted.

"Michael, I don't know why you care, but I haven't been out of this hospital for more than twelve hours ever until my forced vacation this month."

Of course. How could he have forgotten? Her award. Three months of straight work. Matilda had been physically in the hospital every single day. Janet died two months ago. In Philadelphia, a five-hour plane flight away.

Michael closed his eyes. His back wilted against the wall. Matilda had not killed Janet. Likely no one else either.

Then what had Janet seen?

"What's this about, Michael?"

He didn't answer directly. He needed to know. "Do you remember that case? The one with David Eaves? The mixed-up medications and the similar boxes?"

If she was guilty of the same mix-up herself and hiding the mistake, her face didn't show it. "I remember," she said. "Poor David. Did you hear what happened?"

"That he took his own life, yes." He shook his head sadly.

"Poor David," she said again. "It wasn't his fault, of course. I didn't know he blamed himself so."

Now they were getting somewhere. Would she admit her role now, admit that she was the one to make the same error? "Janet saw something. Another doctor almost mixed up the medication. Their warning could have saved my patient." He was fishing, but she didn't know that.

Matilda didn't say anything.

"Janet came to you. You were the chair of anesthesiology."

Matilda sighed and stepped closer. They were alone at the side of the hall. Her body slumped and she reached out to the wall for support. "Michael." The cautious note was back in her voice. "Okay. Yes. Janet spoke to me after David Eaves' mistake. But she wasn't certain, as you know."

He knew it! Matilda was covering up the whole affair, burying her part so no one would know.

"Who else mixed up the medicine? Was it you?" Michael studied her tormented face.

"It wasn't me," she whispered.

"Who was it? Why didn't you say something?"

"It didn't matter anyway," she muttered.

Janet had said the same thing. He couldn't believe this. "Of course it mattered! A doctor knew. A doctor who could have stopped the tragedy to my patient from happening at all. A doctor who was as responsible, if not more so, than David Eaves."

Matilda hadn't killed Janet, but she certainly had a hand in David Eaves' death. Michael was not going to let her off the hook.

Matilda's whole body sagged. "Yes, a doctor knew. A doctor set to retire that very day after forty years of distinguished, flawless service, who assumed he was too old for the job and that he was the only one who would make such a mistake, and it was a good thing that day was his last."

"Rivers? Janet saw Len Rivers?" Janet and Michael worked with him that last day, planned his surprise retirement party. That revered, retiring anesthesiologist was the person Janet had seen?

Matilda went on. "As Janet wasn't certain she'd seen anything at all, I did not chase down Len Rivers at his new home in Sedona. He telephoned me himself as soon as he heard about David Eaves' case, which was almost a year later, since he was well out of the loop. The hospital had already offered the family a very large settlement. No one knew about Rivers' role. Except Janet, Len Rivers, and me. And you, apparently. My biggest regret is that I didn't tell David Eaves."

Michael leaned against the wall. "Len Rivers."

"And, to add to the sadness, Len told me he'd been diagnosed with kidney cancer. Renal cell. His time was up, he said."

Matilda turned to go. "Wait," Michael said. "What was her name? The woman who had the stroke?"

"Her name." Matilda squinched her face. "Her name. My gosh. I can't believe I can't remember."

That made two of them.

# Chapter 65

While he was thankful his mother was fine, after yesterday's scene about his father Michael was loathe to see her awake. He had one more patient to see anyway, eighty-two-year-old Evelyn West. She said she'd retired from accounting before she started to make mistakes, but she still did math puzzles. Len Rivers had assumed he made the medication mistake because he was old. Michael doubted either of them had ever made a true mistake. Len realized his error and tossed the drug. David Eaves, decades younger, had not.

Evelyn would go home soon, once she could pass her exit parameters, getting in and out of a chair and bed, walking with a walker, safely maneuvering stairs, etc. Her pain was manageable. She was progressing well. He'd miss her smile and her sunny attitude. Seeing her was a high point.

"Dr. Baker!" Her whole face broke into a grin. "I'm ready to practice stairs today. I was still too nervous to try them yesterday."

"You're doing great. You only had surgery Friday afternoon. You'll get there."

"I know, I know. I'm ready today to give it my all."

Michael laughed at her enthusiasm. "Don't go too fast."

If only all his patients could be like this. What a joy his rounds would be. She'd flown through her surgery and recovery without a hitch.

Michael saw Tony, the physical therapist, in the hall. "Just saw Evelyn West. Let me know if there's any problem with her PT."

"Will do." Tony held a brown leather folder in his big hands, and he made a notation on a sheet of paper.

Michael still felt her glow and couldn't help adding, "She's a delight, isn't she?"

Tony just raised his eyebrows. Michael hastened to explain. "I mean, she's always in a good mood, ready to do anything we ask, nothing but smiles, even though I know her knee hurts."

"Yeah." The guy's low voice didn't sound impressed.

"Well, she's *my* favorite patient, at least. Maybe you have more like her, but right now, I don't." Michael left him outside her room and steeled himself to see his least favorite patient, who wasn't even his patient.

He retrieved the flowers and set off for his mother's room. She loved chocolate and he kept her in a steady supply at home, but she was still NPO so the flowers would have to do. He always had trouble with Mother's Day cards because none conveyed the complicated sentiments he felt. He had no card today.

Yesterday his mother taunted him that his father was alive. He had always been alive. But not for long. Who knew what mood she'd be in today.

A little too excited a mood, that's what.

"Stinky, Stinky! You're here! What beautiful flowers. My favorite. Thank you." She laid the calla lilies on the bed next to her. "Guess what? Dr. Hal said I can start clear liquids again today. He thinks the radiology drain is really helping, and he bets I can eat real food tomorrow. The gods are smiling on me, Stinky!"

He flinched. This was a reference to a childhood picture book where lucky things happened out of the blue. When

Michael was young, he believed the gods were smiling on him, right up until the day he first overheard his parents' sordid fighting. Then he knew no one was smiling on him.

His mother practically bounced in her bed. "Can you believe it? Tomorrow, Stinky! Tomorrow!"

Hopefully this was true. With her, it was always two steps forward, one step back.

"Juice and broth and popsicles. All for lunch. Ooh la la." She smacked her lips and clapped her hands.

"That's great, Mom. Happy Mother's Day. Look, I've—"

"Tomorrow I can order anything I want off the low-fat menu. That's what he said. I'm starting with toast. Crunchy. Chewy. Warm. I can taste it now! How many pieces do you think they'll bring me? More than two, I hope."

He had to get her mind off food. He needed information. Good thing he hadn't brought chocolate. He dove in before she started dreaming about butter versus jam.

"You were absolutely right, Mom. Someone in this hospital is sabotaging me. Chrissie. My patient in the ICU. And Janet and the anesthesiologist in Boston. And now even Katherine Pierce."

That got her attention. He was prepared for her to mock him and tell him he was the one sabotaging himself. He underestimated her. She would never think that. She was his biggest cheerleader.

She'd never doubted him even when he doubted himself.

"Katherine Pierce, too? I knew it! I knew it, Mikey!"

"I need you to try to remember something. I left my coat in here the other day. I need you to try to remember everyone who came into this room while the coat was here."

She wrinkled her forehead in concentration. "I remember your coat. But Mikey, so many people come each day, I can't remember who was here when." She squinted at him and shook her head. "I'm sorry."

Just what he expected. "Okay. How about any day? Tell me everyone who comes into your room."

"Hoo boy. Let's see. There's Nurse Mildred and Nurse Evan. Nurse Bob hasn't been here in a while because I fired him."

"Yes, I know." The shadow in the parking lot loomed large in his mind. "What about Brent Williams?"

"Dr. Grumpy? No. The only doctors are Dr. Francine and Dr. Hal. Dr. Hal! Do you think he might let me start with real food tonight if I keep my lunch down? Then I could order dinner-type food instead of breakfast. They make a great lasagna here. Hard to believe it's low fat. Do you think they have lasagna on today's menu?"

He needed her back on track. "Anyone else?"

"Hmm? Right. Anyone else. Well, Gerta was here when she brought my clear liquids last time, but that was some time ago. She'll be back today! Do you think they have cranberry juice? They don't always."

"Mom. Think."

"I know, I know. But I can't wait for Gerta." His mother's eyes widened. "Mikey, Gerta. Did you ever talk to her?"

He had to admit he had not. Now his mother's theories weren't nutso anymore. Gerta would be next on his list.

"Who else comes in your room?"

"Well, Tony the Torturer and the other physical therapists. Mostly Tony now. I miss Don and Carlotta. Why do they have to give me the new guy?"

"New guy?" Michael had just seen Tony, upstairs with Evelyn West.

"*Only* guy these days. The others abandoned me."

"How new?"

"Oh, Stinky, I don't know. He wasn't here the last time I was admitted and now he is. Chrissie called him Tony the Terrible, and I agree."

His mom was last in the hospital shortly before Michael moved home four months ago. So Tony started sometime after that.

"Wait. Mikey, I just remembered something. I meant to tell you. Tony's from Boston! Do you think it's Tony the Terrible? Is he the one?" His mother sat upright.

"He's from Boston?" Michael tried to squelch his excitement.

"Evan made the most delicious looking Boston cream pie. Chocolate dripping off the top. Turns out it was mostly from a box. I bet I could make it. Maybe I will."

"Mom! Tony's from Boston?"

"He sure is. Bob confirmed it. And Tony was jumpy yesterday talking about Chrissie. Suspicious, all right. Good thing I added him to my suspect list!"

"That's right. You have a suspect list. Let me see it." Michael should have paid more attention to her. She turned out to be right.

"I *had* a suspect list. Somebody stole it! The very somebody behind all this, I'd wager." His mother nodded so vigorously, he thought she might dislodge her feeding tube.

"Your list of suspects is gone? Are you sure?" Michael surveyed her bed table, covered in papers and markers. "It's not here somewhere?"

"Look all you want, Stinky. It's not here." She made a show of shuffling the papers around. He had to admit, he didn't see the sheet with the thick columns and Chrissie's name. Though in the dark room, who could tell? His mother claimed she could see in this light. She credited carrots, but really it was the bright lights she hated, and she'd say anything to keep them off. She probably couldn't see any better than he could.

Her hands stopped abruptly. She threw her head back and cackled.

"I knew it! Look at this! Mikey! I know who killed Chrissie!"

Michael's heart thudded. His mother held her hand high, waving a green pamphlet as if it were the golden ticket.

"What is that?"

"It's proof, Mikey. Proof."

# Chapter 66

Michael grasped the pamphlet and lifted it close to his eyes to read in the dim light. " 'Your Knees and You.' What is this, Mom?"

"Chrissie had one, too. On the day she died. Tony brought this to me after one of my physical therapy sessions. Chrissie told me he was going to bring her back a pamphlet. I went off for my CT. It was right there when I got back, next to the Reuben sandwich. Chrissie was suddenly sick. And Tony had been back to see her while I was gone!"

"Tony the physical therapist? I read his note. It was from hours earlier." Michael had scoured Chrissie's chart enough to remember every note, every time stamp. No one had seen her after the nurses' rounds three hours before. No one who charted, at least.

"I know. He must have come back. I saw the pamphlet. The pamphlet proves it."

Michael's head spun as if he'd had a drink. He sat on the edge of his mother's bed and held her rail for support. Could Tony be behind all this?

"The sandwich was there, too. You have to talk to Gerta. Maybe she saw something. Maybe Tony poisoned the Reuben sandwich."

Michael's excitement crashed. This whole cockamamie idea of his mother's was based on the notion that Chrissie was murdered, not that she'd died of a fat embolism. Which he one hundred percent knew she had. Nothing else gave that respiratory compromise, that petechial rash. The ME was so convinced, he'd declined an autopsy. That was not unusual, but telling nonetheless. Michael had allowed himself to get caught up in his mom's wacky theories, but Chrissie died because she had a complication of a broken leg. Period. End of story. No amount of wishful thinking was going to change that.

His mom must have noticed his waning enthusiasm. "I know you blame yourself for Chrissie's death. It wasn't you, Mikey. It was Tony. I know it was," she said.

"Maybe," he said.

"He was here when your coat was here. I remember it distinctly. He was looking up his passwords on a card in his shirt pocket and I said you did that, too, and he said he didn't know you were my son."

"What?" The password! The guy had access to his password!

"Chrissie. Me. Tony the Terrible worked with both of us. What about your Antibiotic Man? Don't let him near any of your other patients, Mikey."

Michael's emotions plummeted again. How had he forgotten? How had he been so stupid?

Reginald Stark's antibiotic order was changed well before the day Michael left his coat behind. Tony could not have changed the order.

Was Michael right about any of this? Or was the whole thing much simpler? He left his computer on, and someone accidentally changed the order thinking it was a different patient. Michael was responsible.

Slumped on the edge of the bed, his emotions on a roller coaster up and down, up and down, his mother all a gaga in her quest to clear his name, Michael's mind flashed to another time he was responsible. A blame he had carried for thirty-five years.

His song floated through his mind. *I know you and you know me. Will we be friends forever? I know your secrets and you know mine. Will we be friends forever?*

His mother believed in him. She'd do anything for him. She was blind to what he really was.

He thought he'd escaped.

He knew what he was capable of, and underneath, so did she.

It was impossible to escape when they shared a secret.

# Chapter 67

When Michael was ten, a stormy night left them in the dark and without a ball game to watch. It had been a good day. His father taught him a curve ball and a slider. His mother made fried chicken and they ate it outside on a red checked picnic blanket under the apple tree he loved to climb. Then the wind kicked up and the picnic blanket blew into the air and his mom and his dad both grabbed it at once and ended up in what his mom loved to call a smooch. Fat raindrops fell and Michael's feet slipped as he climbed down from the tree, but his dad was there and steadied him until he was safely on the ground.

His parents moved to the front porch and sat on the steps to watch the storm. Seattle rarely saw thunder and lightning, but this storm had it all. Michael sat with them until they grew loud from the liquor. He disappeared to his room and closed his door and waited for the ball game. His dad promised it would be a doozy.

The lights went out. Michael didn't know this meant no ball game until he heard his dad shouting and his mom shouting back. He stayed in his room with the door shut tight. The house shook with a crash that was not thunder. He crept down the stairs. His mom sprawled on the ground and a chair lay on its side.

His parents had shouted before. Often. But that was it. Never anything like this.

"You want some, too?" His father only growled like this when he'd been drinking.

Michael's mother vaulted from the floor. She seized Michael's hand and pulled him to the hallway toward the door. His father beat them to it.

He slammed them against the wall and rammed his fist toward their heads. His mother ducked her body over Michael's. His father's fist shattered the plaster above them. They scrabbled away and by the time he freed his hand, they had backed into the kitchen.

"Keep quiet," his mother whispered. "If anything happens to me, run as fast as you can."

The kitchen was dark, and the rain hammered at the window. Lightning flashed and the blade of a knife flashed in his mother's hand high above him.

His mother held the big chef knife she'd used to chop the chicken. Michael hid behind her, his head pressed to her back.

Why was he hiding? He should be the one protecting her. He was ten. It was time to end this. He shifted slightly.

"Stay put," she whispered. "Don't antagonize him."

His heart pounded so loudly he barely heard his father's threats as he drew closer. His father filled the kitchen doorway, blocking any hope of an exit. Michael clutched his mother's waist. Her legs were shaking so hard he thought she would fall over.

She held the knife high. His father wouldn't try anything while she had the knife. And if he did, his mother would protect Michael. He was certain.

His father stepped toward them one slow step at a time. He crept so close Michael could see the grass stains on his pants.

His father stood there, the knife inches from his face. Time stopped and Michael's breathing stopped and the whole world stopped.

His mother's arm fluttered down. To her side. Not to his father.

"You're useless, even at this." His father laughed at her, laughed at the two of them, cowering in the kitchen.

He whipped around and walked away. He left them there, recoiled against the counter.

He left.

Michael snatched the knife from his mother's hand. He sprinted across the kitchen and reached his father in the hallway. He raised his arm and plunged the knife into his father's back.

His father pitched soundlessly forward. He planted a hand on the wall to catch himself.

Michael pulled the knife out with two hands. Blood spattered on his face, on the wall. His father whirled, his eyes bugged and his mouth open in surprise.

Michael slashed the knife down to stab again.

"Mikey!" His mother's shout filled the hallway. Her hand held his arm.

Michael strained against her, struggling to get to his father.

His father clutched his side. Blood seeped through his shirt. He stumbled to the door and down the steps and into the storm. Lightning revealed his lurching form, but then darkness swallowed him before the thunder crashed.

His mother, who screamed at the tiniest provocation, remained silent. Scarily silent. His heart still raced. His body wanted to run upstairs and hide. He ground his teeth together to keep from screaming himself.

Blood dripped on his face and clotted in his hair, warm and sickening. The knife was red, and bits of fabric and tissue clung to its edge. His bare feet rested in a pool of blood, squishy and sticky under his toes. So much blood. Michael's stomach heaved and he vomited the chicken picnic.

His mother lifted her skirt and wiped his face. Within minutes, she was down on her hands and knees cleaning the vomit, scrubbing the trail of blood, all without speaking. She followed the red path onto the porch and the front steps and out into the downpour to the sidewalk. That storm, with its torrents of rain, so unlike Seattle's misty drizzle, that storm had already washed the blood away. His father had disappeared into the dark, rainy night and so had the blood.

"Don't say a word," his mother said. "I'll take care of it. If it comes to it, I'll take the blame."

He never said no. He never asked questions. He stood numbly as his mother stripped off her bloody clothes and hurled them into the washing machine. He let her strip his. She put him under the shower and led him to bed.

The next morning the bleach smell was the only indication that anything had happened.

He never ate fried chicken again.

His mother told people his father had left them, the few people who asked. Which was part of the truth.

His dad didn't have a job and had walked away from his parents two decades before, so there was no one to miss him. Only Michael.

Was he alive? Was he dead? If he was alive, would he come back?

The three of them could have recovered from his dad's drinking, his threats, his shouting. They could have limped along as a family, like they'd done before.

But not after what Michael did.

His father had turned away from the kitchen. He was leaving. He hadn't hurt them. He posed no further threat that night.

He was retreating when Michael attacked. He saw Michael raise his arm to thrust again.

This was the true story buried in Michael's brain. He

would have killed him. He thought he had. Michael lived with that his whole life. He was capable of murder.

Though Michael scampered to the window every time he heard footfalls on the front steps, he knew his father would never come home to them. He would never return while Michael was there. Michael was the reason. He alone was responsible.

# Chapter 68

Michael staggered from his mother's room and down the hall to the computer station, blessedly empty on this Sunday morning. He dropped into a chair and stared at a blank screen. All these years he'd kept his mind a blank. All these years he'd known, but he had hidden his secret deep in a file in his head behind passwords and firewalls and much more pleasant stories of the night his father left.

His father was alive. The idea was still so new. Michael had not killed him. He had not used all his ten-year-old strength to plunge a knife into a vital organ and kill the man who first to showed him a book with a skeleton in it, setting off a life-long love of anatomy and bones.

All these years he believed he killed his father. On good nights, he'd play the odds and tell himself it would be statistically very unlikely that a child's stab could kill a grown man. He analyzed angles and tried to predict what part of the body he'd hit. The kidneys? The lungs? The back? How tall was he when he was ten? What caused all that blood?

On bad nights, he was certain he'd killed him. Hit the aorta, and his father bled out before he made it to the end of the street.

Mostly though, he replayed the story of his father tousling his hair. "It's for the best." Or the story his mother told. An argument. No fist. No knife. A sanitized version.

It's the story he told Janet.

Only Michael and his mother knew the truth.

He'd stabbed his father as he walked out the front door and then tried to stab him again and again.

He was ten. He'd known exactly what he was doing.

That's why his father never came back.

It was almost easier to believe he was dead. That that was the reason. Not that his son had stabbed him in the back, the epitome of shouting "I hate you, and I hope you die and never come back."

Michael had the proof now. His father had recovered. He'd stopped drinking. But he hadn't come home. He made a new home.

And Michael and his mother had been tied irrevocably together. His song said it all.

*I know you and you know me. Will we be friends forever? You know my secrets and I know yours. Will we be friends forever?*

The last line lines were his alone, never sung aloud.

*You'd die for me. I killed for you. We'll have to be friends forever.*

Michael slammed his fist onto the desk.

Michael was the reason his father left. Just like he was the reason Reginald Stark was in the ICU. Michael had sat at this very computer. He would have written his note with all the time in the world and logged off in peace, but his mother had trouble with her IV. Instead he had to rush to finish the note in between clinic patients when his mind was on a million other things.

Wait a minute.

Michael squeezed his eyes shut to remember. He'd been writing his notes. Evan interrupted him and motioned him away so they could speak in private. Then they walked to his mother's room.

Had he logged off his computer? Or left it on, a sitting duck waiting for someone to slide over and change an order? Someone with evil intentions.

Because, sitting next to him at the computer station, taking up more than his share of the space and bumping elbows as Michael tried to type, was Tony. Tony from Boston. Tony the Terrible.

# Chapter 69

Michael punched his password into the computer. JS and that dreadful date when they broke up, plus an exclamation point. His fingers slackened on the keyboard. This was not a good password. He couldn't type this every time he logged in.

The computer flashed on. Michael pulled up Reginald Stark's chart and scrolled back two weeks to before he went to the ICU. When he was just a man recovering from a new knee. Michael saw his own notes there and those of the nurses. Bob, Evan, Mildred. And the physical therapist.

There it was. Tony *had* been Stark's physical therapist. He'd seen him every day. He'd known about the pneumonia. If he carried a grudge, he was one seat away from a computer left on begging for an order to be changed. A change that would clearly send this old smoker into a spiral.

Michael racked his brain. Did he know Tony? Had he ever seen him before? In the hospital in Boston? In the ICU with the woman who had the stroke?

Had he seen anyone there, any family? He'd always visited early, before his day began. He didn't remember meeting family. She'd come alone to her appointment, a vibrant, healthy woman with a sore hip who loved to dance. She thought she could get an injection and had never considered a hip replacement. When he explained her options and how transitory the pain relief would be from an injection for her bone-on-bone disease and how relatively easy a hip replacement was, she decided on surgery.

Of course she had family, but he couldn't remember them. And he couldn't remember her name.

Squeaking in the hallway broke the silence of the floor. The code cart wheel squeaked. That code cart had been for Chrissie, less than two weeks ago.

This squeak wasn't the code cart. The cart that passed was multi-tiered and covered in plates with opaque covers and pushed by a hunched, gray-haired woman in a hair net.

"Gerta?" Michael said. He'd seen her countless times before but never knew her name before his mother.

"Yes, dearie, that's me." Her voice was high and thin.

"I'm Dr. Baker. My mother is a patient here and she speaks of you fondly."

"And who might that be, dearie?"

"Margaret McGillicuddy. Madge."

"Oh, yes! Madge! 721. NPO. I haven't seen her in a while since she's not eating. No one else in that room."

Michael was surprised by this plethora of accurate information. "Yes. That's her." He hesitated, then plunged right in. "She has this strange idea. About her old roommate."

"Chrissie Johnson? Regular diet?"

"Oh, my gosh, you remember her?"

"Of course, dearie. Delightful young thing. Such a shame."

Michael breathed deeply. "My mom has a strange idea about Chrissie's sandwich."

"Is this about the sauerkraut?"

"What?"

"The Reuben sandwich. The kitchen was out of sauerkraut. I wanted to tell the girl, but the physical therapist was with her, and I didn't want to interrupt. So I just left the sandwich there, a Reuben sandwich without sauerkraut."

"The physical therapist? Tony?"

"That's the man. The new one. He was leaning in close, so I slipped my sandwich onto the table and skedaddled."

"What time was this?"

"Dinner time. Five thirty? Six? Did she complain to your mom about the sauerkraut? I hate to think that that miserable sandwich was the last thing she ate. Because the next morning she was gone. Gone gone."

Gerta pushed her squeaky cart away. The back of Michael's neck prickled. His mother was right. Tony was the last one with Chrissie. Tony was in a position to change Reginald Stark's antibiotic order.

Michael sucked in his breath. What if David Eaves hadn't committed suicide? What if Tony had pushed him from the roof? And strangled Janet and then tracked Michael down as the last person involved in his mother's tragic case. Set out to ruin his career and his life. Then finish him off.

Tony had been at Chrissie's code. Tony could have been the one to write the anonymous note.

He could easily have given his mother the alcohol. He was in and out of patient rooms all the time. He certainly knew she was an alcoholic.

Was Tony the person Michael had seen on the roof with Katherine?

David Eaves and Janet were dead. Michael had no doubt that Tony's ultimate goal was to kill him, too. How many innocent people would he kill first?

Where was Tony now?

# Chapter 70

Michael jumped up, knocking over his chair. It clanged to the floor, sending echoes down the quiet hallway.

He'd last seen Tony upstairs. With Evelyn West. Lovely, tiny, old Evelyn West.

Michael punched the computer to log off. He raced to the stairs and took them two at a time to the tenth floor. This floor was busier, and he had to push past a gurney and a transport tech to reach Evelyn's room.

Her bed was empty.

"She's out getting PT," said her roommate.

A brown leather folder sat on Evelyn West's bed table. Tony must have left it.

Michael unzipped the heavy zipper and flipped it open.

"I think that belongs to the physical therapist," the roommate said.

"I know," Michael lied. "He asked me to bring him something." If his mother were there, she'd tell him his face was drained of color and the red spot was on his cheek. But she wasn't there.

He rustled through the pages. Green pamphlets on knee pain, shoulder exercises, core strength. A few sheets on outpatient PT and a list of local rehabilitation facilities. Then he saw what he was after. What he only then realized he was looking for.

An old menu with thick black lines and columns and names. In his mother's handwriting, Tony's name in Chrissie's column.

Michael dashed to the nurses' station, which was thankfully bustling. Francine was there and raised her hand in a wave. Michael concentrated on the nurses.

"Anyone know where Evelyn West is? She's with Tony, the physical therapist. Did anyone see where they went? She's in danger."

"Danger?" a tall nurse asked. "They're doing stairs. They're in the south staircase. What danger?"

Michael didn't answer but bolted down the hall toward the far set of stairs. An army of footsteps followed him, but he reached the door first and flung it open.

He stepped back in horror. Others crowded in, the nurse, Francine, the transport tech.

At the top of the long staircase, an entire flight above Michael, Evelyn dangled at the landing precipice. A safety belt circled her waist, held in place by Tony. She was in the middle of the landing, and her arms were far too short to reach the handrail on the wall. She leaned precariously, and Tony leaned, too, the belt in his large hand. If he let go, Evelyn would plummet down the stairs. Almost certainly to her death.

"Call Security!" Michael shouted, and the nurse turned and fled.

"Michael, what's going on?" Francine's voice was calm, but her eyes betrayed her. She was as scared as he was.

"It's all over, Tony," Michael called, willing his voice to stay as calm as Francine's.

"Dr. Baker?" Evelyn West for once had no smile on her wrinkled face.

"What are you talking about, doc?" Tony's voice was gruff, just like earlier that day when Michael relayed that Evelyn West was a favorite patient. Of course he'd target her.

"I know about Chrissie Johnson."

The man's face collapsed. His arm slackened. Evelyn shrieked as she dropped six inches before Tony tightened his grip.

"What do you know?" Tony's stare was intense. Michael's eyes flitted between Tony and Evelyn West and her dangerous angle.

"I found the suspect list you stole from my mother."

"Confused old woman. That doesn't prove anything." The big man broke his gaze and regarded Evelyn West as if just remembering about her. Evelyn's eyes were wild, but she remained silent.

"I know you were the last to see Chrissie. You came back to give her a pamphlet."

"So?"

"She was fine and then she was very, very sick. What did you do to her, Tony?"

"I didn't do anything." Tony's words were barely audible. He dropped his eyes to the belt in his hand.

The concrete steps loomed cold and hard between them, each edge a sharp corner. Michael pried his eyes back to the two people at the top, the big man and the tiny, frightened woman. Evelyn gripped the belt with both hands, though that wouldn't matter if Tony let go.

"Don't do it, Tony." Michael kept his voice steady, but all he wanted to do was scream and bound up the stairs.

The stairwell was silent. Michael heard himself breathing, heard Francine breathing.

The door jolted open. Two large men in blue uniforms crowded in.

"What's going on here?" The older security officer stepped past Michael to the bottom of the stairs.

"He has a grudge. Against me. He's going to drop her! He's already harmed two patients here! He killed two people before this, in Boston and in Philadelphia!" Michael knew he sounded desperate, even a little disturbed.

Evelyn West whimpered.

"Michael, what are you saying?" Francine spoke for the first time.

"Doc, you've got it wrong!" Tony shouted, his voice low and powerful.

"Let's everybody calm down here," the older officer bellowed.

"I'm not harming nobody. I didn't do anything. You're as confused as your mom." To prove his point, Tony hauled Evelyn up, wrapped an arm around her, and stepped back onto the landing. "We're just practicing stairs."

"Sir, let her go." The officer took a step forward.

"If I let her go, she will fall." Tony didn't budge.

"Let her go," the officer said again.

"If he lets her go, she will fall," Francine said.

"Don't let go!" said Evelyn West.

"Enough of this." Tony pivoted and lifted Evelyn in one motion. He cradled her in his arms and started down the stairs. "I'm taking you back to your room."

# Chapter 71

"Stop him!" Michael said to the security guard.

"Everyone clear the stairway," the security officer yelled. "Sir, that includes you."

"This is my patient, and I'll stay right here," Michael said.

"I'm not going to do anything," Tony said. "Let me carry Mrs. West to her room. Then you can talk at me all you want."

The security officers buffeted him as they walked down the hall. Michael felt small among these three huge men. Tony rested Evelyn West on the bed and said, "Let's go." Security led him to the break room, motioned Michael in, and shut the door. Tony slouched on the couch. The two security guards pulled up chairs facing Tony. They indicated a third chair for Michael, but he preferred to stand by the door.

"Tell us what's going on." The older officer addressed this to Michael.

"My patient died suddenly and Tony was the last one to see her. Another is seriously ill due to an order Tony wrote. Tony moved here from Boston, where a doctor and a nurse are dead, and their deaths are linked to a woman who suffered a terrible tragedy due to a medical error. I believe she is Tony's mother, and that's why Tony killed them."

Michael said all this calmly. He thought his explanation made sense. The expressions of both security officers said otherwise.

Tony jumped to his feet, hands up. "Whoa, whoa, doc. What did you say? What are you talking about?" There was no denying Tony's Boston accent as he said this. How had Michael missed it earlier?

"Are you or are you not from Boston?" Michael said.

"Yes, I'm from Boston. Twenty years ago. I left after my mom died. Like I said, twenty years ago."

Michael sat down hard on the one remaining chair. "Your mom died twenty years ago?"

"In a skiing accident. I was right out of college. I moved out here then. Got cousins here."

Tony's mother was long dead. Tony was not related to the Boston deaths.

To be certain, at Michael's insistence, he provided details of his whereabouts when David Eaves and Janet died.

Tony sounded calmer and calmer. It was Michael who resonated absurdity.

"But you did steal my mother's suspect list." Michael heard his shrill voice.

"Suspect list?" one security officer said.

Before Michael had to explain that one, Tony broke in. "Yes. I took her list. And you're right. I saw Chrissie Johnson just before she died."

"There! I knew it." Michael didn't mean to sound so jubilant, but it was the first correct thing so far, maybe the only correct thing.

Tony's voice was flat, soft. "It's my fault. It's my fault she died."

Michael's mother was right. Had been right all along.

The security officers glanced at Michael, then Tony. "You'd better explain yourself, sir."

Tony sighed. "The day she died, I went back to give her a pamphlet of exercises. This was late afternoon. She didn't look well. She wasn't breathing right. But I thought it was pain. It's always pain, making people breathe heavy, making people not want to do their exercises. I thought it was an excuse, that she could work around it. I thought she wasn't trying."

Tony's large hands flew to his face, his fists digging into his eyes. Tears fell to his cheeks. His body shook as he tried to choke back his sobs. His words came out in pieces.

"I told her it was normal. I didn't know she was sick. I'd never seen an embolus."

He was crying harder now. The security officer pushed over a box of tissues. Tony took some ragged breaths. "I thought she was just breathing fast. Not fighting to breathe."

He wiped his nose. His voice cracked. "Then I hear the code, and it's Chrissie. I was there. I saw her. She was dead. And nothing the docs did could bring her back."

Michael remembered that code, all of them trying desperately to get her breathing, to get her heart to start.

Tony's voice was clearer now. "I never told anyone how she looked that afternoon, how breathless she was. It's eating me up. I see her lying there after the code. Dead. Pale and dead. At night, I see her. That poor girl. I told her the breathing was normal, for Christ's sake. Then I saw my name in big red letters on the list your mom made, and I panicked. I took it."

His chest shuddered with another sob. He looked right at Michael, his eyes anguished, his voice gravelly. "If I'd told somebody, would she have lived?"

# Chapter 72

Madge couldn't believe what Mikey was saying. *Creature Friday* played in the background, and its ominous music heightened the intensity of Mikey's story. Mikey had rushed in right as the seemingly innocent pensioner renting a room upstairs was about to stab the naïve landlady, but Madge dragged her eyes off the television and gave Mikey her full attention. Especially since Mikey thought Tony was innocent.

Tony might be a good physical therapist who wanted to strengthen Madge's bad knee, and he might be a man who loved his mother and remembered her Boston cream pies fondly, but that didn't mean he wasn't a killer. She had to set Mikey straight.

"He did it. I know he did. Tony's the one." If Madge repeated it over and over, Mikey would have to listen to her.

"I'm telling you, Mom. He roots for the Boston ball teams, but he hasn't been back in years. He didn't kill Chrissie. He didn't change my patient's antibiotics. We had it all wrong. We had everything wrong. He's only guilty of feeling guilty."

What was Mikey talking about? He could be dense sometimes. "No doublespeak. Plain English," she said.

"He was the last one to see Chrissie alive. When she died, he was devastated. If he'd alerted the nurses, would she have lived? We'll never know. Likely not. But it's possible. He felt responsible. Guilty. That's why he took your list. That's all."

"Are you sure?"

"Mom, you're giving me a headache."

"Just like Dr. Hal. He actually had to leave work early yesterday. You'd never do that." Though maybe he should. Mikey looked awful, spread across the chair, legs splayed, arms akimbo, completely deflated.

"Mom, listen. I don't have a lot of time. They want me out of the hospital in an hour. They're only letting me come to say goodbye to you, then I have to leave."

"What? *You* have to leave? Not Tony?"

"Yes. He didn't report Chrissie's symptoms, and he took your paper. But I called Security and fed them a lunatic tale about murders on the East Coast and nefarious goings-on here." Mikey straightened in the chair and leaned forward, his words terse. "I got caught up in your ludicrous ideas, and now look. I'm suspended pending further investigation. Security called Phil, and he decided. He actually came in to tell me. Too much on my mind, he said. Take some time off. Clear my head. Phil does not like drama."

"Oh, Stinky!" What had they done?

"I have to stay off hospital grounds until further notice. I actually tried to call you because I'm already supposed to be gone, but you didn't pick up."

"I switch the ringer off during *Creature Friday*. Who's going to call me anyway? Just you. And you come in person. Surely you're allowed to visit me?"

"No. I can't. Not until they decide I'm not a nutjob, not a threat. I think they're rethinking what happened to Katherine, wondering if I was involved."

"Katherine?"

"She still doesn't remember anything."

"You said she slipped." The music from *Creature Friday* soared into a crescendo, then faded into an eerie final minor chord. A red splotch materialized on Mikey's already pale face.

Oh, no. What had he done? She didn't slip because of him, did she? His explanation at the time had been unsatisfactorily brief, but Madge had had other things on her mind. George. Now she had all the time in the world, but Stinky was leaving, maybe never to return.

Whatever it was, it wasn't his fault. She knew Stinky.

"Tell me what happened."

His voice was empty, but his words were sharp. "You, Mom. That's what happened. Ever since I came home, it's been one thing after another. I'm about to lose my job." He shook his head and spoke louder. "You don't remember, do you? You don't remember drinking at home, so drunk on admission you told Francine I had the cutest bottom and you would know because you cleaned it enough since I was late to potty train. We had a good chuckle over that. She said you were full of stories that night, telling everyone in the ED I failed physics in high school and had to take it again over the summer, and that I don't eat fish because I got a bad shrimp when I was fifteen and never tried anything wet again. You blacked out the whole evening. You don't remember drinking, right here in the hospital, embroiling me in your filth, catching me up in your fantasies. You don't remember anything."

How could he say such things, and on Mother's Day, no less.

"And Janet." His voice was quieter now. "I let her go. I couldn't believe she loved me. That anyone would truly love *me*, without all my accomplishments. My whole life I worried, about you, if you were alive, if you were sick, who might find out what you were, what you might do next to embarrass yourself, embarrass me. I didn't think she could love *me*, the whole me, only the me I became once I left *you*. You can't comprehend what my life was like. You don't remember."

Mikey was breathing hard, and his face was red. He wasn't being fair.

She did remember some things. She remembered what she'd done for him all those years ago. She'd do it again if she had to. She had never let that secret go, no matter how much she'd had to drink.

Her chest heaved. She was breathing almost as hard as Mikey. Why did she get like this? He could shove the knife in and twist it and she could only lie there and take it. She'd lived her own life all these years. She held down jobs. She paid her bills. She listened when others were low. She was a good person. He didn't see it. He didn't know. He was always talking her down.

Why did seeing Mikey make her feel so inadequate?

Was it because he felt so inadequate himself?

"Mikey, I know my drinking affected you. I am so sorry. But look how you overcame it. Look what you've become."

He was shouting again. "What I've become? I've been fired. I screwed it up. Just like I screwed it up with Janet."

"Mikey—"

"I let her go because I felt defective." He stopped. His breath came in short pants. His voice shuddered. "Why couldn't I help you quit drinking? Why wasn't I enough to make you stop?"

What? What was Mikey saying?

She did remember. She remembered it all. How many times had he implored her, his blue eyes full of tears. "Mom, please stop. Do it for me."

"Michael, it's time." Francine stood in the doorway. How long had she been there? Her voice was gentle and her eyes concerned, and she glanced over her shoulder and then back. "I saw Security down the hall. You want to go before they get here."

Mikey nodded. He pushed himself off the chair as if it were an effort, like George had pushed himself up off the porch steps three weeks ago.

"Goodbye, Mom. I'll call." His voice was tired now.

"Stinky!" She had to make him see. She was the only one who knew his secrets, knew what tortured him. He was hard on her, but he was harder on himself. Since that night when he was ten, he shouldered a lifetime of burden and guilt. He thought he'd killed his father. He thought he should be able to get her to stop drinking. But he was not responsible for George. For her poor decisions. For her inability to stay sober.

He bent to kiss her forehead. She pulled him close and whispered, "You didn't do any of these things. Not now. Not ever. My drinking had nothing to do with you. No one can get someone else to stop drinking. Only I can do that."

"Maybe, Mom. Maybe."

She tightened her grip on his arm. "And you didn't kill him, Stinky. You didn't kill your father."

His voice was just as soft. "But I tried. And I may as well have. For us, the result was the same." He shook himself free and disappeared into the hall.

Francine smiled sadly and twisted her hair. Madge reached out her hand to beg her to stay, but she disappeared as well.

Madge's hand thudded onto the bed table. A colored marker dropped to the floor and rolled under Mikey's abandoned chair.

Mikey was in trouble. Again. Well, Madge wasn't going to just lie there. She pushed the papers into a tidy stack, a clean blank sheet on top, and started over, lines and columns and names and suspects.

Mikey was wrong when he said there were no nefarious goings-on. Mikey was going to be fired, and he hadn't done any of this. Which meant someone else had. Not Tony, apparently. But someone else.

Madge wasn't inadequate. Mikey wasn't inadequate. He wasn't defective. Madge was going to prove it.

# Chapter 73

Michael drove out of the hospital parking garage, maybe for the last time. He had to admit it to himself. Phil thought he was a kookhead because it was true. He'd left all this behind him twenty-five years ago, this drama, this craziness. Now he was right back in it. His mom was clouding his judgement. How had he ever allowed her to convince him that Chrissie's death and Reginald Stark's trip to the ICU were anything other than what they appeared, his own fault? That David Eaves' suicide and Janet's death had anything to do with each other or with him? That anyone had been on the roof other than Katherine and him and an imaginary shadow? It was his mother's doing.

He had accused an innocent man. No wonder Phil sent him home.

He had shouted at his mother. Whatever he thought, whatever demons he carried, he should have kept it to himself. He was angry at himself, but he took it out on her.

He glued his eyes to the street in front of him and off his rearview mirror. No need to add to his paranoia. Finally, involuntarily, he glanced up.

No. It couldn't be.

The old blue car was behind him, one back and nearly hidden by a pickup truck.

This was pure coincidence. *Eyes back on the road.* The route between his house and the hospital was a common east-west corridor. Anyone who lived near him would take this street all the time.

He made one stop on the way home, carefully signaling as he pulled into the parking lot. The blue car traveled on. So there. If the guy were out to get him, he'd get him right there in front of the liquor store.

Michael left the store with a glass bottle in a paper bag and stashed it carefully under the front seat. How many times had his mother come home with just such a package?

He drove over a hill and Lake Washington appeared, gray water matching the gray sky. He knew the morning sun wouldn't last.

Why had he ever moved back here? His life was just fine in Boston. More than fine.

His eyes danced again to the rearview mirror. His breath caught. The blue car was there, cresting the hill.

This was no coincidence. This was not paranoia.

Michael sped up. He careened around the corner of his own street. He jammed the garage door opener on his sun visor. He could see his building's garage door down the street. It was solid and closed and not budging. He jammed the button once more. Finally! The door glided slowly up.

*Come on! Come on!*

As soon as it was high enough, Michael zipped under. He hit the button again to close it, and the door reversed. Just as slowly. Michael swiveled in the front seat and willed the door to slam closed. It drifted down at its own turtle pace. The blue car came into view as the big door shut.

Who was in the blue car? Why were they following him?

How had David Eaves really died? Who had murdered Janet?

Was the answer outside?

Michael pulled to the side and turned the engine off. He eased his car door shut, padded to the large garage door, and peered through the grating. The blue car was parked across the street.

It was time to find out what was going on.

He flicked the button at the side of the door. The garage door rose, and the blue car came slowly into full view.

The car was old and battered, but shiny and clean. A man sat inside.

Michael stared at the man and the man stared at Michael. He wore a hat low over his eyes, as old and battered as the car.

Michael's muscles were on full alert, itching to sprint. He directed them toward the car and strode over. The car door opened, and the man stepped out. Michael stopped in the middle of the street.

Who was it? The man from the roof? Had he tried to pitch Katherine off and now he'd come for Michael?

No one else was around. The low clouds and gray sky cast a gloom and a hush.

The man lifted his arm. Was it empty? Did he have a weapon? Michael's muscles screamed "run," but he stood his ground.

The man took off his hat. He held it in front of him in both hands. His head was down. He raised his face, and Michael knew who he was. They had the same eyes, the same mouth, the same hair.

He could be looking at himself in thirty years. They were identical.

How many times as a boy had he longed to see this face? Had wished his father would appear on his doorstep? Waltz back into their lives and pick up as if nothing had happened? As if Michael hadn't chased him away with the thrust of a knife, attacking him on the retreat, stabbing the man in the back and straining to stab him again and again.

He really was alive. All these years Michael was certain he'd killed him. He had been ten, and he didn't know how to know. All that blood must surely mean the man was dead. Michael waited for the police to come, to cart him away, to cart his mother away. Days and weeks went by, and no one came to their door. His mother never said anything and as the years passed, their secret grew a shell so hard he never asked.

Had she called every hospital? Contacted the police? Searched the newspapers for a story of his death? Michael never knew.

He created an alternative story to fit his needs, one where his dad tousled his hair and told him it was for the best.

Deep inside he carried the rotten truth in his rotten core. Now, back in Seattle, back with his mother, their secret had rotted his life.

His father twisted his hat in his hands and didn't look Michael in the eye, even when Michael walked closer. His features stood out in his gaunt face, the skin pulled tight over his cheekbones and forehead. His jacket was a size too big. This was the cancer's toll.

"So," Michael said.

"So," said his father.

The man Michael waited for his entire life was standing in front of him. Michael was taller and looked down at the father he'd hoped would save him from an alcoholic mother, from fending for himself for dinner after dinner, from making up excuses for the neighbors, from vomit and filth.

"Mikey—"

"Michael."

"Michael. I saw you at your mother's before she took sick. I've been following you."

"I know."

"I was going to talk to you. I was going to..."

Michael waited, but his father didn't finish his thought. Instead, he said, "You're a doctor. You've done well for yourself."

"Yes."

"Me, I never really stuck with anything. I've sold TVs and stereos and books, hardware and tires. I've worked construction and worked security. I've tried it all."

Michael couldn't stand it, this superficial chatter. "I didn't mean to hurt you," he said. Though of course that wasn't true. The threat had passed, and Michael had stabbed the man as he walked out the door. He would have stabbed him a hundred times over if not for his mother.

His father finally held his gaze, his deep blue eyes piercing Michael's core with their pain. He had hurt his father. He had played it over in his head so many times. Now the man could tell him himself.

His father's inhaled and his chest rose and fell. He stood silent, his eyes fixed on Michael's. Then Michael saw the tears.

His father said, "I never thought you had. I was the one at fault. I knew if I didn't get out of there, I'd have blood on my own hands."

His dad was the one at fault? Not Michael?

"You never came back."

"I couldn't come back. I wasn't safe around you while I was drinking. Then, when I wasn't drinking, I met Lois. She never knew the other side of me, the dangerous side that came out when I drank. I liked that. If I came back, you two would always know what I had been. I wasn't strong enough for that."

"I thought you were dead. All these years, I thought I had killed you. Or that you stayed away because of me. That you didn't come back because I stabbed you."

"You stabbed me, all right." He lifted his jacket and his shirt and twisted his body. A jagged scar ran down his side.

Michael's eyes were riveted to his skin, the thick, heaped scar. He dragged his eyes away and to his father's. His dad grunted. "Best thing that ever happened to me."

"What?"

"I was so sick, I couldn't drink. I had a lot of time to think. When I recovered, I wanted to start over, a clean break."

"I missed you. I watched for you every day."

"I missed you, too. And your mom. I loved her. I loved you. But I didn't love myself when we were together. I worried I might slip back. Hurt you."

His dad shoved his shirt down. "I felt so thankful that I was the one to end up with the scar and not you."

"I have scars," Michael said. "When you recovered, you could have come home."

"Yes. I could have. When I finally gave it all up, more than anything, I didn't want to be around anyone who knew about the other me."

Michael bit his lip. Michael knew about his father's other side and still waited an eternity for him to return.

"My life here was hell. You could have helped me."

"I know. Believe me, I thought about that. I thought about you. I've carried that guilt all these years. That's why I'm here. Your mother told you, I'm sure. I'm dying. I only have a few months left. I want your forgiveness."

"Forgiveness?"

"Yes. Your life could have been different. And your mom's. She could have gone back to law school, been someone. Not like me. I don't want to take that to my grave."

"You have a new family now."

He smiled fondly. "Yes. Lois and Parker."

"A new son."

"Yes. Parker's not a doctor, of course, but he's made his way. Computers."

"He's my brother. I'd like to meet him."

His father's face clouded. "No. Oh, no. They don't know anything about you. I don't want my two worlds to meet. I want Lois and Parker to keep their pure memory of me."

His dad still wasn't strong enough. His mother had been right. Coward.

All these years, Michael had had a different idea of what his father would be, if he were alive. This small man before him was not the dad he imagined.

His father was dying. He'd returned for one reason. He needed to hear the words. Michael could do that for him. For himself.

"I forgive you. I wish you only peace in these next few months."

"I bless you for understanding."

Understanding? Understanding that his father took the easy way out, a clean slate, as he said? That he left Michael, a little boy, to hold things together, to pick up the pieces, over and over again? Michael was still picking up the pieces, decades later.

"Your mother wasn't quite so forgiving."

Michael would actually like to have seen his mother's reaction.

His mother. She'd been there for him, through thick and thin, through nightmares and pre-performance jitters, through asking his first date to the prom and through losing Janet.

A month ago, when Michael searched his mother's house for bottles of alcohol, he found a folder tucked high on a shelf in the basement under a dusty box of old Christmas ornaments. They'd given up decorating for Christmas so long ago, the folder must have lain there, forgotten, all that time.

The folder held four pieces of paper. An acceptance letter to the University of Washington Law School for Margaret McGillicuddy. A copy of a letter to the school asking for a leave of absence due to a difficult pregnancy and a letter back granting one and wishing her well until her return. The final letter copy was dated two years later, from his mother, stating she wished to withdraw from the law school, that she didn't want to continue to take up a spot when she knew in her heart she would never come back.

He'd been so intent on finding alcohol that the full meaning had not sunk in.

His mother had given up her career. No wonder she was so keen on Janet continuing hers.

His mother had sacrificed her life for him. She even covered up a potential murder.

His song said it all, those words he wrote when he was young. *You'd die for me. I killed for you. We'll have to be friends forever.*

When he was a boy, he thought he could get his mother to stop drinking. He tried, so many times, so many ways. When she couldn't, he took it as a sign that she didn't love him enough to stay strong against the bottle.

His father had left him. His mother loved alcohol more than him.

But of course she loved him. Of course he was loved. Was loveable.

His mother had tried a million ways to show it. He measured her love by one thing, the one thing she truly wasn't strong enough to fight.

"You can go back to your family now," Michael told his father. "I have to get back to mine."

# Chapter 74

All these years, Michael had concentrated on one thing about his mother. The alcohol. He couldn't see past it, because even days or weeks without it were fraught with the worry it would soon be back, out of nowhere, when his guard was down. Taunting him that her love was only so deep against its pull.

She was right. Her drinking had nothing to do with him, and he was powerless to stop it. He always had been.

He stood in the street and raised his head to the sky. The clouds were low, but the light was pearly and the green of the leaves intense.

The alcohol blinded him to the good memories. How many times had they sat in the kitchen when he was little playing rummy, his favorite card game? Raked the leaves into a tidy pile and then switched over to a leaf fight? Experimented with dressing recipes to make the perfect Caesar salad?

His mother had been fun. He had forgotten the fun.

Or he'd been too much on edge to recognize it. Waiting for the next binge, and later, when the binges ceased and the daily drinking began, just getting by until it was time for him to leave.

Even then, even in her buzzed daily state, she was never mean. Not like his dad. In high school she let him borrow the car whenever he wanted, no questions asked. When he hit a post and cracked the side mirror, she didn't yell. She only said,

"Pay half." When Molly Esteban's mother called screaming about the two of them alone in the basement, his mother didn't scream. She told him to treat Molly with respect and follow the house rules, specifically Mrs. Esteban's forbidding of boys downstairs. When he failed physics, she found money for a tutor to get him through the summer session.

Instead of concentrating on the nights they had no dinner, he should remember the nights they had, and his mother serving him the larger piece of pot roast, offering him a chocolate bar while she had none. He unquestioningly accepted her word when she said she didn't want any.

His mother loved chocolate. She offered him hers because there wasn't enough for two.

When he brought Janet home for the first time, he worried and fretted and prepared Janet for the worst. But his mother was sober for the entire three days, until the very end. She was charming and warm and welcoming. His heart swelled as the two of them bent their heads over the photo album and his mother told stories of his past. They sat on the front steps with lemonade as the sky turned orange, and his mother discovered more about Janet's childhood than he ever knew. She brought them breakfast in bed, knocking politely before she entered and closing the door discreetly as she left.

On the third day, though, his mother broke down and opened a bottle and spilled wine on Janet's white summer dress. Then she vomited on his shoes. That's all he remembered of the weekend. He'd forgotten the rest until now.

His mother was his mother. She was flawed, but she loved him. How could there ever have been any doubt of that? She loved him. And he loved her.

# Chapter 75

Michael's father drove away, his old car backfiring as he turned the corner. Michael went right in to telephone his mother, but she didn't answer. She must have forgotten to switch her ringer back on. He could call the nurse and ask for help. It was Mother's Day, after all. But... The nurses had all raised their heads as he walked out, trailed by Security. They wouldn't take kindly to too many of these requests and he was bound to need more favors soon. He'd try again in the morning.

He let the lizard out, and Frank trundled behind him.

"Good to see you, Frank. I've had quite the day." Frank wasn't the most responsive conversationalist, but it was better than talking to himself.

"Since I'm not going in tomorrow, I'll start the weekend now." Michael laid out his glass and the ice. He pulled the scotch bottle from the paper bag he'd retrieved from his car and set it on the table. He smiled at the lizard, popped the cork, and poured a small amount.

"You might think the weekend is over," Michael said. "Because tomorrow is Monday. Never you fear."

He lifted the glass. "To my father's health. Not that I'll ever know what happens to him. Just like before." He quickly downed the drink and poured another, more this time.

"You should have been there, Frank. You should have seen him. My father." The tegu twisted onto his back then flipped onto four legs. "Can you believe it? I feel like a huge chunk of my life was based on a lie. A gnawing secret that didn't need to be a secret." He crunched an ice cube.

"My mom would have kept that secret forever. I didn't need to move home."

Frank swiveled his head.

"All right. My mom needs me. She may be embarrassing, and she drinks far too much, and she has a big imagination, but she's stood behind me. She's the only one who believes in me now. She would do anything for me. It's been that way my whole life. She's responsible for much of what I am today."

He sipped his drink. "You look a little concerned, Frank, like you think I won't do the right thing. I'm here for her." He swirled the glass and the ice clinked comfortingly.

"Who knows, I might even move home." He smiled ruefully. "Might have to, if I lose my job."

The lizard yawned.

"All that guilt I felt. All that loathing. I thought I'd killed my father. I knew I'd tried, at least. What kind of person tries to kill their father? So much guilt. But not now. He was alive and well and living a fine life without me. Without us." He finished the drink and set the glass on the table.

"I forgave him, Frank. What a relief. I hope he has peace. All these years I thought I needed *him* to forgive *me*. What a waste of emotion. What a waste."

Frank climbed onto the couch. Michael leaned his head back. His eyes blurred with tears. He sat there crying, his hand on Frank's strong, smooth back. Frank lay next to him, unmoving under his hand.

By the time Michael stumbled to bed, the scotch bottle was half empty and the lizard had long since departed for his crate.

Michael awoke the next morning with the sun streaming in. He let Frank out and the lizard scampered to the kitchen, making it clear breakfast was overdue. Michael trudged behind him, his head splitting. The bright light hurt his eyes, and he pulled the blinds. He dropped strawberries in Frank's bowl. Even the refrigerator light was too much, and he stood gratefully in the dark. No wonder his mother wanted the bright lights off. He gulped a glass of water and tried not to move his eyeballs.

Frank finished his strawberries and looked up.

What now? Michael had nowhere to go and no one to see. In his regular life, there was no free time. He was always busy, always needed. He was used to visiting his mother in the morning, as he had every morning for four months, rushing before he went to the hospital, and more recently, rushing in between other patients. He couldn't fathom starting the day without her queries.

He dialed her room number, and again the phone rang and rang. Morning was a busy time on the ward, and he didn't want to disturb a nurse. He'd call the nursing station later to have them check his mother's phone.

Before he could set the phone down, it rang in his hand, a loud jangle that almost made him drop it. Could this be his mother?

"Hello?"

"Oh, Dr. Baker, I'm so glad to talk to you. I just heard what happened. I'm so sorry!" This was Robin, his MA. What exactly had she heard? How was the department spinning this?

"Dr. Perkins called a staff meeting first thing to tell us both you and Dr. Pierce would be out for a while. He said both of you had taken ill. Are you okay?"

His throat tightened. He couldn't speak. She sounded like she cared. Aside from his mother, he didn't have many on his side.

"Dr. Perkins said he needed all hands on deck to reschedule your clinics and your OR cases. I took care of yours."

Just like Perkins to sugar coat this.

"I rescheduled everything for the next three days. Do you think you'll feel better by then?"

Three days? No way he'd be back in three days, the way his career was going. He might even be in jail. He looked to Frank for guidance.

"The way Dr. Perkins was clicking that pen, I thought things might be bad. You are okay, aren't you?"

He had to say something. Keep the whole department from wondering why he was suddenly missing.

"Yes, thank you. I'm fine. Touch of a bug. Katherine may have the same."

"Oh, that's fine, then. Do you need me to do anything else?"

"Well, actually..." Could he ask her to help him with his mother? Turn her ringer back on? Help her to call him?

"It's about my mother."

"Is she still here? Oh, yes, please let me help." He explained about the phone, and Robin said she'd head to the hospital as soon as she was on break. "I made cupcakes again. Maybe I'll take her one."

"You'll be her hero. Today is her first day of solid food. She loves chocolate."

His mother's first day of solid food, her most exciting day ever, and he would miss it.

His head ached. But poor Katherine. Her head must really be hurting. He wanted to check in with her, but he didn't want to jar any of her memories.

Something jarred in his own memory. Something about his mother. And headaches.

And Hal.

His mother said Hal had gone home early with a head-ache. The very day Katherine was attacked on the roof. The very day his photo in the lobby was defaced. KILLER.

Hal was there at every step. He knew about the antibiotic order almost as soon as Michael did. Maybe before. He was there the day Michael's mother found the two little liquor bottles.

Hal was never sick. He'd certainly never go home with a headache, leaving someone else to have to take his shift.

Forget about David Eaves and Janet. They were red herrings. Cascadia was the place. Ever since Michael had come to Cascadia Medical Center, his life had crumbled. He blamed his mother. He blamed his past.

Michael had left Seattle and soared in his career on the East Coast. Now he was back, and he was sinking.

Hal had never left. His life was the same.

Because Michael won the scholarship.

# Chapter 76

Michael grabbed his phone and punched the number for the hospital operator. "Please page Dr. Hal Dexter. I'll hold on."

"Who's calling, please?"

He hesitated. "Dr. Michael Baker."

Did he detect a change on the other end of the line? That was ridiculous. The hospital operator would not know he was suspended. Still, he imagined he could see the operator's eyebrows arch. "Hold on, Doctor."

Why hadn't he seen it earlier? His mother had been right all the time. He had an enemy. He just showed up in the guise of a friend.

Hal finally came on the line. His voice definitely sounded guarded. Did he know Michael had put it together?

"Mike. Hello. It's you. What's up?"

"You sound a little wary, Hal."

"I heard we won't be seeing you at the hospital today."

Michael had no doubt Hal knew everything that had transpired yesterday. He must be delighted. Michael had gone off the rails, accused an innocent man, gotten himself fired. Sooner than Hal could have hoped.

"I think you know why I'm calling."

"Your mom? I saw her this morning. She's doing fine. She ate full liquids, and I haven't heard anything about her throwing them up, so I'm planning on solid food for lunch."

"No. Not my mom. My life."

"Mike. I'm so sorry. I should have called you. How can I help?" Hal actually sounded sincere, like he wanted to help. He'd sounded this way before. The day Michael won the scholarship.

They'd arrived for final interviews together, Hal with his mother, Michael alone because his mother was hung over. After thirty minutes each of grueling final questions about their future plans, the committee sat them down in a small, dark room.

"Congratulations, Michael Baker. You've won the scholarship. Full tuition. And Hal Dexter, you are a most promising young man as well. You should be very proud of yourself. We've got a thousand dollar check for you."

Hal's mother cried. Hal shook his hand and said, "Good for you, man. You deserve it."

He'd sounded as sincere then as he did now.

"Hal, I know it was you. Writing the note to Phil. Changing the antibiotic order. I know why you left early yesterday. You paged Katherine Pierce and you—"

"Mike! Stop. Listen to yourself. You are not your mother. She's poisoning your mind."

"Did you poison Chrissie's sandwich?" The words were out before he thought about them. The words were wrong. They sounded just like his mother. Chrissie had died of a fat embolism. That was a fact.

"Mike. What the hell?"

Hal hadn't poisoned Chrissie's sandwich, but that didn't mean he hadn't done all the rest. "Admit it, Hal. You've had it in for me ever since the scholarship. You wanted to go to Penn, and instead you were stuck here. Now I'm back, too, and you're trying to destroy me."

Hal's voice was quiet and sharp. "No one has to destroy you, Mike. You're destroying yourself."

Michael collapsed into a kitchen chair. He had no words left.

Hal's voice in his ear grew louder. "You want to know about the scholarship, Mike? I'll tell you about the scholarship. In high school, your mom wasn't the only one with problems. You just never noticed. My mom had cancer. Cancer, Mike. She was diagnosed right before the scholarship results, and she was facing six months of chemotherapy. She wasn't doing that alone. Some of us like our mothers, Mike. I wasn't going anywhere. I needed to be with her. So when we had the final interview, I told them. I withdrew my name."

"You withdrew your name?"

"Yes. I didn't want the damn scholarship. I didn't tell my mom. She would have forbidden it. But I wasn't leaving her. Good thing, too. She had a rough course. But she came through. She was never the same. But I've been here for her. That's why I'm such a homebody."

Hal paused. His rapid breathing was harsh in Michael's ear. His words were harsher. "You want to know where I was Saturday? The day I left early? The *only* day I have ever left early?"

Michael was certain he did not want to know. But Hal's voice was loud enough, even with the phone away from his ear.

"I thought I could work, muscle through, but I couldn't. Francine was kind enough to come in early. I was marking the day my mom died, Mike. In May, two years ago, and this year that was the day before Mother's Day."

# Chapter 77

Frank eyed him as he finished the call. Michael dropped the phone on the table. "I just accused my only friend."

The phone rang, the screech causing him to jump to his feet and his head to pound again. Was this Hal with more to say?

"Michael Baker?"

He didn't recognize this voice. Was it the police, saying Katherine Pierce had accused him of trying to throw her off the roof? He locked his knees to keep steady.

"Yes, this is Michael Baker."

"Michael, it's Tom Roberts. Anesthesia. What's this I hear about you being in Seattle now? Followed Matilda, eh? We sure miss you here. Matilda, too."

Of course. Tom Roberts from his old hospital in Boston. They'd had many cases together over the years.

"Tom, how are you? Yes, I've been here four months." Suddenly Michael's headache was gone. His tension and doubts slipped away, talking to this familiar voice from the past, from a place he was respected, where his very competence wasn't questioned, where his integrity was without doubt.

He leaned against the kitchen wall and breathed deeply. Maybe when all this mess at Cascadia was over, he'd go back to Boston. He hadn't been much help to his mother, despite his best efforts. Hell, his mother could come with him.

"What can I do for you, Tom?"

"Well, I guess it's what can I do for you? We got your message on the department phone, and then Marcus told me you talked to him this weekend. I figured that's what your message was about. That case of David Eaves."

It took Michael a moment to understand what Tom was saying. The call to the anesthesiologist seemed an eternity ago. Did it even matter now? Michael had incriminated Hal, of all people. He'd accused a staff member of double homicide on the East Coast. He'd been relieved of duties and sent home. What was he thinking? How could anything that happened in Boston possibly be related to anything that happened here?

"Sorry if I'm wasting your time, Tom."

"Not at all. It took me a while to look things up, but I do have some information. I'm in charge of M & M now."

He might as well hear what Tom had to say.

"I remember the discussion that day because it could have been any of us. Sticks in your head. So I knew right away which case you asked Marcus about. I dug through the M & M files and found the report. We didn't hear any names at M & M, but it's all in the record. It turns out I know the patient's daughter. Grace. She's a doctor, and she and I went to medical school together, used to be study partners."

"She's a doctor?"

"Yes, and I think that's why there was no threat of a lawsuit. Though I think I remember a hefty settlement. Quite deserved. Hell of a case. A tragedy."

"Yes." Michael felt the kitchen growing smaller, the walls closing in, remembering the woman who loved to dance and then the small body on the bed in the ICU, unable to move or speak after the wrong anesthetic and the stroke.

"Well, I called her."

He called the patient, the woman who had the stroke? Michael stood there mute.

"I called the daughter, Grace. My old friend. We'd lost touch after medical school, but I'm going to a conference in Philadelphia next month, so I used that as an excuse, and she remembered me. She's one of those people who makes you feel like you're the only one in the world when she's talking to you. It was the same on the phone. She asked me a lot about my life, but we finally got to her."

"Philadelphia?"

"Yes, that's where she lives."

Michael must have made a grunt or some other noise because Tom went on.

"Her mother died. Just this year. She had the stroke two years ago, but she died a few months ago."

Michael slipped to the floor, slowly sliding down the wall until he sat on the tile with his legs bent. He pushed the phone against his ear, so tight he could feel its warmth.

"Grace told me the whole story, seemed like she really wanted to talk about it. I guess Grace's sister is a nurse, and she stopped working and took care of the mom full time. Sounds like her mom's situation was pretty ugly, but the sister wanted to do everything for the mom herself, didn't want her to go to an assisted living facility. That's what Grace wanted because the mom needed round-the-clock care, couldn't do anything, couldn't eat or talk, couldn't bathe, diapers, the whole shebang. There was enough money for it because of the settlement. But her sister wouldn't hear of it, putting her mother in a 'home.' When the mom died, the sister was a mess, and Grace took her in to try to help her. Her sister even started looking for a job again, but the next thing you know, she was hell-bent on moving west."

"West?" Michael could barely get the word out.

"Yes. Darnedest thing. She moved to Seattle."

# Chapter 78

Madge sat up eagerly and surveyed the empty tray in front of her. The clear liquids had gone so well, Dr. Francine had taken out her feeding tube last night. Madge was woozy with excitement. She'd eaten a full liquid breakfast, a veritable feast of rice porridge and yogurt and applesauce. Dr. Hal said if it stayed down, which so far it had, she could eat solid food by lunch! Real food! Something crunchy!

Such a momentous day and Stinky had to miss it. He would call at least, surely? The telephone remained silent. Sometimes that boy could be so negligent.

Well, he clearly had a lot on his mind.

If only her suspect list didn't end in a big zero once she got to Janet and the anesthesiologist in Boston. She had her grid all filled out, with Bob's name in thick black marker, Evan's name also prominently displayed, Mildred's in smaller letters, and even Dr. Francine and Dr. Hal. Although Dr. Hal couldn't be a murderer. He was an old friend. Plus, he was feeding her food. And it couldn't be Francine, either, because Madge caught the tender way she looked at Mikey when he wasn't looking back. Mikey was a thick-headed numbskull.

Anyway, these people were perfectly reasonable murder suspects until you got to Janet and Mr. Anesthesia. Madge tapped her colored marker against the sheet of paper. She just didn't have all the facts. She needed Stinky to sort this out.

"How was breakfast?" Mildred was so stealthy with her soft shoes, Madge's graph was right out in plain sight. Look where that had gotten them with Tony the Terrible.

"Splendid, splendid." Madge flipped her list over.

"What do you have there? Is that about Bob? Is it a complaint?"

How did she know Bob was on the list? Madge flicked her eyes down and was horrified to see Bob's name staring up at her, clearly visible on the other side of the paper. The marker had bled through. She'd written his name all in capital letters, and BOB on one side was the same as BOB on the other.

Mildred glided to the door on her soundless shoes. She closed it firmly and floated back to Madge's bedside.

"Miss McGillicuddy..."

So it was Miss McGillicuddy now and not Madge, hmm?

"You and I have known each other a long time. You know your brain can get squirrely sometimes."

Squirrely? Where was she going with this?

"Meaning that not everything you think is happening is happening."

The woman was out to gaslight her. Implying that Madge was not in full control of her faculties. Madge knew all about this because of the old movie that played once a year on *Creature Friday*. A noise escaped her mouth.

"Don't give me that harrumph sound." Mildred stood directly over her. "Bob is a good man. I know you have some reservations about him, but I can assure you they are unfounded. Now his job is in jeopardy. Because of you and your accusations. Time will show these accusations are as meaningless as the accusation leveled by your son against one of our physical therapists."

Now she was attacking Stinky!

"I have great admiration for your son and his surgical skills. I don't listen to the things people are saying about him.

But I do know that right now the two of you are causing too much trouble for too many people."

Madge had had enough of this. "Are you trying to say something, Mildred? My squirrely brain is having trouble keeping up."

Mildred leaned in close. Her voice was a whisper, but Madge heard her clearly. "Withdraw your complaint against Bob. No one will take it seriously anymore anyway. Because I hear Bob's isn't the only job in jeopardy."

# Chapter 79

Michael sat on the kitchen floor and gripped the phone. Frank paced in front of him, back and forth in the small kitchen.

"Her name, Tom. What was the patient's name?"

"Eleanor Lake."

Yes. Eleanor Lake. Everything about the woman came flooding back from their one visit in the office. Small with blonde hair sprinkled with gray, she had laughing eyes and a sparkling joie de vivre that was obvious when she talked about dancing, a ballroom dancing class and even competitions. And when she talked about her daughters. Now he remembered. So much pride when she described her two children, a doctor and a nurse. One small, one tall. "My oldest wanted to be president, but I think nursing is just as good, don't you?" she'd said.

Did Michael know anyone named Lake? Any nurses? His mind was foggy, but no one he knew at the hospital was named Lake.

"That's all the information I have. I hope it's what you were looking for."

Michael grunted again and Tom must have taken it as a "yes."

"Well, don't be a stranger if you're ever in town," Tom said. "Take care."

The phone went silent. Michael dropped it on the floor.

Lake. He didn't know anyone named Lake.

*Think. Think.*

He didn't know a nurse named Lake, but he knew someone with a doctor sister. Someone who didn't believe in retirement communities, let alone an assisted living facility.

He staggered to the other room and his computer. He found the Boston obituary for Eleanor Lake. There it was, in black and white.

Survived by her daughters, Grace Lake and Alice (nee Lake) Smith.

Michael's medical assistant was Robin Smith.

Smith.

Frank's front feet dug into Michael's leg. Frank stood on his back legs and stretched his head up to meet Michael's eyes.

Michael's mouth was so dry he could barely speak. "I know, Frank. Where is Robin Smith now?"

# Chapter 80

Madge watched Mildred swish out of the room. She whipped her paper over and selected a red marker and rewrote Mildred's name in letters as large as Bob's. Maybe those two were in cahoots. That would be something.

Could Mildred really be a killer? Could Bob? A killer of beautiful young people like Chrissie and Janet?

Madge examined her list. It was fine to have the victims' names lined up in a neat column like in the detective shows. It was another to actually ponder the people those names represented.

Chrissie had sat right in this room and regaled Madge with stories of Frank, who turned out to be a lizard. Madge must have missed this crucial detail with all her pain meds. Chrissie said he liked mice, but Madge envisioned a cat and mouse chase until Mikey told her what he found in Chrissie's freezer.

And Janet. How Madge loved Janet. Because Janet loved Stinky and Madge could see it in every tilt of her head when he came in the room and every touch on his arm when they sat side by side and every gleam in her eye when she teased him that his sneezes came in threes.

Chrissie and Janet were real people and condensing their lives into names on a victim list minimized the full flesh and blood of their joyful existence.

Madge crumpled the sheet of paper into a tight ball and threw it across the room. Who could have done these terrible things?

What was their motive? How did Stinky play into this?

Whoever it was, they thought Stinky had done something terrible himself, or they wouldn't be after him.

"Mrs. McGillicuddy?" Someone was calling from behind the beige curtain.

"That's *Miss* McGillicuddy. I'm not married." They really should put this on the very front of her chart. Madge shouldn't have to be the one to say it ad nauseum.

"Oh, excuse me. I'm so sorry. *Miss* McGillicuddy." A head peeked around the curtain. "May I come in?"

"Of course you can come in. Everybody else does."

A tall woman stepped into the room, a frosted cupcake in her hand.

# Chapter 81

Michael stared at his computer. Robin Smith started work at Cascadia well after he started. About two months ago, right after Janet was murdered. It had to be the same person. She'd moved from Boston to Philadelphia and then on to Seattle. She was the perfect medical office assistant, competent and skilled and able to predict his every medical need. Because she was actually a nurse.

Could she have written the order to stop Reginald Stark's antibiotics? She clearly hadn't liked the man. She called him an a-hole. It was as close as he'd come to hearing his mild-mannered medical assistant swear.

Robin had easy access to Michael's personal office computer, and that morning of the chaotic clinic, he was positive he didn't sign in and out each time between notes and rushing off to the next patient. He almost never did. He was in his own office, for Christ's sake. He'd set the thing to time out after ten minutes. She could easily slip in after he wrote Stark's note and change the order. With Reginald Stark's lung history, she would know she was signing a fatal command.

And the page to Katherine? How did she know his computer passcode?

Then Michael remembered. He'd spilled coffee, and Robin changed his coat for a fresh one. His passwords were in his coat pocket.

Was it Robin on the roof, too?

All this time he thought Robin was his ally. His only ally. He was down to none.

He found his phone and dialed and asked for Hal again.

"Mike?"

"Hal, don't hang up. I need you to check on my mother for me."

"Mike. I'm kind of busy here. I saw her this morning and she was fine, like I told you."

"But could you go see her again?"

"Sorry, no. I'm swamped. I'm down talking to the radiologist right now, then I have to go to the ED."

Michael's hands were two tight fists and his fingernails ground into his palms. "Hal, okay, if you can't see her, listen. She's in danger. Call Security and have them get up to her room right away."

"Mike, I—"

"It will come better from you than from me. They'll listen to you."

"I can't, Mike."

He had to make Hal see. He blurted it all out. "It's my medical assistant, Robin Smith. She followed me here from Boston and has killed two people already and is going to kill my mother."

"Mike, take it easy."

"Don't tell me to take it easy. Call Security!"

"Man, listen to yourself. First the physical therapist, then me, now your MA. You've gone off the deep end."

Michael slammed the phone down and the connection broke.

Frank jumped and scurried away.

"You're leaving?" Michael said. "Well, you're right. I'm on my own."

# Chapter 82

The drive to the hospital was another forgotten blur. Michael pulled up to the garage gate as he had done every morning for four months. He greeted Raymond with a hearty hello. Raymond peered down from his booth, his eyes shifting left and right.

"Dr. Baker. You're not supposed to be on campus. We got an email alert. I'm supposed to call Security if I see you."

Damn, damn, damn.

So much for Michael calling Security himself. Or counting on help or goodwill gestures from anybody else. He was definitely on his own.

"It's a big misunderstanding," Michael said. Raymond was so nervous, Michael's own voice shook. *Steady, steady,* he told himself. "I'm coming in to talk with them about it. I'll just telephone instead."

Relief cleared Raymond's troubled face. "That's a good idea. Telephone. Goodbye, Dr. Baker."

"Goodbye, Raymond. My best to your wife." He backed his car out, embarrassingly forcing a car behind him to back out, too. He drove down the street and around the corner. He parked and stepped out and doubled back, staying well out of sight of the parking garage.

He joined a large family entering the lobby, bowing his head away from the cameras. He stayed hidden behind them until peeling off at the stairway. He stared at the lobby wall and his gut wrenched. Where his Doctor of the Quarter picture belonged was a blank space. His picture had already been removed. It might never hang there again.

It didn't matter. All that mattered now was what was going on in the room at the end of the hall.

He ducked into the lobby staircase and started up, seven flights to his mother's floor. He eased the stairway door open, eye pressed to the crack. Hal was in the hallway. Michael immediately closed the door again.

A fleeting thought passed through his head. If Francine were on duty, he could ask her for help. And she'd give it.

Not Hal, though. And he'd known Hal forever.

He waited a full minute, then eased the door open again, heart thumping. The hall was empty. Hal must be in a room. Hopefully not his mother's room.

Michael stepped out of the stairway and sprinted toward his mother's door. He heard voices nearby and scrambled to turn the knob and slip inside. He closed the door quickly but softly behind him. As he'd hoped, the curtain was drawn, so no one in the room could see him.

His mother's distinctive perfume filled the air, so she was definitely there. The bright overhead light was on, so she must not be alone.

"You are so right. He's so kind and patient. I'm lucky to work with him. You must be very proud." This voice was Robin's, and she sounded as sweet and guileless as always.

"Oh, I am, I am. Stinky means the world to me. Oops. I'm not supposed to call him Stinky." His mother laughed, and then Robin laughed. They were having a fine time.

Michael hesitated on the other side of the curtain. What was he thinking? This was Robin. His trusted medical assistant, who made cupcakes for the clinic and called him at home to check on him. Not Alice, or whatever the obituary had said. So what if their last names matched? Smith was a common last name. The commonest.

What was going on with him? Robin was the only person in this hospital who believed in him. Now he was about to accuse her of attempted murder and double homicide? Like he had Tony?

What proof did he have of anything? He'd already made two false accusations, Tony and Hal. He couldn't afford another.

"And do you have family, dear? Husband, children?" This was his mother, asking everything about everyone like she always did.

"No, I'm happily single."

"A nice girl like you?" his mother persisted. Michael grimaced, but Robin actually responded.

"I was married. For a very short time. Only thing worthwhile I got from him was his name. I was happy to give up my father's."

"Smith, you said, right?" How did his mother remember these details about people? She was truly amazing. "What was it before?"

*Come on, Mom. You can do it.* His mom was just chattering in her normal fashion, but right now it was crucial. Would Robin confirm what had to be the truth, the only explanation for everything that happened?

Robin stayed silent.

"McGillicuddy is my maiden name. I went back to it when my husband left. You'd think I'd be happy with Baker, such a nice, simple last name. You don't have to spell it out like McGillicuddy. What was your maiden name, dear? Was it complicated?"

*Good job, Mom. If anyone can wheedle out information, it's you.*

Michael held his breath. Would Robin answer?

Seconds slipped by. Then Robin spoke.

"Lake," Robin said. "As a girl, I went by Alice. So, Alice Lake."

Michael's arm lurched out for support, hitting the door and causing a thud. He quickly opened the door and shut it hard, as if he'd just arrived.

"Hello?" he called. He brushed opened the curtain and stepped into the room.

"Stinky!" His mother positively glowed. "Look who's here!"

Robin smiled, too. "Dr. Baker! I thought you were sick."

Michael looked from one happy face to the other. From his loving mother to Alice Lake, whose mother was dead. Who was here to see to it that he and everything he cared about was dead as well.

# Chapter 83

Madge was excited to see Mikey, but he wasn't supposed to be there. His face was a nervous wreck, so he was clearly aware of his breach. Would Security burst in and haul him away? Or was he allowed back in now?

She kept her tone light. "I'm just meeting your medical assistant. She fixed my phone ringer."

Robin beamed. Madge leaned over to show Mikey the phone, but she only managed to slip down into the crease of the bed.

"Help me sit up, will you?" She meant this for Mikey, but Robin was right there, adjusting her pillows and hoisting under her arms like a pro. Robin held onto the flat hospital pillow. "This one's useless." A woman after Madge's own heart.

"She brought me a cupcake," she told Mikey. "She made them for the whole surgery clinic. This one was meant for you, but now it's mine. I haven't eaten solid food in weeks, and I am definitely starting with this."

The cupcake sat in front of her, a deep, dark chocolate cupcake, so brown it looked black, covered in bright yellow frosting. She'd eaten a finger swipe of frosting before Mikey showed up, but he didn't need to know about that. Hmm. The cupcake was actually Mikey's. He wouldn't want it back, would he? She snatched it up and inhaled its chocolatey aroma.

"Now, Mom, maybe a cupcake isn't the best first food to put in your stomach. You're supposed to stick with low fat, remember?"

"Pish tush," Madge said. The frosting had been a little bitter for her tastes, but the chocolate cake smelled fabulous.

"It's made with pumpkin," Robin said. "It *is* low fat."

Thank the Lord. A low-fat chocolate cupcake. Madge ripped the wrapping from one side. "It's such a work of art, I hate to eat it." She grinned at Robin. "But I will."

Mikey's face had gone white. Oh, for heaven's sake. She hadn't eaten in weeks, and he was begrudging her a low-fat chocolate cupcake. You'd think she was about to guzzle a hamburger with French fries from the expression on his face.

"It is beautiful," Mikey said. "Robin makes the best cupcakes. The colors remind me of that delicious superhero birthday cake you made for my twelfth birthday."

Madge stared at Mikey who stared right back at her. He had a smile on his face and a red splotch on his cheek.

That birthday cake had not been delicious and she and Mikey both knew it. Mikey was lying. Which meant there was something wrong and he didn't want to say it straight out. Something wrong with this cupcake.

The cupcake must be poisoned.

Good thing she hadn't taken a bite. Just that frosting. Which had tasted funny.

If there was something wrong with this cupcake, there was something wrong with Robin.

"That it does, Mikey." She set the cupcake back on the table. "It's so pretty, I think I'll save it for later."

"Are you sure?" said Robin.

Madge nodded. "Mikey's right. I should practice with toast first."

"Well, it will make a nice dessert after lunch," Robin said.

"You must need to get back," Mikey said. "Thank you for

coming over to see my mom. And for the cupcake, of course."

"You're very welcome. It was my pleasure. I actually don't have to rush back. It's not so busy today, with two doctors out."

"Oh, yes," Madge said. "After the roof garden."

"No, no," Mikey said. "She's out sick."

"It's okay," Robin said. "I heard about her accident."

"It could have been so much worse," Madge said. "The gods were smiling on her."

Robin sucked in her breath and with it all the air in the room. The silence was so silent, like a space vacuum in the sci/fi pictures that came on after *Creature Friday*.

Robin blinked her eyes. Her face transformed like the werewolf transformations in the older movies before modern animation, a frame-by-frame shift in the woman's expression from benign bringer of sweet treats to a sinister, threatening beast. Robin's mouth twisted into an ugly frown and her eyes disappeared as her brow furrowed. All she needed was scraggly fur.

"Dr. Lake got what was coming to her."

"You mean Dr. Pierce," Madge corrected her. Who was Dr. Lake? Madge prided herself on knowing all the hospital staff, and she'd never heard of a Dr. Lake.

"No. Dr. Lake. Dr. Grace Lake. She hit that precious head of hers. They say she'll be back to work soon. She didn't hit it hard enough."

Uh-oh. This beast was unhinged.

"Robin, are you thinking about your sister?" Mikey's tone was the gentle "You've had too much to drink and I'm going to help you to bed" tone Madge had endured so many times.

The werewolf snarled. "Don't talk to me about my sister."

Madge had been right all along. Someone was out to get Mikey and that someone came bearing cupcakes.

# Chapter 84

Madge squirmed as the wolf woman squished her pillow into a tighter and tighter ball. "Where was my sister when Mom needed her?"

Madge licked her dried lips and watched froth form at the corners of Robin's mouth. Spittle sprayed as she ranted. "When Mom's diaper needed changing and Mom had to avert her eyes from shame? When Mom winced as I turned her every four hours to keep her from getting skin ulcers? Grace never saw the sadness when Mom dribbled pureed food on her chin or the mess when she sputtered her nutrition shake all over her clothes. Grace didn't see the loads of stinking laundry or the endless trips to the pharmacy or the accidents in the bed. Grace wasn't there."

"Oh, my, dear, that does sound difficult." Madge wanted to calm this woman down, because her voice was a growl, more and more animal-like. Had Robin even heard her?

"My mother was grace and beauty and elegance. Until she was reduced to a shriveled shell of her former self, her body giving out and her mind warped by illness and indignity.

"And you know what Grace's solution to the whole thing was? A nursing facility. Could she not remember how proud Mother was? She never appeared in public without her hair perfectly coiffed, her makeup in place, her blouse ironed, her shoes polished, her back straight, and her head high."

The werewolf's red eyes bored into Madge. What was she implying? Madge had porridge on her pink frilly nightgown and yogurt in her hair, leftover from her exciting breakfast, but that was no reason for this murderous look.

"Mom never let on that her black eye was from Dad because we didn't air our dirty laundry in public. But what would Grace know about that, since she was born after Dad died? Grace never knew the fights, the fear, the trying so hard to be quiet and perfect and do nothing to upset Daddy. Grace never heard his words of contempt and loathing. She never knew a slap. She only knew the love of our mother."

Hmm. George was never this bad, but this was reminiscent of Mikey's life. Madge opened her mouth, but Robin was shouting now.

"And how did she repay it? Grace the precious doctor would never dream of giving up her career to care for Mom. The irony was, Mom would never have wanted that either. But me, the nurse, well I could do it."

The monster was on a roll.

"And I did. But all I heard was, 'What Grace say?' or 'Grace coming?' That's what Mom would painstakingly spell out on her alphabet board with her one good hand."

Like Mikey running to the front door window every time someone knocked. Madge could picture his disappointment when no father appeared, even though she, Madge, his mother, was right there.

Robin's voice rose. "Grace, Grace, Grace. Grace the baby, ten years younger and so much cuter. Grace played piano beautifully. The gods were smiling on Grace. She won the Latin competition and the state poetry contest and got into her first-choice college. The Gods were smiling on Grace. All my life I heard that quote from that damned picture book. Why couldn't my mom tell the truth? The gods weren't smiling on Grace. Grace put in the effort, she wanted it, and she had the charisma and confidence to try. Everyone loved her because she was a golden child with golden hair, smart, sweet, charming, graceful. Why couldn't Mom just say it? 'Good for you, Grace. Another job well done. I'm so proud of you. Unlike your sloppy, big, gawky, unmotivated, insecure sister with the dark, twisty hair who reminds me of our dark, twisted past.' "

The werewolf took a breath, and the vomitus-spewing ceased. Now she hissed.

"Mom was so careful to treat us both the same. Well, the truth came out in the end, didn't it? Her final, painful, painstaking message. 'I want Grace. Tell Grace I love her.' "

# Chapter 85

Madge sat absolutely still so as not to disturb the beast. Mikey edged forward. He spoke again in his gentle voice. "I'm very sorry about what happened to your mother."

The werewolf recoiled as if the sun were rising. "What do you know about sorry? What do you know about watching Mom deteriorate into a shrunken body of skin and bones and contracted muscles? About the letters she pointed to on the alphabet board spelling 'No food' and 'Want to die'? The letters were ephemeral. Only Mom and I knew what they said."

Oh, this poor thing. "Your mother was very lucky to have you with her, dear." Madge thought her words would soothe. The bared teeth of the werewolf told her she'd miscalculated.

"Lucky? *I'm* the one who recommended she see someone about her hip. She was stoic, but I could see her pain. I wanted her to have a hip injection. A safe, simple injection. I'm the one who researched. I'm the one who found Dr. Michael Baker, the best in Boston with so many good ratings." She sneered. "Dr. Michael Baker who talked her into a hip replacement."

She dug her fingernails into Madge's pillow and screamed at Mikey, "My mother would still be alive if it weren't for you!"

Whatever this woman was talking about, Madge would worry about later.

Madge had learned to keep her mouth shut, but Mikey

spoke again. Couldn't he see how agitated Robin was? "I'm so sorry. It was a terrible accident."

Uh-oh. Shove those words back in Mikey's mouth.

"Accident? Accident? You mean no one is responsible? No one is to blame? You are wrong. It was no accident. No 'systems error' letting everyone off the hook."

"You're right. I'm sorry. I didn't mean that." Mikey said it loudly, but Robin didn't hear.

She shrieked, "You think the anesthesiologist was not to blame because 'the system' screwed up and made it too easy for him to make a mistake. Is that it? A mistake that left my mother to slowly wither away, lying in her own waste. No one is off the hook. *You* are to blame. And you will pay."

If Madge could stand, she would grab Mikey and run. Instead, Mikey took another step toward this seething monster.

"I'm doing this for my mother." Robin's voice was low now. "I could never do enough for her. *I* was never enough. Well, all this is for her. She'll know it was me."

Mikey was too close. He didn't know the dangers a werewolf posed, how fast they were.

What if Robin attacked Mikey? Or stole the cupcake back? This poisoned cupcake held the evidence that would clear Mikey's name.

Madge eyed the myriad of buttons on her bedrail. Why did there have to be so many buttons? Which was the light switch? All she needed was the element of surprise.

A werewolf could see in the dark, but so could Madge.

# Chapter 86

Michael inched closer to Robin. She held the pillow, and she was an arm's length from his mother. In one fell swoop she could lean over and smother her.

Was Robin thinking the same thing?

She was the one. She had killed Chrissie and Janet and maybe David Eaves. She sent Reginald Stark to the ICU and Katherine Pierce to the emergency department. He'd figured it out. The game was over.

How many more could she hurt before she was finished?

A mother for a mother?

"I loved my mother. You barely tolerate yours." Her words were loud and clear, and Michael saw his mother wince.

Robin was big. She was strong, strong enough to lift Katherine, at least. Surely he was stronger.

"Where's your love, your gratitude? I promised my mother I would take care of her forever. That's what I'm doing."

Michael's own mother fumbled with her bedrail.

Robin held the pillow aloft.

Michael lunged.

The room pitched into blackness.

Michael crashed into the IV pole, and it toppled over. His head snapped back as he hit the wall. He thudded to the floor, the disconnected IV fluid raining down on him.

The dim overhead light flickered on. He pulled himself up using the edge of the bed. Robin stood quietly to the side. His mother was covered in blood.

"Mom!"

His mom waved her arm, spewing blood across the bed. "It's okay, Mikey. It's okay. It's just my IV. It came undone."

He grabbed her arm and pressed his finger against the IV site, clamping the blood flowing out through the open catheter.

"Hold on." He pulled the IV out and kept his finger in place to stem the bleeding. He sensed motion next to him. "You hold on, too." He gripped Robin's arm in his bloody hand. "You're not going anywhere." He glanced at his mother's bed table, now sprayed with blood. "Where's the cupcake?"

"Mikey, I have it!" his mother said. "I have the cupcake. The proof. I nabbed it while the lights were off."

Thank God. Finally, he'd have evidence. He was certain the cupcake was poisoned.

"Fools. There's no proof there." Robin's entire demeanor had changed. She shook herself free and stood up straight, accentuating her tall stature. Her voice was sharp. "There's nothing in that cupcake, and if there is, they'll never find it. So you have nothing."

"But it's poison," his mother said. "Like the Reuben."

"What are you talking about?" Robin looked truly perplexed. "You are a crazy old lady."

"Hey!" Michael shouted.

"And you. You don't even care about your mother. I'm doing you a favor."

Michael placed his free hand over his mother's and squeezed. "That's where you're wrong," he said.

Robin continued, her voice clear and cool. "Either way, if you start talking about a poisoned cupcake, you'll just be a desperate doctor on the edge, spouting more crazy theories. Plus, Dr. Perkins said Katherine Pierce is getting her memory back, bit by bit. She'll remember about you soon enough. You'll be arrested. You'll be finished."

She stood calmly, her face serene, her confidence unmistakable.

Was she right? If the cupcake contained no discernable poison, he would indeed be a driveling fool once again.

He felt any composure slip away. He straightened and lunged at her. He tripped on the IV pole and whacked his knee on the bed table. "You're not taking me down," he bellowed. "I'll find a way. I'll get you."

Bright lights illuminated the room.

"What's going on here?" Hal stood in the doorway. His eyes swept the room, and Michael's gaze followed his.

Blood spattered the wall, a garish red dripping down. A pink puddle of blood and IV fluid soaked the floor. Michael stood in the puddle, his hands covered in blood. His mother sat upright in the bed, also bloody. Robin stood outside the fray, completely clean except for one bloody handprint on her sleeve.

"Hal. What are you doing here?" Michael was immediately on guard.

"You hit the nurse call button. Mildred came, but she heard you, Mike, and she asked me to help." Hal's tone was terse. He crossed his arms.

"Dr. Hal! Thank goodness!" His mother dug around in the bloody blankets and retrieved the yellow and black cupcake, now crushed. She pointed a shaking, red-stained finger at Robin. "She brought me this. It's poison, I say. Poison."

"Lord help me," said Hal.

"Mom's right, Hal," Michael said. "This is my medical assistant. The cupcake was meant for me, but when I wasn't there, she brought it to my mom. She's hell-bent on destroying me."

"Dr. Baker, I don't understand what you're saying." Robin's voice was back to normal, innocent and believable. "I'm only here because you asked me to come help your mother with her phone. What you're saying is nonsense." She wheeled around and started toward the door. "I have to get back to work."

"Mike, you know I have to call Security." Hal said. "You can't be here."

Michael stared from Robin's retreating back to Hal's determined expression.

That would be that. Robin would walk out, Katherine would come to, and no amount of screaming about a man who jumped or a strangled woman was going to get him out of this mess. Robin was right. He was finished. There was nothing he could do about it.

"Wait!" His mother pounded her hand on the table.

Hal sighed. "Miss McGillicuddy—"

"Robin, do you admit that you brought me this cupcake?" His mother had taken on the aura of a detective in the denouement of one of her murder mysteries.

"Yes. I bring them to the office all the time. There's nothing wrong with the cupcake." Robin shot an exasperated look at Hal. "You can have it tested if you want. It's just a cupcake."

The cupcake was now crumpled and squished in his mother's bloody hand. She held it aloft, like a falconer about to release a bird of prey. Hal's eyes and Robin's eyes were riveted. Yellow frosting and dark cake oozed between his mother's fingers. It was just a cupcake. There was no way to prove anything.

"We'll see about that." His mom ripped off the wrapping. She bit into the cupcake and swallowed a third in one bite.

Michael gasped. He knocked the cupcake from her hand. It smashed against the wall, adding a yellow and black smear to the red splatters.

His mother licked a finger. "That was pretty good." She smiled. "Delicious, in fact. Much better than the frosting. Which, gentleman, I already sampled before all the brouhaha."

She laid her grimy hands on the bloody table and caught Michael's eye. "Remember your song, Stinky. Remember your song."

Michael knew what she meant. He knew what she'd done.

*I know you and you know me. Will we be friends forever?*

*You know my secrets and I know yours. Will we be friends forever?*

*You'd die for me. I killed for you. We'll have to be friends forever.*

His mom was willing to die for him. To clear his name.

# Chapter 87

Michael dropped to his mother's side. "Mom! No! Spit it out!"

"I'll be going now." Robin was to the door in a flash.

Hal put out his arm. "I think you'd better stay."

Robin was indignant. "She's fine. Look at her. I'm leaving."

And she did look fine, aside from the blood everywhere. His mother lifted her face to his and whispered, "I love you, Stinky."

"I love you, too, Mom. You've done everything for me. Always."

"Miss McGillicuddy, how are you feeling?" Hal called from where he blocked the door.

"Pretty good right now, Dr. Hal. Pretty good. Well, maybe a little nauseated."

Then her eyes rolled up and she flopped back onto the pillow.

"Mom!" Michael grabbed her wrist. "Heart rate's about thirty. Hal, call a code. Get a cardiac monitor. And atropine!"

"Come back here! Stop her! Code blue!" Hal bellowed down the hall.

The room filled with nurses, the code team, and security officers, who dragged Robin back with them.

Hal jumped into action, shouting out orders and giving the drugs.

Mildred pointed to Michael. A security officer seized him and pulled him away from the bedside.

"Wrong guy." Hal glanced up just long enough. "Take her." He gestured with a syringe toward Robin, who had shrunk in the big security officer's grasp until she looked small and scared.

"It must be a beta blocker, with this heart rate and this blood pressure," Michael said to Hal.

"That's my guess, too. Good thing we were here. She wasn't on a monitor. If she'd eaten that cupcake on her own, the nurses would have found her dead and we would have assumed she'd had a cardiac event, some arrhythmia. Without seeing the numbers, we wouldn't have suspected a thing."

Michael gazed at his mother, ashen and sweaty. Hal's atropine was working, and her heart rate was already increasing. He whirled on Robin. She was also ashen and sweaty.

"How could you?" he said.

"How could *you*?" she replied.

# Chapter 88

Michael held his mother's hand as Hal watched the monitor. The security guard held tight to Robin, but she shook her head and lifted her chin and addressed Michael in a low voice he did not recognize.

"We've met before, you know," she said. "On the day of the surgery. You don't remember because you were focused on Grace, the doctor. Everyone does. Even though I was a nurse."

Michael tried to remember that day and Eleanor Lake's family. David Eaves did the talking, the explaining, clinical, factual. All Michael could add was, "I'm so sorry," but those words were never enough. He didn't remember Robin. She was right. But he didn't remember her sister, Grace, either. He was consumed by the tragedy.

"Well, I remember you," Robin continued. "When my mother died, I knew who was responsible for her pain, her indignities. You had scarpered to Seattle, but no matter. The anesthesiologist could go first, the man who injected the wrong medication. I followed him from the hospital and through his daily routines, work, gym, takeout food. I joined his gym and caught his eye and suggested a drink at his place. I cooked up an omelet from the few ingredients he had. Then I shoved him over the railing."

The security guard whipped his head around. Mildred was filming everything on her phone.

"You'd think I would feel better. But I didn't. I spiraled and perfect Grace had to take me in. Oh, she was kind about it, because perfect Grace only sees the good in people. 'You cared for Mom for so long, you forgot how to care of yourself.' That's what Grace said. I let myself get talked into staying. I looked for a job. And that's when it happened."

Michael dropped his mother's hand and gulped. "Janet?"

Robin didn't hear him. She was in her own world, her story pouring out. She didn't care anymore.

"A cute blonde nurse toured me around the hospital, extolling its virtues and saying how much she enjoyed working there. She looked familiar, but then every petite blonde looks familiar because of Grace. 'Where do you work now?' the cheerleader said, and I told her I'd taken some time off, that my last job was in Boston, and she gushed that that's where she was from, but she was very happy in Philadelphia. Then she told me the Boston hospitals where she'd worked, and it clicked."

All eyes were on Robin, even Hal's. Michael's mother's vital signs were much better.

"That girl didn't look familiar because she looked like Grace. She looked familiar because she was the nurse in the room when Mom was injured. The nurse who'd told us there was a problem, and come with her to this private room, and the doctor would be in soon to talk. Grace tried to pry more out of her, saying she was a doctor and asking her what was going on. That nurse wasn't talking. So we waited. And waited. Waited to find out that our lives had changed forever and our mother would never walk again, let alone dance, never speak again."

Michael didn't want to hear anymore. But Robin's voice was loud and clear, far louder than the monitors.

"That bubbly Philadelphia nurse had been in the room. And there she was, living her life, happy. She'd said so herself. Well, I could take care of that. I asked her about the shifts and about public transportation, and she volunteered that her shift ended at seven and bus service was great, but the worst part was a shortcut through the alley after dark to meet the bus. She met me instead, her lanyard dangling from her thin neck like an invitation."

Michael put his hands over his ears, but he couldn't block the words.

"Her surprise and her pleading eyes were a salve. Just what I needed. Not like David Eaves. He stood at the balcony railing, a drink in his hand, a smile on his face, happily enjoying an evening with a new acquaintance one minute, and dead the next. There was no redemption for me in that. I wanted more suffering. More ruin. So I came here."

"Chrissie Johnson? That innocent girl?" Mildred said.

No, Michael knew that couldn't be true. Chrissie had had an embolus.

"Not her. She was a boondoggle. I had nothing to do with her. But I found out about her tragedy when I called her room to schedule the follow up appointment and the nurse, probably you, told me the code had just ended. It fell into my lap. A sign. So I started with Reginald Stark. I had been there when the call came from radiology about that awful man's pneumonia, and Dr. Baker, ever the helpful teacher, taught me about antibiotic choice. As if I didn't already know. He never signs off his personal office computer. Why would he? He's the only one who uses it. So later, when I saw Reginald Stark's chart open, I stopped his antibiotics. Let that man suffer."

Robin had ingratiated herself and become indispensable. Michael's staunch advocate. His one true supporter even as his life cracked around him. She was the crack.

She raised her voice and nodded toward Michael. Her arms were held tightly by Security. "You self-destructed better than I hoped. Lost the chairmanship. But then they gave it to Katherine Pierce."

Robin's snarl was back, and Michael strained to hear her. "A woman doctor. Like Grace. Small, blonde, perfect. Like Grace. Why was she now chair? What had she done that was so special? Just because she was there when you fell apart? Like Grace being the favorite because she was born after our father was gone?"

"So you lured her to the roof pretending to be me." Michael's stomach tightened at all the destruction.

"A win-win. Get you. Get Katherine Pierce. Because Katherine Pierce is just like Grace. Grace would be next. But first you."

The cupcake was meant for Michael. Robin had loaded it with beta blocker. Was it her own blood pressure medicine? Her mother's heart medicine? Whoever's it was, Michael would have eaten the cupcake at his desk, then slumped over with a slow heart rate and a bottomed-out blood pressure. People would assume he'd had a cardiac arrest. They'd call it a tragedy, but perhaps secretly thank it as a tidy solution to their problem. He was a stressed-out middle-aged workaholic who drank too much coffee and thought once-a-week basketball and the occasional run counted as exercise. No one would suspect a drug in the first place, and even if they did, standard forensics panels didn't cover beta blockers. Even if someone specifically asked for it, few beta blockers had tests. She wanted to kill Michael. And she would have succeeded.

But his mother ate it instead.

# Chapter 89

Madge was the hero.

Stinky was saved and Robin had told all, and nurses kept coming by the ICU to effuse about Madge's bravery. Gerta brought a big piece of chocolate cake from the kitchen and said it was a new item on the low-fat menu because it was made with fruit puree and not oil. Madge ate it, but just to be polite. She was a little wary after the whole chocolate cupcake incident, but she couldn't live without sweets her entire life, so might as well start now. It wasn't very tasty. When she got home and was back on a regular diet, she'd make a whole chocolate cake just for herself. With oil.

Francine brought two lemon bars in wax paper baggies, and Madge gave them both to Stinky. That's who they were for, anyway.

Big Tony showed up and awkwardly hemmed and hawed at the end of the bed while she and Mikey made small talk. He finally said, "I get now why you went bonkers in the stairway. No hard feelings." Then he and Mikey shook hands, which was good, because Madge didn't need Tony the Torturer taking any aggression out on her.

Even Nurse Bob stopped by. "Looks like you both had good reason for being weird. So, okay."

The boy chaplain visited early one morning. He held her hand and she didn't snatch it away. It was somehow calming.

He didn't seem quite so young anymore. "You are a remarkable woman. Life is precious, and you chose to sacrifice yours. Yet here you are, and thank the Lord, because you are needed and loved. You will face more choices when you leave the hospital." He sat next to her, quietly. She let him. When he left, he said again, "Life is precious. Don't squander yours."

Mikey told her about what happened in Boston, the unfortunate drug mishap and the lady with the stroke. Robin's mother. The werewolf clearly loved her. But even Madge would not want love shown through murder. No mother would. The poor woman.

Stinky had stayed by her bedside all night that first night and had to ask Francine to feed Frank on her way to work. He even gave her his key code. And Madge knew how persnickety he was with his passcodes.

"That Dr. Francine sure is nice," Madge said. "Makes lemon bars, too."

"Yep," Stinky said.

"Shows how much she likes you if she's willing to visit a scary creature like that. I'm sure she'll take good care of your lizard."

"Uh-huh."

"Probably take good care of you, too."

"I can take care of myself, Mom."

"I know, I know. More fun to be taken care of."

He smiled at her and took her hand again. "You always took good care of me."

Who was this boy's mother? Give her a medal.

Would Mikey ever move home?

Hopefully not. It was nice to have him around, but she didn't need him underfoot. She had her own life to lead.

Gerta told her the university offered classes to senior citizens for a pittance, a special program that was dirt cheap. Any class, as long as it wasn't full. Even law classes. Not for a degree, but for interest's sake. Madge had some catching up to do.

"Dr. Hal said if you hadn't been Stinky-on-the-spot when I ate the cupcake, I might not be here now. You saved me."

"You saved me. And you know it." His voice held respect.

Yes, she did know it. And so did he. And that's what mattered most to her.

Her keen ears picked up the chime of the baby bell in the hallway. Did Mikey look wistful?

"I do like children," she said. "I'm good with children. Stories, bubbles, swings. If any children were to come my way, from two busy doctors perchance, I'd be delighted to take care of them."

"Enough, Mom."

He didn't say no. There was hope yet.

Babies. Maybe she'd have a celebratory glass of sherry when she got home. Why not?

Mikey's blue childhood eyes flashed into her mind. "Mom, please stop drinking. Do it for me."

She'd let him down for all those years. She wasn't strong enough. Was she strong enough now?

After all, she didn't want to die. How many times had she heard from the doctors that her next drink could be her last? She never believed them. And anyway, so what?

Now she had come close to "her last." She'd almost died. It put a whole new spin on things. The young priest was right. Life was precious. Stinky was precious. There might be babies.

"You should get some rest, Mom. You're still healing from your pancreatitis and now this." He bent down and kissed her forehead. "I love you. I want you to get better."

So precious.

# Chapter 90

Michael slid next to Francine at the computer station. He smiled and she smiled, but then she frowned. "I have to tell you something. It's pretty chilling."

"Okay," he said, but he didn't know how much more "chilling" he could take.

"I heard this from the security officer who sat with Robin until the police came. His father is a patient of mine, so I've seen him a few times this week." Francine lowered her voice. "Your cupcake wasn't the first time Robin used a beta blocker."

As if she could read into Michael's soul and his long-standing fear, Francine said, "When she was ten, she didn't know its power." Francine paused and twisted her hair around her finger. "She killed her father."

Michael thought of Robin at age ten. He thought of himself.

Francine said, "Here's the story. One day Robin's father couldn't remember if he'd taken his blood pressure medicine. Her mother said, 'Don't take another. It might be dangerous.' The next day her father threw his plate on the floor because the roast was overcooked, and Robin ran to the bathroom to hide because, unfortunately, she knew what came next. There on the sink was her dad's medicine, and all she could think was 'too dangerous, too dangerous.' "

Michael understood what Francine was going to say. He sat back and closed his eyes.

"Her mother sported a new black eye and Robin sported a pocket full of beta blocker. She crushed it up and put it in her father's coffee, and he yelled that the coffee was too bitter but he drank it all. Then had a heart attack while driving to work, crashed, and died instantly."

Francine took a deep breath. "She said she wanted to make him sick, to gain a respite from his anger. But she actually told the security officer that what happened was even better."

So that's where they were different, Robin and Michael. Michael's deed haunted him forever. He regretted his action almost immediately. Robin was still happy with hers.

Francine continued. "Her mother might have known, though. When they were cleaning out her father's things, her mother saw the bottle and lifted it to the light and tilted it this way and that. She never opened it. She never counted the pills. But Robin believed she knew. Robin had done it for her. To stop the pain. They never talked about it. Soon after, Grace was born, and the new baby took over their lives, and, sounds like from Robin's standpoint, her mother's love."

Two ten-year-old kids living in troubled households. Two mothers, doing their best.

God, was he lucky he had his life and not Robin's.

# Chapter 91

Michael pushed his mother's wheelchair out the door of the room at the end of the hall and bade it good riddance. One week ago his mother almost died in this room. May he never have another patient in room 721 again.

Mildred, Evan, and Bob lined the hallway and waved goodbye as well, quite enthusiastically, Michael noted.

Francine waited by the nurses' desk. She motioned Michael aside and said, "Guess who's coming out of the ICU today and is back on my list? Reginald Stark. He's doing very well. He'll be out of the hospital in no time."

"Thank goodness for that." What a relief. Thank goodness for the ICU team.

"What are you two whispering about? Secret plans?" His mother craned her neck.

Francine smiled. "No secrets."

"I will miss you, my dear. Until next time."

"Next time? No, Mom, no next time," Michael said.

"It's always nice to see you, too, Miss McGillicuddy, but hopefully 'next time' can be outside the hospital," Francine said.

"Maybe you and Mikey could stop by for a nightcap after your date this week," his mother said.

Poor Francine ducked her head and blushed.

"Shh. Mom. The whole hospital doesn't need to know."

Michael shrugged at Francine and wheeled his mother away, toward the elevator.

She dropped her voice then and whispered at him. "It's been more than a year since Janet. I'm very sorry about what happened. I liked her. She was good for you. Francine will be, too."

Janet, the love of his life, knew him better than anybody. That's what he thought, but that wasn't true. He'd hidden his secrets from Janet. His mother knew him better.

He drove her to his house and settled her on the couch.

Frank circled around her, his tongue flicking in and out. His mother didn't flinch.

"I'll make you some lunch, then get you home, and later I'll bring over groceries. You can make me a list." He gave her paper and pencil.

"The last time I had paper and pencil, I made a suspect list. But Robin was never on it. Didn't you have *any* suspicion, Stinky?"

"None," he said. "I thought she was on my side."

"I'm glad she confessed. And while I'm sorry Dr. Katherine is not feeling perfect yet, I'm glad she and Dr. Perkins chose you to run the department in the meantime."

"Me, too. He is happily retired, and Katherine is better all the time. We talk every day. You'll be happy to know, I am convinced she is by far the best person for the job. Patient. Empathetic. Great ideas. They should have chosen her initially. I think part of the problem was that she was on the choosing committee. Too modest to put her own hat in the ring. She'll make a much better chair than me."

"Better than you, Stinky? I don't believe it."

Was this her dry wit again? Probably, but it didn't matter.

When Katherine came back full time, Michael would be in charge of the patient experience. That's all he ever really wanted, anyway. Let Katherine take care of the administrative headaches. He had his mother to take care of. He had Francine.

Michael had finally unpacked his office boxes, filling the bookcase with medical books from his past and his red glass Clinician of the Year award from Boston. He had unwrapped a framed picture and put it in the center of the desk, a photo of him as a seven-year-old on the swings, his mother on a swing next to him. He added a photo of Frank. He hung his picture of Mount Rainier on one of his four windowless walls and admired how cozy the office felt.

His condominium was not as cozy. Yet. Michael's mother sat on his sleek leather couch in front of his sleek glass coffee table facing the painting on the wall, the dark canvas with slashes of red. It would be relegated to his office soon, to be replaced on this wall with a new painting.

Francine had shown it to him the night before, at dinner at her apartment. They'd had two dates in a week, but this was the first time back in her apartment since the spring party. The canvas sat on an easel covered with a sheet, and she unfurled it dramatically. The sheet landed on his head and covered his eyes and he waited, laughing, for her to untangle him. She lifted the sheet and he kissed her and smelled her lemony scent.

How had he gone four months without seeing what was in front of him?

Francine twirled him around to face the painting. On the easel sat a replica of the picture they'd admired in the art gallery, a valley of loosely painted wildflowers with snow-covered Mount Rainier in the background. Francine's was actually prettier than the one they'd seen, the colors more vibrant, the mountain more majestic.

"Wow," he said.

"I painted it from the photo I had. It's yours for a small fortune, like the one in the gallery," she said.

"Sold," he said.

"Actually, you can have it for nothing, because I have

nowhere to hang it." She indicated the small apartment, which had furniture or windows on every wall. "I mean it. I want you to have it."

"How about we trade it for a weekend trip to Mount Rainier?"

She beamed at him, and he beamed back.

His mother interrupted his memory. "Francine said you might go away for a weekend. I'll feed the creature."

Good Lord. At least Francine knew exactly what she was getting into.

He left his mother on the couch and headed for the kitchen. Frank trotted in ahead of him.

"That's her," Michael told him. "That's my mother. Never mind about the 'creature' comment. I can tell she likes you. And don't worry. I'll tell her about your tail."

Michael made two sandwiches and carried them in on a tray with two glasses of milk. He stopped so abruptly, the milk sloshed over.

His mother had found the short glasses and had set them on the coffee table next to the bottle of scotch he'd tucked away in the hutch in the corner.

"Mom! You almost died!"

She tilted her head and blinked innocently. Her tell. She lifted the scotch bottle. "I'll drink to that, Mikey. I'll drink to that."

Then she turned it over to fill the first glass. Nothing happened. No liquid poured out.

"I dumped it," she said. "I dumped it all. The gods are smiling on us."

"No, Mom. The gods aren't smiling on us." Michael handed her the milk and raised his in a toast. "You did that all by yourself."

Thank you to Lyle Sorensen, MD
for orthopedic specialty medical advice.

## About the author

Susan McCormick is a writer and doctor who lives in Seattle. She graduated from Smith College and George Washington University School of Medicine and served as a doctor for nine years in the US Army before moving to the Pacific Northwest and civilian practice. She writes an award-winning cozy murder mystery series, *The Fog Ladies*, and she wrote *Granny Can't Remember Me*, a lighthearted picture book about Alzheimer's disease and dementia, and *The Antidote*, a middle grade to adult medical fantasy. Susan is married with two boys, and she loves giant dogs. Visit her at:
https://susanmccormickbooks.com

Thank you for purchasing
*The Room at the End of the Hall.*

Please consider leaving a review.
It helps more than you can know.

9 780999 861877